WILD KINGDOM

Anne Rouen

DEDICATION

To all my friends in the Outback.

PROLOGUE

Mid-June 1990 – End of May 1992

Laura stood by her husband's grave, gazing blankly at the red rose she was about to lay on the casket, oblivious to the chilly wind that whipped around her ankles and tugged at her skirt. It was her second funeral in two days: the first had been that of her best friend, and she wondered how she was going to stay on her feet for the remainder of the service and then make it home, let alone survive for the rest of her life.

A pale, fragile figure in her black coatdress and cloche hat, she appeared bewildered, as if she could not believe that fate could deal her such a blow. Her shocked parents, who had flown over from England to support her, hovered about her helplessly. They would soon have to return to their tourist-management position at a castle in Somerset, and she would be completely alone, except for her great-uncle who lived in North Queensland, over two thousand kilometres away from her home here in Adelaide.

As if she didn't have enough to contend with, a week later, just after her parents had reluctantly returned to their commitments in England, she received word that her beloved great-uncle Jonas had also passed away. In a haze of misery, she learnt that he had left his property in the Gulf and all his interests to her. Too battered by grief to bother, she signed all the documents sent by the solicitors without reading them: a circumstance she would one day regret, although now she cared for nothing except how to get through each painful and guilt-ridden day.

Soon after, her friends Anne and Bill gave her a job in their busy delivery business, not because she needed the money, but to try and take her out of herself. Accepting with gratitude that they cared, she did her best to carry out their wishes. For two years, she struggled, forcing herself to get out of bed and dress every morning to present herself at work, instead of lying with her face to the wall, but things didn't get better. Only the fact that Anne had told her she wanted time away from their business to spend it with her children prevented Laura from giving her notice, however much she loved her friends. So, she forced herself to go on, getting up and going to work, despite the black despair that loomed over her every waking minute.

Then, one night, she had a dream: Uncle Jonas was at his front gate, beckoning her. Standing beside him was another man, tall and athletic, wearing a wide-brimmed hat, an open-necked shirt and denim jeans—the uniform of the Outback. He stood relaxed, one hand resting on the gatepost, yet confident, as if he owned the world. Laura could not see who he was because he was turned side-on, a silhouette against the setting sun. Puzzled, she stared at the proud, ruthless profile; the untamed line of his jaw; the strong column of his neck; feeling that she should know him. But even though she didn't recognise him, she knew instinctively that he was a man who refused to submit to the shackles of civilisation: imperious, independent, indomitable, a master of his own wild kingdom. A man like her great-uncle Jonas.

He reminded her so vividly of Polaris that she felt her nails bite into her palms with the force of emotion sweeping over her. *Polaris!* The place of her dreams, of fabulous holidays with her great-uncle in the vast, magical world beyond the Divide: the world they called the Gulf.

And now she could think of Uncle Jonas without the pain—of all the wonderful times she had shared with him—and longed with all her being to be back there, safe and comfortable.

She wouldn't admit it, even to herself, but it was the dream that decided her—took her out of the dreadful apathy that had gripped her like a boa constrictor for two long, lonely years—rather than the disquieting letter she had from Uncle Jonas's solicitors: a sort of psychological catalyst.

Suddenly decisive, no longer paralysed, Laura resumed her maiden name of Neumann, wrote to Uncle Jonas's solicitors asking them to wind up their administration of the estate and pass it over to her, and gave her notice to Bill—all within the week. 'I will stay until you get someone, but I would like to go as soon as possible to have as much time as I can before The Wet.'

Bill had told her to go straightaway, as his wife could help him out until he found someone. 'And, Laura?' His eyes held a far-sighted gleam. 'I am not one for making predictions, and I hope you find the answers you're looking for, but I believe you will find your destiny at your, what is it called, Star in the North?'

'Polaris. One of the biggest stations in the Gulf. And all of a sudden, not making any money. I want to find out why.'

'Go for it!' He kissed her cheek. 'And good luck. Come round for dinner tonight. Anne will want to say goodbye.' He turned back. 'What about Oscar? Do you want us ——?'

'No.' She smiled. 'He can come with me. I wouldn't know what to do without him, really. And he has lots of relations flying about up there that I am sure he would love to meet.'

He rolled his eyes. 'Budgerigar heaven, eh? He's a dear little fellow. We're going to miss him.'

'Oh, well … I've had to do *something* to stop your drivers teaching him how to swear.' A cheeky smile hovered on her lips. 'A bit drastic, but …'

He laughed. 'Get out of here.' Watching her walk away with new life in her step, he thought it had been the first time he had seen her smile in over two years. *And it feels good,* he told himself. *Real good!* He gave a little grunt of pleasure. *By Jove, Anne will be pleased when I tell her.*

Chapter One

Early June 1992

Midmorning on the fourth day of her journey, Laura turned off the road from Cloncurry to Burketown and pulled up before a sagging gate. She drew in her breath at the state of it. The top hinge hung rusting and useless beside a drunken signpost whose faded and peeling black lettering forlornly announced the name of the station. Never had she seen it in any condition but white and solid with crisp, bright lettering. Uncle Jonas always said that a front gate said a lot about its owner. He would never have allowed it to have fallen into disrepair while he lived.

She stepped out of her four-wheel drive, feeling tired and more than a little depressed, dragged open the gate and drove through, then, with difficulty, closed and latched it. A little zephyr played with her hair, but otherwise the day was warm and mild with a hint of dust and a very bright sun. *This is how I remember it,* she thought, breathing deeply of the dry, earth-scented air as she wrestled with the gate. *A typical dry-season day, far away from the cold rain of an Adelaide winter.* Her depression lifted momentarily and then resettled. Oscar seemed similarly affected. He hadn't spoken for quite a while. She sighed. It had been a long haul and it wasn't over yet. There were still many kilometres to cover between the front gate of Polaris and the smallish dwelling that passed for its homestead.

She drove on, seeing neither man nor beast. The land was eerie in its vast loneliness, but Laura knew that she had come home. The road was rutted and potholed, and of necessity, she drove slowly. When she passed the turn-off to Juliana, the neighbouring station about eighty kilometres away, she knew that she had not much farther to go.

Juliana was another huge enterprise, owned by the Jamiesons. She remembered Mr Jamieson. He had died, too, about five years ago. Uncle Jonas had told her once that only Polaris stood between Juliana and Mr Jamieson's wish to be the biggest landowner in the Gulf. Despite his repeated offers to buy him out being met by Uncle Jonas's constant refusal, they had remained staunch friends to his death, when his son had taken over the management.

Idly, she speculated on what the son, Rick, would be like. He would have to be about thirty-four by now, she guessed, though she had never seen him. Her holidays in the Gulf had not coincided with his, and being eight years older than herself, he would not have had much in common with her, back then, anyway.

Would he be like his father? she wondered. *If so, he would certainly be a man to be reckoned with!* In her mind's eye, she saw Mr Jamieson as she remembered him from her childhood. He was not much above medium height with fine, neat features, yet he made any room he entered seem small. Although grey-haired with his skin weathered into folds like fine leather, he had a peculiar grace of movement and arresting bright blue eyes. Even as a little girl, Laura had been aware that he possessed his own special brand of magnetism.

Vaguely, she remembered lunching at the homestead—a gracious old two-storey building surrounded by trees and cool, green vines—when, long ago, Uncle Jonas had taken her to see the waters of the Gulf of Carpentaria. Mr Jamieson had welcomed them with Outback warmth and hospitality, and Mrs Mac, the housekeeper, had treated them with motherly kindness.

More than an hour after she had crossed her south-western boundary, Laura drew up before the garden gate of a dilapidated old house. Climbing out stiffly and taking her first proper look around, she could hardly believe her eyes.

It had been a matter of twelve years since she had spent her last holidays here, but surely it had not been like this, then? Her eyes travelled over what used to be the front lawn. It was now bare, dry ground with the occasional clump of long, brittle grass. An oleander hedge, straggly and half-dead, and a few hardy old shrubs in the same condition were all that was left of Uncle Jonas's cherished garden.

'If I had my way, Laurie,' he had told her once, long ago, 'I would have this garden and no house. I like to sleep under the stars. Trouble is, it gets a bit rough in the wet season.' And he had chuckled and ruffled her hair.

The memory brought back to her, with renewed intensity, the fact that he wasn't here, and for a moment, she was overwhelmed by shame that she had neglected his gift of love. 'Oh, Uncle Jonas, I've let you down,' she whispered. 'I should have come before.'

Far away in Adelaide, it had been hard to believe that the man who had built these lands into a vast and profitable business was no longer here. But now, faced with all this desolation and ruin, realisation hit her that he was indeed gone. She knew now that all the way from the boundary gate, she had subconsciously expected Uncle Jonas to be waiting for her as he had in years past. Her head bowed in her hands, she leant on the gate, blinded by tears. Something touched her knee and she jumped. It was an old cattle dog feebly wagging her tail and gazing up at her with anxious, blue-filmed eyes: Uncle Jonas's dog, who'd hardly been more than a puppy when she'd last seen her. 'Oh, Bess …' She sobbed. 'How *lonely* you must have been.' Kneeling to put her arms around her, she wept into the blue speckled coat.

Soon, Laura recovered herself and, giving the old dog a pat, dried her tears and turned back to her Land Cruiser to get Oscar.

The budgie regarded her quizzically out of bright black eyes. 'Oscar's a good boy,' he ventured, tilting his head to one side and ruffling his sky-blue feathers.

'Of course, you are, darling.' She removed his cage from the vehicle and carried him to the house—the old dog limping at her heels. 'What do you think of your new home?'

There was a short silence. Then, 'Bloody hell!' swore Oscar, beginning to scold in a harsh little voice, interspersed with chirruping calls to the birds in the trees and sundry comments addressed to his mirror.

Laura laughed. 'I don't think I quite got you away from those drivers quickly enough, you bad boy.' But when she had hung his cage on a hook suspended from a rafter on the verandah, on which Uncle Jonas had always hung his waterbag, and tentatively pushed open the front door, all desire to laugh left her.

At first the door resisted her efforts, then suddenly swung inwards with a loud groan that made her skin prickle. She stepped over an accumulated pile of leaves and debris and into a room festooned with cobwebs and dust. Recoiling, she gasped, then sighed with relief when she realised that the ghostly figure standing in the gloom beside the door was only Uncle Jonas's hat and oilskin coat hanging on the hatstand in the corner. They, too, were covered in spider webs, their colour concealed by a thick film of dust. Gingerly, she removed them from the stand, ornately carved in the form of a tree, which she had much admired as a child, placed them over the end of the bed in his room, went out and closed the door.

Looking about her with horrified eyes, she was forced to admit that this silent, lonely ruin bore more resemblance to a ghost house than the welcoming home of her memories. For one craven moment, she was assailed by an overwhelming desire to turn and run—to get Oscar and Bess and drive away—anywhere, as long as it was away from the dereliction that faced her here.

Her lapse was only temporary. The steel that her great-uncle had long ago glimpsed in her came to her rescue, and biting her lip, she went from room to room—the dog padding behind her.

The tour of inspection did nothing to raise her spirits. The whole house bore evidence of neglect and decay. Everything was thick with dust and grime, and their feet made tracks on the floorboards, which had once been kept polished. Windowpanes here and there were broken, and the gauze screens torn and loose.

Some of the rooms had fallen into such disrepair that it was evident that a carpenter must be employed before they could be used again. Water stains on walls and warped and rotting ceilings were testimony to the fact that, sometime in the last two years, sheets of iron must have come loose on the roof, allowing the torrential monsoon rains into the house.

I would like to know what that so-called manager has been doing all this time, she thought, frowning. *I can't wait to give him a piece of my mind!* This was something that must be seen to straightaway, although it was only June now and several months before the wet season was due to start.

It was certainly going to be a big job to make it home again, but it was characteristic of Laura that once decided on a course of action, she did not flinch from problems or difficulties, and she was determined that this house would be a home again, just as she remembered it.

Standing in the living room—a large, irregularly shaped room that ran the depth of the house that all the others opened off— she saw, not how it was now, but how it had been when she had come here for holidays. Modest, hardly more than a cottage; old and shabby, yet clean and welcoming; with two Aboriginal women, Lily and Mary, who had cooked and cleaned for Uncle Jonas since they were teenagers, welcoming her with wide, shy grins. 'Little Missus' they used to call her. They were good-natured and capable, and she wondered where they were now. Laura could certainly do with some help.

In the end, Laura decided that only two rooms were liveable: the living room, entered by the front door, and one bedroom— the one that had been hers when she had come for holidays.

Somehow, she shrank from using Uncle Jonas's room.

The state of the kitchen made her feel ill—and conscious of a rising anger against the unknown manager. It was obvious that, occasionally, someone had cooked here without bothering in the slightest with cleanliness. The gas stove was black and filthy with a combination of burnt grease and dust, and the sink contained a putrid mass that defied description.

Examining the large bathtub with its ball-and-claw feet and matching pedestal handbasin in the bathroom that had been constructed by enclosing one end of the back verandah, she noted thankfully that once she had removed the leaves and dust, this would certainly be the easiest room to clean. Her lips curved in wry amusement. Evidently, whoever had camped and cooked in the kitchen had not thought it necessary to bathe.

Laura's reflection in the fly-spotted mirror above the basin shocked her, and for a moment, she did not know who this pale stranger with the huge, shadowed eyes and hollow cheeks might be. She pushed back a strand of chestnut hair that had escaped from her ponytail. Then, she shrugged. It had been a long trip, that was all. Tomorrow, she would regain the enthusiasm that had driven her to come here.

She had come because of a dream, but what ought to have brought her was the dwindling income of an inheritance that should have made her a very rich woman. Now she needed to give some thought to who might be systematically robbing her.

Pensively, she returned to her Land Cruiser and took out her vacuum flask and a packet of sandwiches. Then, seated on the front steps with Bess at her feet, she shared her sandwiches while Oscar chattered gaily above her head. She ate her lunch in the bright sunshine with a vista of wide-open woodland stretched before her. This view, at least, was as she remembered it.

The problem of why her profits had dwindled to almost zero occupied her thoughts as she drank her coffee. The way she saw it, it could only be one of a few choices: gross mismanagement, neglect and/or systematic robbery by her so-called manager; cattle theft by professional thieves; or, God forbid, one of her neighbours. Not that she would like to think it of her neighbours, but it was a possibility, however remote. Laura needed to meet them and see how they struck her before she made any decisions about their honesty, one way or another.

She rose to her feet and, calling Bess, went to find the one person who may be able to help her—if he was still alive, that was.

Chapter Two

On her way, she remembered Uncle Jonas's horse. Would he still be here? Twelve years ago, he was a leggy three-year-old, and she had helped Uncle Jonas break him in. Turning back, she retrieved a crust of bread from her sandwich packet and made her way down past the stables to the paddock where she could see some horses drowsing in the shade of a tree. They stood head to tail, in pairs, protecting each other from the flies. She walked closer and called. One of them raised his head enquiringly and then trotted towards her. Yes, it was Ben, recognisable now, as he had been as a three-year-old, by the large, shield-shaped star on his forehead. He accepted the proffered crust and rubbed his head on her affectionately.

'We must go for a ride soon.' Laura determined, then and there, to start riding him again as soon as was humanly possible. *I hadn't realised,* she thought, stroking his silken neck, *how much I have missed having a horse.* When she walked away, he followed, hanging over the fence and whinnying after her before turning to gallop back to his companions.

Laura found the dry creek she wanted and walked along its bank for a short way towards a run-down tin shed built haphazardly of old kerosene tins and small pieces of roofing iron under the shelter of a large tree, which Jackson called his *gunyah*. She walked past, too afraid to call out in case she met only silence, afraid that she would find it abandoned because that could mean only one thing

A soft, burry voice spoke from the shadows behind her: 'G'day, Little Missus.'

Laura spun around to see an ancient, white-haired Aboriginal seated on the other side of his shack with his back against the tree trunk. In front of him was a tiny fire, which he stirred now and again with a stick.

'Jackson! How are you? Oh, I was *so* hoping to find you here!' There was a lilt of gladness in her voice that the old man did not miss.

'Pretty good, Missus.' The seamed mahogany face split into a wide grin, revealing one or two blackened stumps in wizened gums—the fault of white man's flour and sugar. Yet, despite this, Laura was struck by his air of wisdom and gentle dignity. Jackson was very old, but no-one, not even he, knew how old he was. He had been with Uncle Jonas since the beginning and had been his head stockman. He had been a wonderful horse breaker and a legendary horseman. It had been said that the horse had not been foaled that could throw him. Uncle Jonas had often told her of how Jackson had been called to break in a wicked youngster that no-one had been able to tame, and in three weeks, the horse was so quiet that even a child could ride him.

He must have been good, reflected Laura, *to have commanded the respect of Uncle Jonas.* Jonas Neumann had been a great horseman—this Laura had seen for herself.

Jackson had been retired and living here in his *gunyah* down on the creek for as long as she remembered.

'You come home, eh?' he said gruffly, squinting up at her.

'Yes, Jackson, I *have*. I've come home.'

'About time, Missus. I bin waitin' fer ya. That white fella, him no good. Told me, call him Boss. I no call him Boss. Call him nothin'. Him nothin' to me.' He spat in the dust and looked away.

Laura realised he must be referring to the manager. 'You mean Ed Sykes?'

'Yeah, him: that Sykes. No good, Missus.' He shook his head. 'Not like Boss Jamieson. Him pretty good fella. Call him Boss, orright.'

There did not seem to be anything to say to this, so she asked a question instead. 'What happened to Lily and Mary, Jackson?'

'After Boss go, they go to Doomadgee. Live there now. They come home soon, now Little Missus back.'

Laura knew that Doomadgee Shire was the Indigenous lands about three hundred kilometres away. 'Can I get a message to them, Jackson?'

'No need.' He waved a gnarled hand. 'They be back in a coupla days.'

'Oh.' Once again, Laura was left with nothing to say. After a short silence, she asked, 'Where are the men today?'

'Down finishin' spear traps on Clovelly bore, Missus. They back soon. Them fellas don' work too dam' hard. All the hard workers gone now.'

'What do you mean, Jackson? Where have they gone?'

'Well … Some too dam' old, like me. But that nothin' fella, he sack all the others except for Lou. Put his no-good mates on.' He shook his head. 'Good thing you back, Little Missus. But you watch out for him. Him no dam' good.'

'I will,' she promised. 'But why didn't he sack Lou?'

'Wouldn't go. Said he's been livin' down there on the outstation for fifty years, and nothin' short of a bomb's gunna move him.'

'Well, good for him! Has Sykes been stealing my cattle, Jackson?'

The old man shifted uneasily. 'Dam' bad man, Missus,' he said at last. 'But I don't think it's him.'

'What makes you say that?'

'Comin' from up that way.' Jackson waved a hand, looking even more uncomfortable.

Laura drew an incredulous breath. 'Are you saying it's Juliana?'

He shook his head again. 'Up that *way*, Little Missus. But it's not Boss Jamieson.' He raised troubled eyes. '*Can't* be Boss Jamieson.'

'I hope you're right …' Laura noted his worried expression. 'But that remains to be seen, don't you think?'

Jackson looked down into his fire and poked at the embers

with his stick. 'Won't be Boss Jamieson.'

'All right.' Laura heard the note of finality in his voice and knew no more was to be got out of him. 'Thanks, Jackson. I'd better get back now and start cleaning the house.'

'Good-o, Missus. Don't work too hard. Lily and Mary'll do it for ya.'

She left him—a wizened figure, yet to her mind, the embodiment of the nobility of his race—and made her way back to the house.

Laura knew now that it could never be the same again—now that Uncle Jonas was gone. But wandering up to the homestead through his beloved trees, she felt his presence like a softly comforting touch, and it was as if she heard him say, 'Chin up, Laurie. It'll come good.' An image of his dear face sprang into her mind, and she saw again the twinkling blue eyes beneath shaggy eyebrows, the snowy hair above the noble forehead.

'I'll be all right, Uncle Jonas,' she whispered. 'I'm home now.'

When Laura arrived at the homestead, pondering some of Jackson's more cryptic utterances, she heard a fast-driven vehicle with an over-revving engine. Her eyes narrowed as the four-wheel-drive utility squealed to a protesting halt, and she turned as the driver, momentarily obscured by dust, flung himself out and slouched towards her, leaving the door open. His hat was pulled well down, hiding his eyes, but there was a taut, angry set to his jaw as he approached her.

'Who the hell are you?' he demanded. 'And what do you think you're doing here?'

'I beg your pardon?' Laura raised haughty brows.

'You heard me!'

'I don't know that it is any concern of yours who I am. Nor do I appreciate being spoken to like that.'

'Listen, I'm the manager here ——'

'Then, if that's the case, I'd like to know what *you've* been doing to allow the front gate to be falling off its hinges and this house to get into such an *appalling* state of filth and disrepair!'

'Listen, Lady, no woman's gunna tell me what to do! I manage this place, see. And I don't have to answer to no woman that moves in and thinks she owns the place!' He jutted an aggressive chin. 'Who are you, anyway?'

'Just who you said.' Laura's eyes were sparkling dangerously, but her words were soft and deliberate. 'Only—I don't just think I own the place—I *do* own it. The name is Neumann. I take it you are Ed Sykes?'

He nodded, studying his boots in silence.

'And since you're not too keen on taking orders from a woman,' she continued, 'you can finish up today. Come back in an hour or so, and I'll have your cheque ready for you.'

The man stood for a moment, nodded once and turned to go.

'Just a second.' Laura's voice stopped him in his tracks. 'Is that a station vehicle?'

'Yeah. What about it?'

'Leave it here. You can walk down to the quarters.' Laura was dealing him an insult and she knew it, but she was unprepared for the naked hatred she saw in his eyes as he tilted back his hat and stared at her. She sustained his regard for what seemed an eternity, even though her flesh was creeping at the venom she saw there. Then, slowly, the man's eyes dropped before hers, and he turned and walked away.

The tension seeped out of her, but she found she was trembling with the effort of holding those dark, rather frightening eyes. Giving herself a mental shake, she went to get the station books and her cheque book.

Engrossed in her calculations, Laura did not, at first, notice anything outside her books, but the unmistakable buzz of angry voices interrupted her concentration, and she dropped her pen and went to the door.

Assembled in the front yard were a group of men who subsided into an uneasy silence when they saw her. She walked out onto the verandah and let her eyes travel over them, and each one looked away or down at his boots as her glance fell on him.

'Yes?' she queried. 'Can I help you?'

There was a general shuffle before one man reluctantly allowed himself to be pushed forward by his mates. The spokesman cleared his throat and looked desperately about him, as if for an avenue of escape or, perhaps, to gain inspiration for his speech. Eventually, it came tumbling out, staccato-like: 'We came ter tell yer that if yer sack Ed, we're goin' too. He goes, we go! Yeah.' He briefly raised his eyes to Laura's, and she saw a triumphant gleam in their depths before he lowered them and stepped back into the group.

There was a period of expectant silence while Laura considered them.

Her expression suddenly hardened. 'Well, go then!' She lifted her chin. 'Come back with Sykes, and I'll have your cheques ready.'

The quality of the silence changed. The men's faces registered shock and then, incongruously, dawning respect. Without another word, they turned and headed back towards their quarters.

A little over an hour later, Laura was back on her verandah, watching all the hands needed to run a large property depart in a convoy of assorted utilities and four-wheel drives, piled high with swags and dogs.

Chapter Three

With a fluttering feeling in the pit of her stomach, overlain by one of impending doom, Laura sank down on the step, hands clenched in her lap. *Now what do I do?* she asked herself. The muster had to be started, bores and watering places kept in operation, spear traps had to be checked and emptied of cattle, as well as the hundred-and-one-other repair and maintenance jobs required to keep a concern of this size and nature operating smoothly.

I'll have to hire a new team of men. But where do I start? While she thought about it, Laura began the difficult task of restoring the living room to a state approaching cleanliness and order.

By the time another hour had passed, she had managed to remove the worst of the dust and grime from the floor and thoroughly cleaned the table and chairs. She'd taken the old carpet square and hung it over the fence, but she doubted its ability to survive the beating that would be necessary to remove its accumulation of dust. Tomorrow, she must see if the electricity generator in the lighting shed could be brought into operation. It would be handy to be able to use the vacuum cleaner and other electrical appliances she had brought with her, and it would provide lights at night. Meanwhile, she had her gas camping stove and light.

The physical actions of cleaning soothed her taut nerves and allowed her to view her plight philosophically. *The manager's not much loss, anyway,* she thought. *And according to Jackson, his men aren't a lot of use, either. And even if it isn't Sykes stealing stock, and it is just the dry seasons, why didn't he say something to the lawyers administering the estate? I can't give up just because everything is not the way I wanted it.*

After all, if it had been mentioned to the lawyers, she might not have listened to her dream and come here to make a new life. She would still have been in that dark maze, beating on the walls in frustration, haunted by her memories.

She drew the curtain on her thoughts and wielded her broom even more energetically. *By the time I'm finished, this room shouldn't look too bad,* she mused. *At least it will be clean, even if it's not exactly the type of home to feature in House and Garden.*

Laura was industriously knocking down cobwebs with a dust mop she'd found in the broom cupboard when she felt her spine tingle and spun around to find herself being gravely watched by a tall, well-built man. Their eyes met, and for a few seconds, there was an electric silence.

Then, the man removed his wide-brimmed felt hat. 'May I?' He gestured, indicating that he wished to come in.

Now that his hat was off, she saw that his hair was a glossy black and sprang from a broad brow to thickly cover his well-shaped head. His eyes were light—striking, under winged eyebrows—and his lean, sun-browned face, although too rugged to be classically handsome, appeared all the more attractive for its slight cragginess. It was a face that haunted her. Surely, she'd seen him somewhere before? The memory eluded her. *Perhaps he's one of the Polaris ringers come in late?* Whoever he was, she was made blindingly aware of something else: this man possessed a latent sexuality far more potent than mere physical good looks. Arrested, she didn't realise that she had not answered.

He seemed to take her silence for assent because he came into the room, looking at her quizzically.

'I suppose you've come to be paid off, too?' Laura, uncomfortably aware of her grimy clothes and dishevelled appearance, took an aggressive stand.

'No.' The man's lips quirked as he observed her defiant attitude. 'I am quite happy in my job.' His voice was low and pleasant, not quite a drawl. Then, as if he had considered keeping up the pretence as a joke but suddenly thought better of it, he thrust out his hand and smiled, teeth very white against his tan. 'By the way, my name is Jamieson. Rick Jamieson. And you must be Jonas's great-niece. I've heard quite a bit about you over the years. How do you do?'

Laura shook his hand and mumbled a response, feeling remarkably foolish. 'Yes, I am Laura Neumann. I'm sorry, I didn't hear you drive up. Please, won't you sit down.'

He threw his hat on the table, lounged in a chair at its head and looked around, his eyes travelling to the water-stained walls and upward to the gaping hole in the ceiling. 'Oh, hey! I can see you've got your work cut out here. Why didn't you let someone know you were coming? You could have stayed with us at Juliana while this was repaired, and the cleaning done for you. In fact, why don't you come and stay at Juliana, anyway? Mrs Mac will be pleased to have the company.'

'Mrs Mac? Is Mrs Mac still there? I remember her: She was your housekeeper when I used to come for holidays. I would have thought she'd have …'

'Retired? No way!' He grinned. 'Still ruling the roost: as spry and bossy as ever. What do you say? Will you come?'

'Oh, thank you, that is very kind, but I want to stay here. As to why I …' Laura stopped. How much could she trust him? Jackson had seemed hesitant even while he reiterated his belief in the man's innocence. *Does Rick know what has been going on here? He hasn't shown much surprise about the state of this place. How can I tell him that I wanted to find out what is really going on and not some cover-up designed to placate me when he might be the one?* She shrugged. 'I just decided to come. Spur of the moment, you know.'

He raised a sceptical eyebrow. 'I see.'

To cover the awkward silence, she said, 'You don't look like your father.' Silently cursing herself for uttering such an inanity.

He shrugged. 'I take after my mother's people.'

'I never knew your mother.'

'No. She died of cancer when I was eight. But it just seemed to me that she wilted in this climate, like a delicate plant.'

'Oh, I *am* sorry.' Laura felt even more crass.

'Don't be.' He rose to his feet. 'I have had a lot of years to become accustomed to being without her.'

Laura felt a surge of tenderness so shocking in its intensity that it startled her— although his tone precluded sympathy—and heralded another awkward silence. She glanced at her watch. 'I'll put the kettle on.'

'Good-o,' he said, stepping out onto the verandah. 'Hullo, a budgie! How do you do, young fellow? What's his name?'

'Oscar. How do you like your tea?'

'Black, no sugar, thanks.' He continued to talk to the bird for a few minutes, then strolled back inside as the kettle screamed. He sat at his ease: big, kind, faintly amused, filling the room with his presence. Laura was acutely conscious of him as she made the tea and set the table.

'How did you know I was here?' she asked, putting a mug and plate from her picnic set in front of him.

'I didn't.' He nodded his thanks for the tea, a little tremor touching the corners of his mouth. '*Until* I saw your entire station staff passing my front door.'

'Oh …'

'I went down to the gate to see where they were going in such a hurry. And they informed me …' He paused. 'That the new lady boss had sacked the whole lot of them not five minutes after she had arrived. So …' A little thread of suppressed laughter vibrated his voice, 'I decided to come and see this new lady boss for myself.'

'I'm glad you think it's funny.' Laura's tone negated the words. 'It was a shade longer than five minutes, but it didn't take me long to see what kind of men I had to deal with.' Her brows knit, and she gave him a straight glance. 'Besides which, it doesn't seem like much of a reason for you to come all the way from Juliana. I mean, it isn't exactly your business, is it?'

'Don't be silly.' He disarmed her attempted snub, the twinkle in his eyes more pronounced. 'As a matter of fact, I'd say it will be hot gossip all the way from here to Camooweal by now.'

'What do you mean?'

'Just that what anyone does up here is everyone else's business. Haven't you heard of the galah session?'

'Of course I have! I'm not that green. It's the time of day when everyone can call each other for a chat on their radios unless the Flying Doctor has an emergency.'

'That's right. And just what big news, my dear girl, do you think they'll be talking about?'

'I'm not your "dear girl".' Laura bit her lip, bristling at his lazy amusement. *Patronising,* she thought, but her next words were defensive. 'I suppose you think I shouldn't have done it?'

'It's not that I think your judgement is at fault. On the contrary, it was spot-on. It's just your timing that's a little out. The trouble is …' He wrinkled his brow. 'I don't know how we are going to replace them this late in the season. Everyone is mustering now, you know.'

'We?' she challenged. 'Who's we?'

'Well, naturally, I will do what I can for you. That's just being a good neighbour, even if there were no other reason. I'm saying it will be difficult.'

Reason? What other reason? Feeling even more at a disadvantage, Laura said, 'I know it sounds stupid when you put it like that, but I didn't sack them *all.* I sacked one. And the others said that if I sacked him, they would go, too. So, I told them to go. I mean, what else could I do?'

'What, indeed?'

'Are you *laughing* at me?'

'Of course not! I wouldn't dream of it. Which one did you sack?'

'The manager: Sykes.'

'I said your judgement was spot-on.' He took a slice of the brownie she offered. 'Mmm, thanks.'

They drank their tea in a silence that was now more companionable since Laura's wary discomfort had begun to subside in the warmth of his personality and his undoubted approval of her estimation of the manager.

'Tell me: what made you come here alone, like this?'

'I didn't have anyone to come with me,' she parried.

'Yes, but: why now?'

She knew she ought to resent the question. In the light of the letter from her trustees, it was a dangerous one, but it was said in such a warm tone of interest that she couldn't. But what kind of answer could she give? *I came because of a dream? No, never.*

'I don't know. I wanted to see it again, I suppose. I was so happy at Polaris as a child on my holidays, and it's been a long time since I was here. And I've always loved it up in this country. There's something about it, you know?'

'I know. No half-measures out here. You either love it or you hate it.' He regarded her steadily, a hint of warning in his eyes. 'Nor is it for the faint-hearted.'

'Oh, no,' agreed Laura, adding, to avoid being questioned further, 'I met your father often when I was here; he and Uncle Jonas were such good friends. I wonder why I didn't ever meet you?'

'Probably because I was away at boarding school, then at Ag College. After that I spent a year backpacking around Europe. It was interesting but, eventually, I pined for the big country. I came home just after your last holidays here, I think, because I remember Jonas telling us that your family had moved to Adelaide, and it was a pity I hadn't come home a week or two earlier. He thought the world of you.'

'The feeling was mutual. That's probably why I didn't come … before. I couldn't bear to think of it without him.' She raised eyes sparkling with unshed tears to his. 'Did you see him before he …?'

'Before he died? Yes, I was over here that day. He said he felt tired. He died in his sleep, so I don't think he would have suffered. He had his supper, as usual, and the two women found him unconscious in his bed early the next morning when they came to get his breakfast. I called the Flying Doctor but there was nothing he could do. Jonas didn't recover consciousness and died in the plane before it even got off the ground. I think that's why the women left. They came back a couple of months later but only stayed a few days and then cleared out again.' He looked at her kindly. 'Don't grieve too much for him, will you? He lived the kind of life he wanted and enjoyed good health up until the last few weeks. And I think he was ready to go.'

His voice had a gentle, velvet edge, and Laura felt comforted. 'Yes, you're right. Uncle Jonas was a man whose philosophy of life embraced a profound wisdom. I only wish I had the half of it.' She smiled a little tremulously.

'Yes, he was a wise and clever man,' agreed Rick. 'You're not the only one who misses him. He was very good to me when my father passed away.'

'I was truly sorry to hear about your father, Rick.'

'Thanks, Laura. It was very sudden, unexpected. One minute he was there, sitting at the table, the next he was gone—bit of a shock. Jonas helped me a lot. I spent quite a bit of time with him.' He hesitated, fiddling with the crumbs on his plate, then drastically changed the subject. 'Your coming here: it wouldn't, by any chance, have to do with missing stock, would it?'

The question caught her at a loss. She stared at him, shocked and troubled. 'What do you know about my missing stock?'

'As little as you do, I hope,' he assured her. 'We will have to get to the bottom of it.' His expression hardened; he raised his level gaze to hers. 'How long will you be staying?'

Laura began to feel upset. The questioning was no longer friendly and neighbourly but appeared to have a purpose. She sensed that under that easygoing attitude, unbelievable as it seemed, she had got in this man's way. 'Why do you want to know?'

He shrugged. 'Just curious, I suppose. I mean, it is over two years since ——'

'I plan to live here and run Polaris, just as Uncle Jonas did.'

'You *can't* be serious!'

'I have never been more serious in my life!'

'But you haven't thought! You can't have!' He leapt up to pace about the room.

Laura could see that he was really horrified. She was not to know that he saw her as too fragile to take on the huge job she was so obviously unprepared for; that in his mind's eye, he saw another beautiful, delicate woman slowly dying in this harsh environment.

'Yes, I have,' she told him, pushing back her chair to follow him. 'Oh, yes, I *have*.'

'Oh, for God's sake, woman, see reason!' He made a quick gesture. 'You only have to look around you to see that the place is practically falling down.'

'It was good enough for Uncle Jonas!'

'Jonas was a man who had lived all his life in the Outback. His preference was to sleep in a swag under a tree. His staff quarters were of a much higher standard than his own home. When he got those rebuilt, even *he* said that it wasn't worth it to do this one—that it only had to see him out.'

'It has a lot of memories for me. Besides, I can renovate it.'

'Renovate it!' he exploded. '*Renovate* it? The whole thing wants *bulldozing!*'

'There's nothing that a carpenter can't fix,' she shot back.

'Laura, listen to me.' Restored to his usual calm, he moved to take her hands. 'This is a harsh, dangerous land, even for those with experience of it. It gives no quarter and allows fewer mistakes. You came here for a few holidays as a youngster and went home with a rosy dream of it. You've never lived through a wet season where mould grows on the walls, and you can't go anywhere—completely isolated!—for weeks on end. There are no shops for hundreds of kilometres, so you live out of the station store for months. You've never seen a crocodile take a full-grown bullock—and they've got no diet preferences, let me tell you! All living things, including humans, are just food to them. And that's not the *half* of it! Whichever way you look at it, the Gulf isn't any place for a woman. Can't you see that?'

'No!' She snatched away her hands, tilting her chin. 'I *can't!* I used to help my father on the property at Mount Isa before we moved to Adelaide, so I do know something about running a station. All this talk about it being no place for a woman! Other women have managed to live here—and in the days when it really *was* isolated—without phones or fast transport. Do you think that I am any less of a woman than they were?'

'Those women had men to take care of them. They weren't fool enough to come here alone with no experience and think they could run the world. They had pretty hard lives, too—far harder than you might imagine. And, for some strange reason, you choose to deny that I have some say in this matter.' A gleam came into his eyes. 'As to how much of a woman you are, I have my suspicions. Unfortunately, I haven't the time just now to stay and test them out.'

'Oh!' gasped Laura. 'You *arrogant* ——'

He laughed, enraging her even more. 'Sorry, but you did ask for that … Look, have your holiday.' He spoke as if to a wilful, fractious child. 'I'll try to find you a mustering team to get you out of trouble. Then, I want you to think about selling out to me. I'll give you a good price, and you can buy yourself a nice little easy-to-run place in the softer country and invest the rest. You'll have a good income for life.'

Galled by his attitude, frustrated that he wouldn't even try to understand her, she was dismayed to feel a fury rising out of her control. *Well, here's one way he's like his father*, she thought in disgust. *He wants Polaris.*

There was another trait they had in common, but she wasn't prepared to admit, even to herself, that he, too, possessed magnetism in abundance. 'No. I won't sell you Polaris.' She drew herself up. 'It is my home, and I will be staying.'

He gave her a long, hard look, then shrugged. 'Suit yourself. I don't think it will be long before you change your mind. When you do, let me know.' This seeming carelessness was succeeded by something approaching exasperation as he took her by the shoulders. '*Think*, Laura! Do you really believe you can handle this place? Do you know how big it is? How long it takes to drive around the boundaries? Or even where the boundaries are? Half of them aren't even fenced!'

Laura shrugged out of his grip. 'I can find all that out from the maps in the office. I might not be a man, but I *can* read a map!'

'Infuriating, contrary, *wilful* …' Without any warning, he pulled her to him and kissed her, let fall his arms and stepped back, looking as stunned and bewildered as Laura felt.

Laura stared at him. Only the fact that she was pretty sure that he had shocked himself as much as he had her, choked her fury. 'Why did you do that?'

His recovery was instant. 'Love thy neighbour …' he murmured.

'Oh! *Outrageous!*' She almost stamped her foot. '*That* is the worst misquoting of the bible that I have ever heard! You ought to be ashamed of yourself!'

'Not necessarily.'

'What do you mean? You're not going to tell me that this is the normal way you behave when you meet your neighbours?'

'Not in the general way, no. But then,' he reflected, 'there are not many of my neighbours that I would *want* to kiss. Old Conroy, for instance?' He shook his head.

Laura almost dissolved into giggles, but instead said, 'That is not the way to show your appreciation, or whatever it may be, for your neighbour.'

'Oh, I don't know. I was just making a point. If I could get it into your silly little head that you are really not safe here, I think I will have done you a favour. Jonas was a pretty good mate to me, you know.'

Ooh, that is so arrogant! After he kissed me, too! Her breath whistled in indignation. 'Was he? Well to my mind that does *not* give you the right to take liberties with his great-niece!'

'Very true. On the contrary! I must keep it in mind.'

'Oh you…' Laura had to bite her lip. 'You dreadful man! When will you start to take me seriously?'

'When you start talking like a sensible woman.' He grinned. 'You look like a kitten with its fur rubbed the wrong way.'

'Don't push me too far,' she warned—her eyes beginning to smoulder. 'I have claws.'

'Thanks for the warning. I'll remember it.'

But she didn't think he cared, one way or the other. He looked as if he should be easygoing, tolerant, the kind of man you could twist around your little finger. But he wasn't.

'It's impossible to talk to you!' she informed him. 'It isn't just that we're not on the same page: we're not even in the same book!'

'Or even in the same genre,' he agreed. 'You seem to think that life up here is some kind of fairytale.'

Laura ground her teeth. 'Of course I don't! You … Oh! Fairytales are not all sweetness and light. They abound with ogres and witches.' She looked directly into his eyes. 'And *wolves*.'

To her chagrin, he laughed. 'Well … That's something you'd do well to remember, Little Red Riding Hood. And run away from the big bad Gulf as fast as you can.'

'So, I can take it from your attitude that you're not married, then?'

'Do you suppose that I would kiss other women if I were?'

Her lip curled. 'You wouldn't be the first!' She searched around in her mind for the worst insult she could think of in the most cutting tone she could deliver. 'But you're such an arrogant, overbearing brute that I can't imagine any …' Laura stopped because she saw that he had grown pale around the mouth. So, her random gibe had hit home! *I wonder what I said to make him look like that?*

'Your lurid imagination can be of no possible interest to me,' he snapped—his eyes granite chips. 'Listen, I've offered you my help, and you've thrown it in my face. I've also offered to buy you out and that offer still stands. Let me know when you change your mind.'

Laura watched him stride away with turmoil in her heart. Whatever his effect on her, or hers on him, the room seemed empty without his larger-than-life presence.

What have I done? she wondered, miserably. *I've only been here six hours, and I've quarrelled with everyone I've met—except Jackson.*

And now, here she was, a vast property on her hands, the cattle muster about to go into full swing and no-one to do it. And not only that—she'd completely alienated the one person who had it in his power to help her.

Chapter Four

Laura woke very early and, for a moment, did not know where she was. She sat up—her heart racing—then sank back on to her pillows as she remembered that she was in Uncle Jonas's living room. The room was very dark. Through the uncurtained window that only yesterday she had cleaned, she could see a thin red line on the horizon, growing broader by the minute.

Yawning, Laura shifted her feet from under Bess and slipped out of her sleeping bag to stand at the window. At twenty-six, she was tall and slender with an air of fragility that was deceptive. Her face was finely drawn and, in repose, held a grave, thoughtful expression. Her eyes large and thickly lashed of a green-gold hazel; finely modelled cheekbones; classically straight, small nose and softly curving lips all combined to make her hauntingly lovely. Rich chestnut-brown hair, curling softly about her forehead and ears, fell in thick waves to her shoulders. Often, she swept it up into a knot or chignon, which emphasised the delicate planes of her face and the shadowed eyes that told of suffering, past and present.

Breathing deeply and stretching, Laura turned away from the window and went to her luggage. A short while later, dressed in shirt and jeans and sipping a morning cup of coffee, she sat on the verandah steps and watched the sun come up: a molten, glowing orb that almost literally sprang above the earth before her eyes.

How peaceful it was here, away from the bustle of the city. Birds had begun to sing in the trees, and Oscar answered sleepily. Laura uncovered his cage and brought him out onto the verandah. Immediately, he began a long and involved conversation with his mirror friend (or enemy, as the whim took him), and when he tired of this, began to answer the calls of the wild birds.

With a jerk, all Laura's problems leapt to mind. Here she had been soaking up the peace and beauty of early morning without thinking of anything in particular. Now her mind rushed over all the events of yesterday: her encounter with the manager and the station hands; her puzzling and infuriating neighbour; his amused, not unkindly expression; his soft, slow voice; the warmth and understanding in his eyes; the hardness and power of him; his suddenly whitened face …

It had been a long time before Laura had slept last night, and when she did, his face and the feel of his arms and lips had haunted her dreams. She wondered what had happened to make him look as he had when she had fired that random shot at him. *How could I have been so stupid as to lose my temper with him when he was only trying to help?*

But was he? Her brow creased as she tried to remember. He

had put barriers in her way at every turn, had tried to talk her out of staying, had even become half-annoyed with her when he saw that she was determined. Almost as if she had got in the way of something. *That was what made me angry,* she thought. *That and his arrogant assumption that because I am a woman, I am some sort of lesser being, unable to cope with hardship.* Of the snatched kiss and his physical effect on her, she dare not think. But, even so, she regretted her hurtful words.

He'd told her that it wouldn't be long before she changed her mind. Laura's expression hardened, and she tilted her chin. *I'll show him whether or not a woman can handle living out here!* she vowed. He would learn, as had others, that when she set her mind to something, she would do it. That was why she had persevered with her marriage when most sensible people would have long ago given up. She frowned at her painful thoughts and hurriedly pushed them away. Somehow, Laura felt vaguely guilty, as though, perhaps, there were things she could have done to prevent what had happened. But that was ridiculous: how could she have prevented something that she had not been aware of until too late? *But you should have been aware,* said an unwelcome inner voice. *Why weren't you aware?*

Laura shrugged. There wasn't much point in going over all that again. She'd come here to gain a new dimension to her life. *Well, I've certainly done that!* she thought cynically and jumped up to go inside and make herself some breakfast—her mind now fully occupied with the problem of finding a new team of ringers. Uncle Jonas had a radio telephone installed in the office, but he refused to have one in the house, disturbing the peace. He did have a two-way radio set up in the homestead, but until such time as she could start the generator, it would remain silent.

Mid-morning found her in the office, making herself some coffee on the camp stove and beset by frustrations. Two hours on the radio phone had produced no ringers, only the repetition of 'I'm sorry, I can't help you' so that she was almost ready to scream. 'Advertise in the major country newspapers,' she was told. That would mean even more delay. *How long would it take? One week? Two?* Laura just didn't have that much time.

Some things, such as checking bores and fences, Laura could do herself, but if something went wrong with them, she knew she would be useless. And as far as trucking cattle out of the spear traps? Well, she supposed she could drive a truck. But nobody, not even men like Uncle Jonas, tried to load wild cattle on their own.

In theory, Laura knew what went on at mustering time—had even helped Uncle Jonas with some of the quieter cattle. It was quite simple, really: Where water could be controlled in difficult country, special yards were constructed with narrow openings that allowed the cattle to enter and obtain water, but when they turned to leave, the funnel-shaped entrance through which they had pushed their way became a bewildering array of poles. Or spears, as they were called. So, there they stayed until trucked away or taken to nearby yards for branding and drafting.

The country watered by rivers was mustered by a combination of helicopters and men in four-wheel drives or on horses, depending on the roughness of the terrain. Uncle Jonas had always used horses, as he believed that cattle moved more quietly with them and, thus, were more easily handled.

Laura sat sipping her coffee, deep in thought. She could do nothing without a team of ringers and a man to oversee them.

Quickly, she composed an advertisement to be placed in the newspapers and rang it through. That done, she collected some groceries from the store and went back to tackle another room in the house. She knew it had to be the kitchen: she couldn't last for much longer on tinned food heated on her gas burner.

On her way back to the homestead, Laura noticed a billowing dust cloud. Several vehicles were coming along the road. Unconsciously, she braced herself, her hand on the garden gate while she waited for the convoy to reach her. And the thickset, fair man driving the Land Rover in front was struck by the pathos of that slight, lonely figure.

The assorted four-wheel drives rolled to a halt behind the Land Rover, and the fair man stepped out of his vehicle and strode towards her. He was dressed, as most stockmen, in an open-necked shirt, denim jeans and elastic-sided boots.

'Good day, Miss Neumann.' He removed his hat. 'I'm John Riley. Heard you were looking for an overseer and a team of ringers.'

'How do you do?' Laura shook hands with him. 'May I ask where you heard that?'

'Rick Jamieson rang me up. Said you needed a team pretty quick. So, here we are.' His smile and gesture encompassed his men who were still sitting in their vehicles.

If Laura had been noticing, she would have seen that he was a good-looking man of about thirty, with the healthy, outdoor appearance that characterises so many men of the Outback. She would also have seen that he had an attractive smile and friendly, curiously perceptive brown eyes that often saw much more than they were meant to.

But Laura was grappling with a strange reaction to her neighbour: partly resentment at the thought of all the fruitless hours she had spent trying to find a team, when he, apparently with the minimum of effort, had seemed to conjure one out of nowhere; partly a sensation of half-remorse and half-joy that he had cared enough to help her after all that had been said; and, on top of all this, an insane, desperate wish that she could have sent these men back to him, so that he could see that she could indeed manage for herself.

Ashamed of her feelings, Laura knew that she had no choice but to swallow her pride. 'Yes, I do need help,' she admitted. 'I'm so glad you've come.'

'Good. Rick told me to bring some gas cylinders for your stove and water heater and that you'd probably need your generator fixed.'

A phrase popped into Laura's mind: something about heaping coals of fire. Why had Rick been so thoughtful? Was it genuine concern? Or was he motivated by a desire to show her that she needed his help? Whatever it was, thinking about it only served to make her tangled emotions even more confused. 'Yes, the gas has run out. I haven't looked at the generator yet, so I don't know whether it goes or not. Even if there is nothing wrong with it, I expect it may need a general clean up.'

'It's right: Mick will fix it. He's good with engines.' He turned and raised his voice. 'Hey, Mick! Come over here.'

A slight, dark man materialised at his side and was introduced to Laura as Mick Edson.

'Day, Miss Neumann.' He grinned shyly, hat in hand. 'I used to work for your great-uncle.'

'Oh, did you? Welcome back.' Laura returned his smile.

'Thanks. Yeah, worked for him for ten years, I did, before that jumped-up … Sorry.'

'No apology necessary.' Laura gestured. 'In fact, I might just agree with you.'

'You won't be on your own, there.' Her new overseer smiled. 'Mick, hop on over to the lighting shed and get that generator going, will you? And make sure those gas cylinders are hooked up properly for Miss Neumann before you come down.'

'Rightio, John. She'll be jake.' The man, in the same quicksilver fashion, went back to the Land Rover, took out a toolbox, spoke to two of the men and vanished into the lighting shed. The two he had spoken to hauled the gas cylinders over to the side of the house.

'Well, Miss Neumann,' said John Riley, 'we'll go down to the quarters now. It's a bit late to start today, so I'll just send a couple of men out to check the spear traps. I have maps of the area, and I know this station pretty well, so I think we'll get along all right. We'll start in the morning, eh?'

'Yes,' agreed Laura. 'That suits me. But, please, call me Laura.'

'Thank you, Laura.' He smiled. There was a short silence, then he said, awkwardly, 'If you need any help with anything up in the homestead, you know you only have to ask.' That was as far as he could go in offering to help her, even though something about her touched him. Perhaps it was her air of fragility, or his discerning eye had glimpsed something of her tragedy. Whatever it was, he felt an urge to protect her.

'That's very kind of you. But once the generator is working

and the gas is hooked up, I think everything will be right.'

'Rightio, then. We'll get along and settle in. See you tomorrow.'

Laura watched them drive down to the quarters with a sense of a great weight having been lifted from her shoulders. Now, at least, the muster would get under way.

That evening Laura enjoyed the luxury of a leisurely hot bath (instead of a hurried cold one) and a meal cooked to perfection on a now shining gas cooker. The only drawback to her evening was the presence of large numbers of insects that flocked to the lights. However, once the screens were fixed, this problem would become negligible. At least until the wet season, when no amount of screens sufficed to keep out the hordes of tiny invaders. The next thing to do, then, was to find a carpenter or handyman—no easy task out here.

The following morning found Laura deep in conversation with her overseer in her office as they planned the muster. They decided to do the closest paddocks first, which should, by the records, contain the most saleable cattle, and then move on to the outer mustering camps.

There was also the problem, John Riley told her, of an unfenced boundary between Juliana and Polaris. Rick, he said, must be consulted before they started, since it was usual for a team from each station to muster the area jointly and draft out the respective cattle that belonged to each station.

'All right.' Laura rose, ending the meeting. 'Start where we agreed, and I'll speak to Rick about mustering that particular area.'

Apart from the reference to her neighbour, which niggled her conscience, as well as arousing a host of carefully buried emotions, Laura was well pleased with her morning. She knew she should call Rick and thank him for sending the men, but she felt a strange reluctance to contact him again. *I know I'll have to talk to him about the muster, but I'll do it later,* she told herself.

Walking back to the house, Laura called a greeting to Jackson, who responded with a wave of his hand. As she approached it, she thought she heard the hum of a polisher or vacuum cleaner, and her nose very definitely detected a delicious cooking aroma. A presentiment came to her, and she began to hurry, so that Bess, at her heels, broke into a shambling trot to keep up. 'Who is there?' called Laura, rushing into the living room.

A greying curly head appeared around the kitchen door; dark, liquid eyes and shining white teeth in a black-velvet face. 'G'day, Little Missus. I bin got your dinner ready. And by cripes …' She eyed Laura up and down. 'You look as if you need it, too.'

'Oh, Lily!' Laura laughed with happiness. 'I am *so* pleased to see you. Where's Mary?'

'Oh, she bin polishin' floors. I tell her, get rid of dust and cobwebs on walls first, but she don' listen. Them floors was her pride and joy an' she dam' upset when she see them.' Lily shrugged tolerantly. 'Too bad she only gotta do them again after she do the walls.'

Laura laughed again. 'I had the same problem, myself, with the living room. But Lily! How did you get here?'

'Heard you was back, Missus. So, we hitched a lift with a fella from Doomadgee, going south. Then we walked from the front gate.'

'You walked all the way from the front gate? *No,* Lily!'

'Too right, Missus. Dam' long way, too. Took us a coupla days.'

Laura knew that there was a much shorter way to the homestead by foot or on horseback than going around the road. But it was still a long way. 'Oh, Lily! You should have sent me a message from Doomadgee. I would have come and picked you up.'

'No matter.' Lily dismissed the whole thing with a matter-of-fact wave of her hand. 'We here now. You get washed up, Missus, and I get dinner.'

'But …when did you find out I was here?'

'Oh …' Lily shrugged. 'Coupla days ago, in the mornin'. Got a lift straight away.'

How strange, thought Laura. *I was hardly here myself*. The appearance of Mary, bobbing her head and grinning with delight, disrupted her train of thought, and she greeted her and duly admired the shining floor of her bedroom.

When Laura protested that they should rest after their long walk and start tomorrow, they laughed heartily, and Mary found her voice enough to say, 'Aw cripes, Missus, walkin' don't hurt cha. We got plenty of time to rest tonight.'

With the return of Uncle Jonas's cook and housekeeper, Laura was able to turn her full attention to the running of the station. She knew how lucky she was to have two such jewels of efficiency to help her, reared in habits of cleanliness and domesticity by the nuns on a North Queensland mission. Sisters—adopted as a tiny baby and a young toddler after the death of their mother from typhoid—they had been given names reflecting purity, as was usual at the time, and trained specifically for the two positions they held so proudly. Lily, the elder and more outgoing, was the spokesperson; Mary, the shy one with an elusive sense of humour, followed her lead.

Laura knew something of the difficulties besetting the original inhabitants of the land, with successive government policies that were as short-sighted as they were inept. But these two women had seemed to embrace with alacrity the very different roles in life that were forced upon them by circumstance. *And,* thought Laura, *when they'd heard, by some mysterious means, that the evil manager had gone and I was back, they returned, full of enthusiasm, as ever. That tells something, surely?* They had the same simple, carefree outlook on life that they'd always had, that Laura had always found endearing and was suddenly beginning to envy.

After lunch Laura returned to the office to pore over the station books. She found them neat and meticulously kept, and try as she might, she could find no discrepancies in them. It would seem that the drop in production was indeed the result of poor seasons.

Giving up the officework in frustration, Laura went back to the homestead.

'You ready for smoko, Missus?'

'Yes, thank you, Lily.' Laura sat in the chair opposite the one Rick had lounged in when he had come the day before yesterday. She could still see him there, his light eyes full of lazy amusement, his lips just lifting at the corners, his hands … Laura tried to push the thought away, but his image persisted. 'Get out of my life!' she muttered under her breath, causing Lily to jump as she put down the coffee in front of her.

'What's that, Missus?'

'Oh, nothing, Lily. I was just talking to myself.' Laura took a deep breath. 'This coffee smells beautiful. Thank you.'

Peace reigned while Laura sipped her coffee. At the sound of Rick's voice reverberating around the silent room, she gulped, almost scalding her mouth. Finally realising that it was just the two-way radio and not some kind of sorcery, Laura seemed unable to make any kind of move until he said for the second time, 'Juliana calling Polaris. Are you on channel, Laura?'

'Answer it, Lily.' Laura jumped up from the table in an unreasoning panic. 'I don't want to talk to him just now. Tell him I'm not here.' She snatched up her coffee and went into her room.

'Where will I say you are, Missus?' Lily poked her head around the door. 'If he asks?'

'Oh … anywhere. Out on the station.' Laura waved a hand. 'Go on.'

Lily padded obediently to the radio. 'G'day, Boss. Lily here.'

'Hello, Lily. Nice to have you back again. Is your Missus there?'

'No, Boss. She decided to work outside today.'

'Did she? Was that before or after I called?'

Lily rolled her eyes. 'Dunno what time she went out, Boss,' she said with perfect truth. 'Didn't see her go.'

'Okay, Lily.' There was a definite ripple of amusement in his voice. 'Just tell her when she comes in that I'll be over to have a word with her sometime in the next few days. Oh, and by the way, I've sent a carpenter. He's on his way.'

'Rightio, Boss. Good thing.'

'I hope your Missus thinks so, Lily.' Giving what seemed to Laura to be a fiendish chuckle, he signed off.

'What's up with you, Little Missus?' Lily came to the bedroom door to look askance at Laura. 'Boss Jamieson bin a good neighbour to Boss Neumann. Talked on the radio every day. Always came over when Boss was sick. Bin very close, all the time. Even went with him on his last trip to hospital.'

Laura couldn't meet the frank gaze. 'I'm sorry, Lily. I don't know what came over me. I'll talk to him later. But not on the two-way.'

'Good-o, Missus.' Lily's face cleared. 'Phone's better. Two-way's nothing to worry about, though. Unless you want to say something you don't want everyone to hear?'

Laura left it at that, but she was smarting at her own stupidity, appalled by her lack of control. *I'm going straight to the office to phone him,* she thought. *I can't fall apart like this at the sound of his voice.* Like Lily, she began to wonder what was up with her. *I can't believe I'm behaving so ridiculously!*

Chapter Five

Laura dialled the number for Juliana hoping that either the housekeeper would answer or no-one would. But she was out of luck.

'Rick Jamieson,' said the well-remembered, deep, slow voice.

Laura hesitated, almost too long. 'Hello, Rick, it's Laura. I'm sorry I was out when you called on the radio earlier.'

'That's all right. Did the new mustering team find their way?'

'Yes, they did. I am ringing to thank you and say how much I appreciate you sending them. *And* the carpenter: desperately needed.' She took a deep breath as he made a deprecating murmur. 'John said I must ask you about a shared boundary?'

'Yes, we need to have a word about the muster. I'll come over in the morning. Eight o'clock, all right?' At her assent, he added, over a sudden babble of voices in the background, 'Look, someone's just arrived. I'll have to go. Talk to you tomorrow.'

Laura put the receiver in its cradle, feeling as if she'd been cut off. She knew it was ridiculous to suppose that he'd made an excuse because he didn't want to talk to her when she'd, herself, heard the sounds of arrival over the phone. She tried to shake it off. *I should be pleased*, she thought. *Knowing how little I wanted to talk to him.* Inspired by a surge of nervous energy, Laura spring-cleaned the office and checked the supplies in the store before going back to the house.

A little later, the promised carpenter turned up. He was a small, bird-like man with a jaunty air, greeting every project shown him with a cheerful 'No worries, Miss Neumann.'. Then, announcing his intention of starting on the broken windowpanes and screens, he went out to his battered utility to return directly with the necessary tools.

Presently, Laura heard him banging away, alternately whistling happily or making bantering, apologetic remarks to Mary, whose housekeeping he had interrupted. She was astonished to hear Mary reply, 'No matter, Mr Jenkins. It'd have to be better than them insects I sweep up of a morning.' Just as if she'd been back for weeks and not just hours.

Remembering that she had not cancelled her advertisement in the newspapers, Laura hurried back to the office to repair her omission. Then, overwhelmed by the enormity of what she'd taken on, she stayed sitting at the desk, lost in thought, and the time passed unheeded.

Laura did not sleep well that night, and she knew it was worry about her lack of control where her neighbour was concerned. *I must not allow myself to react to his attitude. In the morning, I will be cool and in charge of my emotions*, she vowed. *However angry he makes me, I must not show it. Even if he does laugh at me!* She was determined that there would not be any more childish lashing out with hurtful comments. For her own sake, as much as his.

§

A little before eight, Laura, dressed in her working uniform of shirt and jeans, sat at the table in the living room. She had tied her hair back with a scarf into a ponytail and, not satisfied with her pale cheeks and smudged eyes, had applied a little make-up. She heard Rick's Land Cruiser draw up but sat on at the table, holding her cup before her in both hands, almost as if it were a shield. Aware of her heart thudding heavily when he filled the doorway, Laura thought fleetingly how ruggedly handsome he was as he wished her good morning, and she invited him to come in and sit down.

'Coffee?' she asked, as he stood for a moment, holding his hat.

'Please.' He looked as if he wanted to say something, but Laura was before him.

She stood up and gripped the table, words rushing out: 'Look, Rick, I'm sorry I lost my temper with you the other day. I didn't mean what I said. I was just ——'

One stride and he stood beside her, his hand coming down to cover hers. 'No, don't apologise. I'm sorry I let you get under my skin when I knew you were just hitting out. But we'll cope.' He smiled. 'I know what to expect now.'

'Oh!' Laura snatched away her hand. Then she saw amused understanding in his eyes, knew that he was teasing and subsided. For a moment, she felt overpowered by his presence and, panicking, escaped to the kitchen to make his coffee, very nearly colliding with Lily, who had already made a fresh pot and was bringing it out on a tray with his cup.

'Watch out, Little Missus! You burn yourself! Mornin', Boss.'

'Good morning, Lily. Mmm, the coffee smells good. I see you haven't lost any of your old skills. When are you going to come and work for me at Juliana? Good wages. Good quarters. Mary can come, too. What do you say?' He gave a wink and a devastating little smile that both flustered and flattered her as she poured his coffee.

'Get away with you, Boss! We couldn't leave our Missus on her own. What you thinkin' of, eh?' Lily grinned broadly at his joke.

'You can bring your Missus, too, Lily. How about that?'

'Too right, Boss! Good idea. Mrs Mac might need a hand, eh?'

Rick's brow suddenly furrowed. 'You're right, there, she does. But get her to admit it …'

Lily, about to reply, caught sight of Laura's face, mumbled something about biscuits burning and shuffled away.

Humour lightened Rick's expression. He laughed, calling after her, 'Don't you burn them, Lily! I wouldn't want you to spoil your reputation.' Then he surveyed Laura over his coffee cup, eyes gleaming wickedly. 'The men going well, are they?' he enquired in a gentle voice.

Laura wasn't fooled by the tone. She knew that voice now: in fact, she was beginning to think of it as an iron hand in a velvet glove kind of voice. *Rubbing it in,* she thought. 'Oh, yes, very well,' she returned, as coolly as she could.

'Good. I think you will find they are a good team. Some of

them have worked here in the past. I'll have a word with John later, to see how he is getting on.'

Laura felt her hackles rise. There it was again: the not-so-subtle hint that they needed his hand on the rein, that she couldn't handle them herself.

Rick continued, 'While I'm here, we should discuss some of the business of the estate, and I must point out some boundaries to you. Jonas bought two or three blocks since you were here last, which you probably haven't seen.'

Laura took a deep breath. *I will not—No, I will not!—lose my temper!* 'Look, Rick …' She was careful to modulate her voice: 'It is very good of you to be concerned, but I don't need you to point out my boundaries or discuss my property. I do *not* need your help, and I can manage on my own. And it is really *not* your business.' She stopped, miserably aware that she sounded unbearably churlish, rather than coldly dignified as she had hoped. Also, she knew that it was a lie. Where would she be now without the help he had already given?

Their eyes clashed across the table: Two strong-willed people, each a prisoner of the forces that had shaped their separate lives, brought together by destiny and the unwritten law of the Outback—help thy neighbour. Laura noticed with a little thrill of dismay that the warm devilry had quite vanished from his, though he still smiled, rather grimly, she thought, as he withdrew a long, slender envelope from his shirt pocket and tapped it against his other hand.

'There's no doing anything with you, is there?' He shook his head. 'You're a stubborn woman. And I don't know why you keep on insisting that the Polaris estate is not my business, when you must know quite well that it is.' He handed her the envelope. 'Before we go any further with this conversation, you had better read this.'

She glanced at him in puzzlement, before turning her attention to the contents of the envelope: a folded letter and what appeared to be a legal document of some sort. Opening out the document and beginning to read, Laura received an unpleasant jolt. The document stated that a large holding named Miranda, situated so that it partly adjoined Polaris and Juliana and held in the names of Jonas Daniel Neumann and Richard James Jamieson, was now transferred to the tenure of the aforementioned Richard James Jamieson and Laura Jane Neumann.

The letter to Rick, unmistakably written in Uncle Jonas's copperplate hand, was a real facer. It requested Rick to keep an eye on the manager of Polaris because *I don't like the cut of his jib or his reputation but had no choice when Col got sick. You know the story, Rick: a case of the not-very-good best of a bad bunch.* It also informed him that Jonas had taken the liberty of making him an executor of his will and *a trustee until Laura arrives to take control of her inheritance.*

As to the matter we discussed before, I'll leave it up to Laura. She can sell out to you if she likes. But I'll bet my last quid she won't! I know a filly with spirit when I see one, and I reckon she's got what it takes to make a go of it. It's a pity I won't be around to see the outcome. All the same, my boy, it's a hard life for a woman, and I'll rest easy knowing you'll be around to look after my little Laurie. God bless her. God bless you both.

Laura bowed her head, surreptitiously wiping away tears.

Then she raised brilliant eyes to Rick's. She was very pale. This letter confirmed the closeness Rick had claimed with the old man and raised some complications that Laura would need time to think about, not the least of which was that Rick was so set against her doing what her great-uncle had made clear that he wished. There was also a more subtle, perhaps even sinister aspect to all this that her confused mind was unable to grasp.

'But … but …' Laura's voice failed. She gestured helplessly towards the papers.

Rick's glance held hers. He said in his velvet voice: 'Now, just a minute, Laura. Are you going to tell me that you didn't know anything at all about this?'

Laura nodded, still too stunned to speak.

'Why the hell not? Didn't the solicitors send you all the information?'

'I suppose so. I didn't … I didn't …' Her voice failed once more. She couldn't tell him that she had been just too devastated to care. And the knowledge that he was her partner, at least in some degree, shocked her beyond words.

He got up and strode around the room, his lithe frame eloquent with restless energy and controlled anger. 'I don't believe this!' Exasperation was evident in the quiet tones. 'Do you mean to say that you didn't read the letters the solicitors sent you?'

'N-no. No, I didn't.'

'Not one?' He raised incredulous eyebrows.

'No.' Laura felt incredibly stupid.

He relaxed and sat down again to drop his head into his

hands. 'Oh, Laura, *Laura* … What am I going to do with you? You need a keeper.' He raised his head to regard her quizzically. 'Don't you know better than to sign an unread document? Anyone could have bled you dry! And you wouldn't have known a thing about it until the bank account was empty!'

Since this was more or less what had happened, Laura didn't have any answers for him and sat gazing miserably into her half-empty cup, unable to meet his eyes. *I feel such a fool,* she thought. *I can't bear it if he is laughing at me. And if he's angry, as he has every right to be, what can I say?*

But there was no sign of either laughter or anger in his voice when he rose and scooped up his hat. 'This has been a shock to you; I can see that. I'll leave you now to think it over and get used to the idea. Give me a call when you're ready to discuss it.' He cast her a worried glance, looked as if he would say more, but when she didn't respond, raised his voice as he walked out. 'Thanks for the coffee, Lily. Take care of your Missus, won't you?'

'Yeah, Boss. No trouble.'

Five minutes later, he was back, stepping onto the verandah, a blue-speckled bundle cradled in his arms.

Still traumatised from the revelations of their last encounter, Laura stared for long seconds, unable to take in the significance of what she saw. 'Oh, *Bess!*' She rose shakily to her feet. 'What happened?' She looked at him in accusation. 'You've run over her!'

'No, no,' he soothed. 'Of course I haven't run over her. I didn't even get as far as my vehicle. I found her in the garden. Now, get me a blanket or something to lay her on, will you?'

Laura returned with a quilt she folded on the sofa. 'Is she still alive?'

'Yes, but I don't know for how much longer.' He lay the dog down carefully and examined her eyes.

'I can't believe it. She was okay early this morning when I let her out. Perhaps it's her age?'

Rick shook his head. 'No. See the pinpoint pupils and the way she's breathing? It's a poison of some sort.'

'Poison?' Laura was horrified. 'But, who …?'

'It may have been accidental. In fact, I feel certain of it. Get Lily, will you?'

Lily arrived, visibly distressed and twisting her hands in her apron.

'Has anybody been using any poison around here, Lily? For mice? Or anything like that?'

'Not mouse bait, Boss. But Mr Jenkins, he told me about white powder to poison ants. Meat ants bin terrible bad lately. Then I remember some of that powder in the shed. So, I sprinkle it on a bit of mince, like Mr Jenkins told me and put it on the ants' nest.'

'Have you still got some of the powder?'

'Yeah, Boss. I jus' get it.' Lily returned with an unlabelled bottle, and Rick took it and sniffed the contents.

'Neguvon!' He turned to Laura. 'Quickly, in your first-aid cabinet: atropine tablets! Bring them with some water. We might save her, yet.'

Laura rushed to find the tablets, and Lily went for the water, while Rick carried the old dog onto the verandah. They watched anxiously as he coaxed Bess to swallow two of the tablets with water and laid her head back on the quilt. He knelt there, stroking her—an expression on his face that brought a lump to Laura's throat.

As if aware of eyes upon him, Rick suddenly looked up. 'You'd better get rid of all unlabelled bottles in the sheds, Laura. Storing old poisons that way can be a dangerous habit. And you, Lily, next time you poison ants, you get an empty milk tin, punch holes in it big enough for ants to walk through, put your poisoned meat in there and stamp on the lid to shut it. That way, you'll be sure you only poison the ants.'

'Yeah, Boss. Sorry, Missus.'

'Don't worry, Lily. You weren't to know. Oh, look! She's coming round.'

All eyes turned to Bess, who sat up, swaying groggily.

'Gently, girl.' Rick moved to steady her, and the tip of her tail waved slightly in acknowledgement. In a while, she settled down and appeared to be sleeping peacefully.

'I think she's over the worst of it. Quiet and rest is what she needs now.' Rick stood up, flexing broad shoulders.

'Thank you.' Laura's voice was low. She knew that Bess would have died if Rick had not been here. And she never would have thought of Lily's ant bait, nor known what to do if she had.

Rick surveyed her keenly. 'What are you going to do for the rest of today?'

'I'll have to stay here and keep an eye on Bess, don't you think?'

'I think you should come with me to look at our boundaries.

There's nothing more anyone can do for Bess. We just have to wait for the atropine to take full effect. I think you're better off out of the house, rather than moping about here worrying about her. I'll tell Lily to get Jenky to take a look at her when he comes. He's as good as a vet when it comes to dogs. Come on.'

Regarding him warily, Laura could detect nothing in his sun-browned face other than kindness and understanding. Then, knowing he was right, she agreed. As he said, a morning moping around worrying about Bess would achieve nothing. After all, as she was beginning to acknowledge to herself, there existed no-one more able than Rick to take her mind off things. Whether or not it would be an improvement was another matter.

Chapter Six

'Missus! Missus! You bin forgot your tucker!' Lily ran out to the gate behind them, holding out a basket and a vacuum flask as they walked towards Rick's Land Cruiser. There had already been a short altercation between them as to whose vehicle they would take.

'Oh, how silly of me!' Laura turned at the same time as Rick to take the basket from her. Their hands collided and Laura drew hers back as if she had been stung. The sensation that leapt through her nerves at his touch was rapier-sharp and left her tingling. Badly shaken, she took the vacuum flask and followed him to the vehicle.

If Rick noticed her reaction, he gave no sign, merely holding open the passenger door with his free hand before depositing the basket in the back and striding around to the driver's side to get in and move off. 'I'll take you to the south-eastern boundary of Polaris first. Following that northwards will eventually bring us to the holding we share.'

So unsettled was Laura that she didn't even react to this typically masterful statement but replied meekly enough, 'If we start with the south-eastern boundary, we can go through the stud paddocks first. I've been longing to see Uncle Jonas's lovely thoroughbred mares and foals and the stud Brahmans. I haven't been out there yet.'

'Good-o. I haven't been out that way myself for quite a while, since it is one boundary that doesn't join Juliana.'

The Land Cruiser gathered speed, bouncing over the ruts. Laura glanced at Rick's profile, then at his tanned, capable hands, effortlessly controlling the plunging vehicle.

'Hmm, a bit rough along here. When we've finished the muster, I'll have to get Mick to overhaul the grader and have your roads reformed.'

For a moment, Laura said nothing. She was determined not to argue with him today, after all he'd done for Bess—even if it wasn't his business to repair her roads. But she couldn't resist a comment with a hint of challenge: 'I wonder that you can find the time to show me around the boundaries when you must be in the middle of your own muster?'

He frowned a little at the road ahead—his profile proud and fierce. 'I have very good men that don't need constant supervision. In any case …' He glanced at her. 'I would have made the time.'

'Yes, of course. I'm sorry …' Laura was effectively reduced to an embarrassed and ruffled silence.

How he always seems to be able to put me in the wrong! she thought. *Oh, why can't I accept his help with the same dignity and generosity with which it is apparently offered?* And then she answered herself: *Because he's high-handed and overbearing and managing, that's why! And he doesn't want me here, that's why!*

As time passed, she forgot her resentment, since it was becoming increasingly obvious that the stud paddocks were devoid of their aristocratic inhabitants. Vainly, Laura searched for any signs of the valuable stock, but as they came to each watering point, she saw that the only animals to have drunk there lately had been wildlife such as kangaroos and birds.

'Rick? Where are the studs? You can see that no cattle or horses have been at these waters.'

Rick shrugged his shoulders, started to speak and then fell silent.

Laura gazed at him, wide-eyed. She'd sustained one shock after another today. 'Uncle Jonas's beautiful blood mares, the Star Kingdom stallion, where can they be?' She was really upset now. They were all valuable horses, but more important to Laura, was the fact that Uncle Jonas had been extremely proud of them and would never have sold them.

Rick cleared his throat, met her anxious eyes briefly and turned his attention back to the road. 'It may be that the stock were moved to other paddocks during the dry spell we had last year and not returned. I wouldn't panic just yet. Wait until we finish the muster. Then you'll know for sure whether they are here or not.'

Laura recognised the sense of this, but the feeling of disquiet—of loss—did not leave her. Her fears were not allayed by finding that at a point just beyond the turn onto the boundary, the new six-wire fence was broken.

Rick made a small sound of disgust as they drew up alongside the opening surrounded by tangled ends of wire. He jumped out and rummaged in the toolbox mounted on the back of the four-wheel drive. Climbing out more slowly, Laura saw that he held a pair of pliers, a small roll of wire, and an assortment of steel and chain that she recognised from her past as a set of wire strainers.

Deftly, he set to work unravelling the tangles and joining the ends of the wires with pieces from the roll he had brought with him. In a remarkably short time, the fence stood, shining and erect, and Rick gathered his tools, throwing them back in the toolbox. 'That should do it.' He smiled at Laura. 'Though, it is a bit like locking the gate after the horse has bolted—literally. This may be your answer to the missing stock. You'll have to write to old Conroy, since he won't have a phone or radio on the place, and ask him to let you know if the studs are over there. He might be an eccentric old hermit, but he's an honest one. He will tell you if they are.'

Laura agreed, but her anxiety reasserted itself. *There is something going on here*, her sixth sense told her. What it was, she did not know, but she was reasonably certain that the fence had been deliberately cut, rather than stressed to breaking point. Her lip curled. She knew a cut fence when she saw one, even if her neighbour did not. Watching him covertly, she decided that he did know and, for some reason, was not going to say so to her. If only she could think clearly, but it was impossible in the light of this discovery.

Everyone had heard of cattleduffers. They were not new to the Gulf. Laura knew that a special Stock Squad had been formed as part of the Queensland Police Force to combat this very thing. And poddy-dodging was almost the expected norm between some neighbours where there were no dividing fences, since whoever put their brand on cleanskin calves were the legal owners, but most did it in a fair way, even if ownership was arbitrary. But neighbours normally did not cut fences or steal stud horses and cattle, even if they might accidentally brand a stray calf that came into their herd. Laura did not believe that she would find her missing stock on Conroy's, though she must certainly write to him and explain her problem.

They drove on in silence. Laura, biting her lower lip, eyes unfocused, did not even notice that the new section of fence had given way to a much older one, while Rick was apparently concentrating on negotiating the rough track. Neither of them appeared to be inclined for conversation.

Abruptly, Rick braked, uttering an oath that startled Laura out of her reverie, making her clutch at the dash handle to avoid being thrown forward. 'What the hell?' he growled. Then, 'Are you all right?'

'Yes.' Laura stared at the road in front of her in astonishment.

They had just come over a slight rise, and on the ground ahead lay a tangled mass of wire and posts. Where the fence should have been, there was nothing. They sat in a well of silence while the dust whirled and settled in a veil over the dry grass.

'We'll have to send someone out to repair this,' said Rick at last. 'Otherwise, we'll never get to Miranda today. Besides,' he added with a wry twist, 'it is going to take more than a pair of pliers and a set of wire strainers for this job.'

They got out and walked around the pile of wire and posts that seemed, to Laura's stunned gaze, to have been uprooted and dragged onto the road. 'Rick, what has been happening here?' Her voice trembled with distress. 'What could have done this to the fence? And this is the last of the fattening paddocks and no stock that I can see!' She took a deep breath and waited for his reply, which seemed aeons in coming.

'I don't know, Laura. A stampede, maybe …? I just don't know. This was an old fence, but …'

She watched his profile, wondering again why it seemed so familiar, waiting for him to say more, but he didn't. He simply cast one more cursory glance over the ruined remains and turned back to the vehicle. Some time later, he emerged from his frowning silence to briefly indicate the beginning of the shared property, and Laura keenly studied the lay of the land as they entered this, to her, new territory.

At midday, Rick called a halt on the shady bank of a dry creek. Laura was glad to alight from the Land Cruiser and enjoy the tall trees and the scented air, even though she'd had no say in the matter. Anthills stood like ghostly sentinels here and there through the open woodland, reminding her of how she had feared them as a child when camping out at night. She smiled reminiscently at her younger self and strolled back to where Rick, having scorned Lily's flask, had made a small fire in the rocky bed of the creek and was boiling a billy of water he had taken from a large container he carried at all times on his vehicle.

Since this ritual demanded great concentration, Laura had ample time to study him while he threw tea-leaves into the boiling water, left it on the coals for just the right amount of time, removed the billy from the heat with a stick and tapped the side to settle the tea-leaves before pouring it into two mugs.

Big, kind, generous with his time, he seemed content with his lot, unfazed by calamity, embracing the challenges of everyday life in this wild land with tolerance and humour. And yet, there were undercurrents. He'd made it plain that he didn't want her here. But if she were a thorn in his side, there was no sign of it today. *Does he just want Polaris?* she wondered. *Or is it something more? And if he does want Polaris and wants me out of here: why?* Though she scrutinised his downcast features in the most minute detail, she was no nearer to fathoming either the answers to her questions or his complex attitude towards her when he looked up and caught her watching him.

At the dawn of his slow smile, Laura flushed and turned away, annoyed with herself. 'I'll unpack the basket.'

Rick did not immediately reply but carried the two mugs over, handing one to Laura before seating himself beside her with his back against a tree. It was his turn to study her, which he did unashamedly. 'This brings back memories for you, doesn't it?'

'It does, indeed.' She sighed. 'But it was all a long time ago.' *And Uncle Jonas was here then.* She didn't say it. She didn't have to.

'You know, Jonas and I used to do this often. He was always a great one for his billy tea.'

'I know.' Laura made a discovery. 'You *were* really close to him, weren't you?'

For a moment, he said nothing. Then, 'Yes, he and I were mates, as I told you. We had many a yarn over our billy out in the bush. He was a good neighbour. The best.'

Listening to his quiet words and the gentle tones of his voice, Laura realised that there had been a bond between this man and his old neighbour that had run too deep for words. She understood that Rick, too, already grieving his father, had grieved the loss of her great-uncle, and her resentment towards him softened and waned so that they were just two people united in their feelings for the man who, in his journey through life, had given them both much comfort and wisdom, and in his passing, had thrown them together.

Thus, it was that his next words did not provoke her to the anger that they might have done at any other time. 'Laura, forgive me if I am prying, but I thought Jonas told me—oh, about five-or-six years ago, now—that you were married?'

'Yes,' she agreed in a tight little voice. 'I was married.'

'But you're not now?'

'No, I'm not now.' The long, thick lashes veiled her eyes. *Tell him you're a widow, for God's sake!* said her inner voice, but she couldn't find the words.

'You had a hard time, didn't you?' The velvet tone was back in his voice.

'Rick, I *can't* …' Laura made a move to jump up, but he was quicker, grasping her hand to hold her beside him.

'No, don't run away. I won't ask any more questions. I'm sorry, okay? I didn't realise the extent of your hurt. Will you forget I said it and forgive me?'

Laura nodded, unable to speak, but when she tried to draw her hand away, he held on to it.

'Laura,' he spoke her name softly, his tone persuasive, 'I know we started off on the wrong foot, but do you think that we can forget our disagreements and start again? You see, despite everything, we have to be not only neighbours but business partners, and really, I am only carrying out the last wishes of my old friend Jonas where you are concerned.'

Laura found her voice: 'And yet, despite his wish that I live here, you are against it.' Her eyes challenged. 'How is that carrying out his wishes?'

'If he saw how fragile you look … and you're too thin. I can't see how…'

She made a moue. 'I hope everyone doesn't see what you do. I hope I don't look too haggard.'

'I didn't say you look haggard. You're a beautiful woman, Laura. You don't need me to tell you that.' He didn't seem to notice the slight movement she made to free her hand. 'But you look as if a little wind would carry you away. That's why I can't bear to see you struggling here, alone.'

Laura was touched by the sincerity in his voice. Tears threatened, and search as she might, she could find nothing to say. Rick caring—obviously moved by what he saw as her vulnerability—was far more dangerous to her emotions than when he was trying to reason with her. And suddenly a spark of humour came to the rescue, lightening the moment. 'But I won't be alone, will I?' A little mischievous smile played around her lips. 'Thanks to Uncle Jonas, I'll have a bossy, managing neighbour to keep an eye on me. And to fight with, just to keep things interesting. And just so you know: *whatever* happens, I intend to stay here.'

He laughed. 'I see you have it all worked out. We'd better finish our lunch and get on with it. We still have a long way to go.'

Laura sat silently as they drove along, a little part of her wishing she had not left her old dog. She wondered how she would stand it if she found that Bess was dead when she got back.

Rick slanted a glance at her, arriving at her disquiet with uncanny precision. 'Worrying about your dog? There's no need.'

Laura smiled in acknowledgement. 'I was just wondering if she's okay.'

'I'm sure she'll greet us happily when we get back.'

'I hope you're right.'

'I'm always right.' Rick laughed. 'No, not always, but I am in this instance.' He gave her a provocative glance. 'Would you like to bet Polaris on it?'

'Very funny.'

'I'm not joking.'

'Well, in that case, I'll bow to your better judgement and say no.'

'Very wise.' He braked to a smooth halt in a wide belt of grassland. 'I wanted to show you this. Part of the property can be a little difficult to muster, but Jonas and I decided it was worth it for the good land.'

Laura looked around. Some of the country ran back into rocky scrubland, which had to be mustered by helicopter. Much of it was good grassland, and she was well pleased with it.

'Why did you go into this as partners?' she asked, genuinely wondering, since Uncle Jonas could easily have managed to buy it on his own.

'Well … There were several reasons: I think that Jonas felt that, at his age, he had enough on his plate without it, and at the time, I couldn't handle it alone, having just bought two fattening blocks down south. Neither of us wanted a third party in such a vital spot between our two boundaries since it was unfenced.' He glanced at her to see if she understood.

She did. 'I see. So, you bought it between you. Then, you do think that there could be stock stealing going on?'

'Let us just say that we wanted to make sure there would be less temptation by controlling the land between us. It worked very well with two full teams to muster it. There were no disagreements then, and I don't see why there should be now, do you?' His little wry smile softened the words.

Laura wasn't going to give in that easily. She thought, *Well that all depends on you, my dear neighbour, and remains to be seen.* But she said, 'Hopefully not.'

Her mournful tone made him laugh as he started the Land Cruiser. 'Come on, let's get you home, while we're still getting on!'

The day was far advanced when they arrived back at the homestead, and Laura was thrilled to see Bess barking happily at the gate with her tail wagging furiously.

'What did I tell you?' Rick glanced at her—eyes gleaming.

'I can't tell you how glad I am that you were right.' Her cheeky smile hovered as she opened the door. 'Even if it goes against the grain with me to say it.'

He gave a shout of laughter.

A note of constraint crept into her voice. 'Are you coming in?'

He regarded her speculatively, eyes narrowing a little, challenging her in a way that made her wish that she had phrased her question differently. 'No, I'm sorry. I can't. I must have a word with John Riley on my way home. I'll arrange for him to have your fence repaired as soon as possible.'

Laura was about to retort that she was quite capable of organising the repair of her own fences when he forestalled her. 'By the way, as soon as the boys come in from the first muster, we always hold our round-up. It will be in about three weeks' time.'

'Round-up?'

'Yes, we have a weekend of horse sports: campdrafting, team roping, milk a wild cow, catch and ride a wild horse, that sort of thing. Just a bit of fun where we let down our hair, so to speak. We also have evening entertainment: a band imported at great expense from Townsville, and this time our ball is going to be rather special, as we'll celebrate my cousin's twenty-first birthday. We are still a little old-fashioned out here,' he added with a deprecating grin.

That's an understatement! she thought, watching him under her lashes.

'You'll come, of course. It will be a good opportunity for you to meet everyone. All the Gulf comes.'

'Thank you.' She knew she could not snub him by refusing his invitation, even if it was issued more like a command. *But it would have been nice to have been asked, not told,* she thought.

'Most people arrive on Thursday afternoon and set up camp on a special ground we have prepared for them down near the racetrack. And no-one even thinks about leaving until Monday or Tuesday. It's a *big* weekend.'

'Camping? I don't think …' Laura's brow cleared. 'Oh, yes, I know, I can sleep in the back of my Land Cruiser in my sleeping bag, and I have my little gas burner and light.'

'Who said anything about you camping out? You'll be an honoured guest in my house.'

'Oh, no, don't worry. I'll enjoy camping.'

'You will stay at the homestead.'

'I'd rather not. Thanks all the same.'

'Why not?' He raised black winged brows. 'I think most people would be very surprised if I allowed my neighbour and close relative of one of my dearest friends to rough it alone, sleeping in her car, when I have plenty of spare rooms, don't you?'

'Not if the person liked camping! Anyway, it has nothing to do with others.'

'No, but it's important to me that you stay as my guest. Let us just say it's out of respect for Jonas's wishes.'

'Oh, no! You're not going to blackmail me like that!'

He went on as if she hadn't spoken. 'Besides, Mrs Mac told me that on no account was I to allow you to camp. She said to tell you she has your room all ready and is looking forward to renewing her acquaintance with you.'

Laura gave in. 'I … Oh, thank you. What day should I come?'

'Today, if you like.'

'No, seriously.'

'I am serious. It would be by far the best idea. Surely, you can see that? You can keep in touch with John from there. It will be much more comfortable than this old shack.'

'You needn't disparage my house, if you don't mind!' retorted Laura, catching the gleam in his eye. 'And I'm not going to rise to your bait. So, you can just go home.'

'Stubborn, silly woman,' he countered, eyes full of devilment. He made the words sound like a caress.

He's winding me up, thought Laura. *I'll teach him!* 'Managing, overbearing *chauvinist!*' she shot back, enunciating each word with relish.

'Right,' he acknowledged with a grin. 'Well, now we know where we stand, I'll get on home.' He gave her a little salute. 'I'll be in touch.'

Laura watched him drive away, prey to mixed emotions. *I don't know whether I want to laugh or cry*, she thought, hugging Bess. *Where are we headed with all this trading of insults?*

Oscar woke up from his afternoon nap, flapped his wings and yelled, 'Bloody hell!' Laura collapsed into laughter and went inside, still laughing, Bess at her heels. Some time later, glancing out of the window, she saw that Rick had met her overseer on the road. They were both leaning on the side of one of the vehicles and appeared to be deep in conversation. They seemed to stay there for quite some time; a fact that Laura found troubling, though she didn't know why it should worry her.

This brought to mind her problems that had manifested themselves earlier in the day. Who had cut her fences? Where were the horses and cattle that Uncle Jonas had valued so highly? They represented not only a substantial asset but also much of his life's work. And perhaps more importantly, why had Rick dismissed so lightly their disappearance and the unbelievable state of her fences? As a trustee, he must surely have been aware of the rapid decline in the station profits, mustn't he?

These were questions that had not entered her mind when she

had been with him, but now that she was alone, had begun to assume significant proportions. They were also questions to which, somehow, she alone must find the answers, since Rick had not shown any desire to help her in her quest. It may even be that he would try to hinder her. And this she must bear in mind, no matter what effect he had on her.

§

Over the next few days, most of Laura's energy was taken up with the running of the station, and there was little time for introspection. Every morning, she consulted with her overseer and received a progress report on the muster. So far it had not been good, with few stock coming into the spear traps. He had sent men to ride and repair the boundaries and disclosed that many internal fences had been found in a similar condition.

Up until now, there had been no sightings of the missing horses or the stud Brahmans. While the men were emptying the traps, building others and drafting the cattle, Laura searched daily for the studs but was forced to conclude that they had been long gone. Not so much as a hoofprint showed in the dust of the cattle pads to and from water. The only horses left on the whole place, it seemed, were the work geldings in the horse paddock.

At dusk, Laura returned from these fruitless expeditions tired and dispirited, to find Lily hovering anxiously over the gas cooker and Mary removing the sawdust and debris of the day's carpentry.

§

The following week, Laura decided to explore some of the northern boundary that joined Juliana. This made her think of her annoying neighbour, but since she was fairly certain he was mustering elsewhere, she forgot all about him as she approached the silent majesty of the river: her north boundary. Enchanted, she braked and stepped out of the ute, following a cattle pad that wound through the ti-tree to where the river itself gleamed through the brush.

Laura heard a low moan and, turning upriver to follow the sound, saw a small calf snagged in some half-submerged branches of a fallen tree. The calf cried again with such a pathetic expression in its big, sad eyes that, without further thought, she plunged into the shallows and waded towards it. 'Oh, you poor little thing! Don't worry, I'll soon have you free.'

A short way from the calf, Laura felt a prickle of fear so strong that she stopped to look behind her, but the river was empty, except for a gnarled, floating log. There was nothing to disturb the silence. Turning back to the calf, she suddenly stiffened in terror. *The log! There's something weird about that log!* She looked again. It was floating towards her, not away, as it should be if it were going downstream. And then, she was hit by a paralysing truth. *It's not a log. It's a crocodile!*

Crocodiles: in Laura's experience, they had never come this far up the river, and she hadn't even given them a thought. The plight of the calf had driven everything else from her mind. Mentally, she calculated the distance to the bank and the fast-approaching crocodile. She knew she had no hope of reaching it in time. In a horror of fascination, she watched the huge reptile glide closer: saw its blank, unwinking eye; watched it begin to roll, revealing rows of jagged teeth; tried unavailingly to galvanise paralysed limbs into superhuman action.

'Don't move!' The words cracked as sharply as the rifle shot that immediately followed. The crocodile turned its white belly skyward and floated away from her, down the river. Laura looked around to see Rick seated on a horse, just lowering his rifle. But for that movement, they could have been statues, so rock-still did his horse stand. In one lithe move, he holstered the rifle and swung down from the saddle in time to lift Laura out of the water and set her on her feet on the bank in front of him.

'My God, woman! You're a piece of work, aren't you?' His face, white under its tan, was set in forbidding lines. 'Whatever possessed you to do such a stupid thing? Don't you know better than to go into the river like that?'

Laura met his eyes, too shaken to answer. He had spoken in his usual quiet tone, but there was no sign of his lazy twinkle. His gaze held anger and something else—something she could not define. *At least, he's not laughing at me,* she thought, but it gave her no comfort. On the contrary. She shivered.

'My God!' he said again, under his breath. 'Didn't I say you need a keeper? Why did you do it?' He gripped her shoulders and shook her. '*Why?*'

'The … the calf.' She pointed to a spot hidden from his sight by a tree branch.

'Oh, blast the calf!' He went back to get his rifle out of the saddle holster, cocked it and thrust it into her hands. 'Here, it's loaded. All you have to do is point it and pull the trigger. If you see another croc, shoot it.' Then, wading into the river, he freed the little creature and carried it to the bank.

Laura was vaguely aware of several things simultaneously, as if from a great distance: the calf galloping up the cattle pad, bellowing for its mother; Rick's eyes on hers as he held out his hands for the rifle; the hiss and plop of the river as it settled down again after the unexpected activity; her feet squelching in her sodden boots and, above all, that she owed her life to this man.

'Hey! Don't point that thing at me,' Rick chided her gently. He took the rifle, made it safe and re-holstered it. 'Come on, snap out of it, Laura. It's over now.'

'Wh-what are you doing here?' *Thank him, you idiot!* But she couldn't.

'I've got cattle in the yards up past the ford.'

'My cattle?'

'Yes, your cattle. There's a cow creating because she can't find her calf, so I came back this way to see if we'd left it behind somewhere.' He looked at her closely. 'And no, I won't be putting my brand on them. Don't you talk to your overseer?'

Laura flushed. 'Yes, I remember now. He said you would help if you finished your own muster in time. But I thought you would be down south with him.'

'It was easier for me to do this end, since I wasn't all that far away. *You* might not know what I'm doing here, but you don't have to tell me what *you're* doing.'

'No. And I'm not going to.' Laura was shaken with unaccountable fury. 'It's *my* affair, not yours ——' She broke off, realising that she was speaking with shocking ingratitude. *And I still haven't thanked him!*

'Look, I know you're worried about your missing stock, but you're not going to find them here. The best thing you can do is go home and wait until we've finished your muster. You've already ——'

Laura's skin prickled. She stared at him. 'Already what?'

'Nothing that matters right now. If you're feeling okay to drive, go home.' He shook his head and, it seemed to Laura, deliberately changed the subject. 'I wonder what Jonas would have said to *this?*'

'Oh, that's so *unfair!* I've never heard of crocodiles this far south.'

'Haven't you? But as you've just seen, they're here. Back when you used to visit, they were hunted, some believe almost to the point of extinction. But now they're protected, they're everywhere. One has even been sighted at the Five Ways. And every year it gets worse. Didn't I warn you on your first day?' He looked around. 'Where's your vehicle?'

'Over there. But your horse …'

'He's been taught to ground tie. He'll stand there until I come to get him.' He moved across to scoop up the reins. 'Come on, I'll see you into your ute. Then I must follow up the calf, make sure he gets back with his mother.'

But when they got to the vehicle, Rick had another lecture to deliver. 'Haven't you got a radio in that thing?' He took her by the shoulders. 'Well, *get* one. Understand?' He raised his eyes skywards. 'If you don't, the next thing we'll have is you broken down somewhere and no-one knowing where to look for you. Haven't I got enough on my plate without having to worry about what fool thing you're going to do next?' He turned away, drew the reins over his horse's ears and gathered them on his neck.

Another burst of uncontrollable fury took possession of Laura. 'Bossy, *unbearable* … I wish you hadn't come!' She jumped in the ute and slammed the door.

Rick had a hand on the pommel of his saddle, but he turned back at that. 'Have you got a death wish?'

'*No!* I ——'

'Because *if* I hadn't, you'd be dead by now.' The words were soft and deliberate.

His light eyes held Laura's. In them, she read mockery, anger and, incredibly, hurt. Shaken as she had never been before, she watched him mount his horse and canter away.

Why do I react to him like that? she wondered. *And why couldn't I thank him for saving my life? Really, it was the least I could have done. Could he be right? Do I have a death wish?*

She put her head down on the steering wheel and wept bitter tears. It was a long time before she felt up to starting the ute to drive home.

Chapter Seven

When Laura arrived back at the homestead, Lily greeted her with disproportionate relief. 'That old Jackson!' She shook her woolly curls.

'Jackson? What's he done?'

'Sits there all day, lookin' in his fire.'

'Do you think he does it for comfort, Lily? Surely, he can't be cold?'

'Nar, Missus, not cold. Reckons he sees things in the fire.' Lily's face grew indignant. 'He said you were in danger today. Had me scared outta me boots! Then, just when I was gunna call Boss Jamieson, he said not to worry, that you was all right.'

'It's true, Lily. If it wasn't for Rick being there to shoot it, I would have been taken by a crocodile.'

'By cripes! He was right, then.' Lily opened her eyes in wonder. 'Croc's getting dam' bad, Missus. People gettin' taken where they never used to. You was lucky Boss Jamieson came along.'

'I know.' Laura gave a faint sigh. 'It takes a bit of getting used to.'

Lily looked at her in silence.

'The shock, I mean.'

'Oh, yeah, the shock! Gives me the heebie-jeebies just thinkin' about it. That old Jackson, eh?'

'That reminds me …' Laura gave the cook her full attention. 'There was something I've been meaning to ask you. How did you and Mary know that I was back here on the day I came?'

Lily avoided her eyes, mumbling at her toes, 'Fella in Doomadgee. He told us.'

'Yes, but … How did he know?'

Plainly reluctant to answer, Lily twisted her apron in her hands. 'Lookin' in his fire. Seen old Jackson talkin' to Little Missus. He said, "Go back. Little Missus need you." So, we come.'

'And very happy I am that you did; I can tell you.' Laura glanced at her warmly. In a time when the rest of the station and her inner self were in turmoil, she was glad of the cheerful company and the shining order of her home. She hesitated. 'Lily … is that what they call the mulga wire? How does it work?'

'Damned if I know, Missus. But that's what they call it, all right. Jackson and that fella from Doomadgee say they descend from Kadaicha Man, but I dunno … Anyway, dam' pleased he was right, this time.' Lily closed the subject. 'Dinner be ready in an hour if that's all right?'

'That's fine, thank you, Lily. I'll just take Bess for a walk and go to thank Jackson.'

Lily laughed. 'Jackson don't want no thanks. You'll see.'

Lily was right. When Laura was close enough to see Jackson huddled over his fire, he held up a hand, both acknowledging and forbidding. For a little while, she stood and watched him practise his mental telepathy—a form of communication almost as ancient as the land itself. Occasionally, he pushed the ends of the sticks farther into the coals, causing sparks and smoke to rise in curling wreaths about his snowy head, giving him the aspect of an ancient, exotic wizard.

As Laura turned away, an image of glossy black hair, arresting grey eyes and a ruggedly handsome face etched itself into her mind, and she knew a fear she had never before encountered. *Did Jackson tell me the truth?* she wondered. *Is the mulga wire always right? And would he even know the details that are worrying me about Rick?*

Laura mulled it over on the way back to the house. Rick had offered her friendship, but he might well be her enemy. Laura's properties were running at a loss; as far as she knew, his were not. Rick wanted her land; Laura refused to sell. He was in a position of trust. Had he abused that trust? *I wish I knew,* agonised Laura, wringing her hands as she entered her living room. *I wish I knew!*

'So, Jackson didn't want your thanks, eh? Told you!' crowed Lily, putting a mouth-watering casserole and a freshly baked crusty loaf on the perfectly set table. 'Oh well …' She took the lid off the dish, put down a warmed plate and gave Laura the serving spoon. 'I suppose he don't do no harm.'

§

'Are you there, Laura?'

John Riley appeared in her doorway as Laura was enjoying an early morning cup of tea. It was barely daylight.

Laura invited him in and raised an eyebrow. 'Trouble, John?'

'I'm afraid so.' Her overseer smiled apologetically.

'Well, when did anything on the land ever run smoothly? Would you like a cup of tea?'

'You can say that again! To both questions.' He grinned. 'Thank you. I would love some tea.'

Laura rose gracefully from her chair to bring him a cup and saucer. When she'd poured his tea and passed him the milk and sugar, she said, 'Now you can tell me what's wrong.'

'It's the bores on Polaris South. They've all broken down. Every single one!' He shook his head. 'I can't believe it!'

'Good heavens! One or two, I could understand, but … all of them?'

He nodded, worry clouding his frank brown eyes. 'Old Lou on the outstation called up last night to tell us. You know Lou, don't you?'

Laura nodded. Her lovely smile dawned. 'Oh yes, he's been the caretaker down there since before Uncle Jonas bought it. He went with it, I think. I believe he refused to be sacked?'

'That's true. He'll be there till he dies. Greeted Sykes with the shotgun, apparently.' He gave a grin. 'But we're not saying anything about *that!* Mick's going out there just now, but he says the bores will all have to be pulled before he can find the trouble, and of course, he'll need help. Lou's getting on a bit and his eyesight is going. If only they were flowing bores like we have everywhere else. These subartesian bores are a lot of trouble for the amount of water you get, but it is imperative we get them going in the next couple of days. The storage tanks are getting low.'

'Yes. We can't let the stock run out of water. There's no permanent surface water down there, is there?'

'Not a drop, I'm afraid. There's nothing to do but send men out there today.'

'Yes, I see that. It means we will have to interrupt the muster.'

'That's what I've come to talk to you about. Can you ring Rick and ask him if he's got a couple of men to spare for a few days to pull the bores and make sure they're all pumping properly? Then, we'll just leave a man behind with Lou, in case anything happens while we're mustering. That way we won't get behind schedule. The men won't like to miss the Juliana round-up.'

'*No!*' Laura almost shouted, startling both of them with her vehemence. 'I mean, there's no need for me to ask Rick for help. I'm sure he needs all his men at the moment. I will help. What can I do?'

'Well, I …well, I suppose you could drive for Mick. You know, pull up the rods and columns with the vehicle. That would leave the rest of us free to continue the muster. If you're sure?'

'Of course, I'm sure. There's not much to it, is there?'

'No, it isn't hard, except that you have to be precise: watch the man at the bore head, do exactly as he signals, keep him safe— that sort of thing.'

'That's all right. I'm a careful driver.'

'I know you are.' He hesitated, fiddling with a teaspoon. 'There's one more thing. Would you consider going to stay at Juliana until we finish the muster?'

'Stay at Juliana?' She looked at him as if she couldn't believe her ears. Then the fight went out of her, and she seemed to slump. 'You've heard about the crocodile.'

'Yes, you had a lucky escape, thankfully. Don't worry, the alert has gone out. We don't want to lose anyone. But no, that's not it.'

'What then?' Her face hardened. 'Because your reason had better be good.'

He spoke with quiet dignity, bringing a flush to her cheeks. 'There are several reasons, and they're all good. Two of the spear traps have been found empty—with the rails cut! I have sent a couple of men to repair them.'

'You're sure that the rails have been cut?' Laura was breathing fast.

He nodded. 'There's more. Two days ago, the truck broke down. Mick says it has been tampered with. And on the last mustering camp, our drinking water was contaminated with kerosene. When you add these to cut fences and broken-down bores, it all points to deliberate sabotage of your muster. And that's another problem: whoever is doing this knows you're here alone when we're out on the mustering camps.'

'But I'm not alone. I have Lily and Mary.'

'Do they sleep in your house at night?'

'No, they have their own cottage.'

'You've answered yourself, then. Please, Laura, you'll be safer at Juliana. I—we—would like you to consider it for your own sake.'

Laura's lips curled into a small, bitter smile. She thought she had a pretty fair idea who was doing the sabotage and why. She told herself that she was safe enough as long as she kept beyond the reach of a certain dynamic personality. Was there nothing he would stop at to show her that she could not manage? 'We? Who's we?'

'Well … Rick and I—that is. Rick offered to have you stay at Juliana, and I thought it was a good idea.' He was startled by the flash of anger in her eyes at this reference to her neighbour, but those amazingly thick lashes came down over them so swiftly that when she next looked at him, he thought he had imagined it. 'Look, there are all kinds out here. You know yourself how hard it is to find ringers. If a man does his job and behaves himself, no-one asks any questions. There's everything from young blokes looking for adventure to bad men trying to hide from the law. There *is* cause to fear for your safety. Please, Laura …'

Laura was regarding him coolly. 'There is no need to worry about me, John, though it is kind of you. I believe that I will be quite safe here. Mr Jenkins put locks on all the doors and screens before he left. Please, just go and do your job.'

Her overseer seemed to bite back some kind of retort. 'Very well, Laura.' He rose and picked up his hat. 'I'll be off, then.'

Watching him go, Laura felt a little sorry that she had spoken so sharply to him. He was not a man who had ever presumed on her goodwill, and she sensed it was genuine concern that prompted him to make a suggestion that she felt he had been rather reluctant to tender. But it definitely seemed as if he ranged on the side of her neighbour when it came to women in the Outback.

After my last encounter with Rick, he may not want me at Juliana, she thought. *Perhaps, I've given him enough grief to wash his hands of me? I've stopped him laughing, anyway!* Laura tossed her head, but at the back of her mind was a lurking shame for her ungrateful outburst at the river, though she refused to admit it.

Working swiftly, Laura packed her swag and a few sets of clothing and personal necessities, leaving the care of Oscar and Bess in Lily's capable hands. It was a relief to have something concrete to occupy her mind for a few days, and she was ready to set off as soon as Mick arrived with the bore-pulling gear.

Lou, at the outstation, was touchingly pleased to see her and gave them tea and damper on their arrival. 'Leave the gear on the verandah, Mick,' he commanded, as he saw them off to start the repairs. 'I'll take it over to the cottage for Laura. And if you fix number one bore today, we might all get showers tonight. Hooroo.'

Unfortunately for Laura, she had plenty of time for thinking during the slow, laborious task of pulling up endless columns to find the problem, and then putting them all back down again. It was a seesaw process of forward and reverse, which at times required precision driving, but in the main, was most uninteresting. 'No wonder they're called bores!' she muttered in exasperation as she put the ute into gear for about the five-hundredth time.

By the end of the week, all the bores were pumping smoothly. In every case, a small bolt had been found wedged between the buckets and the outer wall of the pump, effectively jamming them all. Obviously, a case of deliberate sabotage since the bolts were new and shiny and had not fallen from the windmills.

Laura knew it was ridiculous to believe that Rick was at the bottom of her troubles. Her heart told her that a man like him would never stoop so low, however much he wanted to prove his point. But her heart had been wrong before: dangerously wrong. It had caused her to make the biggest mistake of her life—one that still flayed her.

Laura didn't know whether she could trust Rick, but she knew beyond doubt that she couldn't trust her heart.

Chapter Eight

Enjoying the luxury of her own bed after the better part of a week in a swag, Laura was engrossed in a mystery novel when all the lights went out, and she was left in pitch darkness. Her skin prickled into goosebumps. And, since her heroine was in such a precarious situation that she would never sleep for wondering what was going to happen, Laura decided that, rather than go out and wrestle with the generator which had probably run out of fuel, she would use her gas camping light to finish the novel.

Feeling for her torch, Laura flung a satin wrapper over her pyjamas and padded out to the pantry to find her light and some matches. She had just lit the lamp and was in the act of picking it up from the living room table when she heard footsteps on the verandah. Fear touched her heart. It was late, after midnight. Just as she realised she hadn't remembered to lock up, she swung around to see a dishevelled man leaning on the doorpost.

The man's mouth twisted into an ugly leer. 'Well, if it isn't the high and mighty *Miss* Neumann … Forgot to lock your door, did you? Tut, tut.'

'Who are you? What do you want?' Laura's heart was pounding. She grasped a chair back for support.

'Don't you know me, *Miss* Neumann?' Again, the sneering emphasis on her title, but this time he slurred his speech.

Laura realised he must be drunk. She hid her fear behind scornful words. 'I don't invite drunks into my home. I don't know you and I don't care who you are. Just get out of my house!'

'Not until I've done what I came for. You made me eat dirt, and I'm here to return the favour.'

It couldn't be! Laura could not believe that the filthy, unshaven tramp facing her could be the same arrogant manager who had so infuriated her on her first day. But then she looked into the bloodshot eyes and recognised the expression. 'Ed … Ed Sykes?'

'That's right, Missus. Ed Sykes. I hear Boss Jamieson's got his eye on you. I don't reckon it'll hurt him to take my leavings.'

Laura threw the chair at him and screamed, turning to run as he lunged at her. But he caught the chair and flung it aside. Surprisingly agile for his condition, he made a grab at the collar of her robe, hauling her backwards as she tried to get out the door. The belt gave and her wrapper was dragged from her shoulders revealing silk baby-doll pyjamas. Cruel fingers bit into her arm, spinning her around to face her attacker.

'That looks better,' he leered, jerking her into his arms and trying to force a kiss on her.

In real terror now, she tried to fight him off, but drunk as he was, she discovered him to be incredibly strong; the stench of stale beer and cigarettes nauseating her to the point of faintness.

The next second, a tornado slammed through the door, dragged Sykes off Laura and hurled him across the room. *Rick!* she thought in a daze. *How can he be here?* She watched in disbelieving silence as the man scrambled to his feet and ran for his life. Rick, in hot pursuit, tripped over the chair and sat up cursing. Oscar, woken by the commotion, shouted, 'Bloody hell!' then fell silent under his cover.

'You're so right, mate!' Rick leapt to his feet and rushed out, but there was no sign of his quarry, and after a quick look around, he came back, firing up the generator on his way.

Laura was standing where he had left her, leaning against the wall—an odd, exhausted expression on her face. 'You've come to my rescue again. Are you psychic, I wonder?'

'No.' He turned off the gaslight and stooped to pick up her dressing-gown. 'It was Shirl from the roadhouse at the Five Ways. She heard Sykes boasting about having wrecked your muster and that he was coming back for you. She took him seriously enough to ring me. I got John out of bed on my way. He'll be out there, somewhere. We were hoping to catch Sykes before he got this far. Here, put this on.' He wrapped her in the robe, then looked down into her face. 'Oh, my poor girl, come here.' He folded her in his arms. 'It's over now.'

Laura met his gaze and was lost. How comforting was his embrace; how warm and tender the expression in his eyes. She lifted her face for his kiss.

There was a flurry of movement in the doorway behind him. 'What you doin' with our Missus this time of night, Boss?' demanded a disapproving voice. 'This is a woman's camp.'

Rick let Laura go and swung round. 'Lily!' His arms and

eyebrows flew up. 'Don't you skewer me with that thing!'

Laura made a choking sound. Lily—attired in a bright red woolly dressing-gown, elastic-sided boots, curls confined in a hairnet—was holding a garden fork, prongs levelled at Rick's midsection and pressing into his shirt. Mary, similarly dressed, except that her gown was electric-blue velvet, carried a shovel like a pike.

'Heard a scream and a crash.' Lily kept him covered. 'Thought we better come. If she wants you here, Boss, why did she scream?'

'Lily, it was Sykes. Rick got him off me.'

Lily lowered her weapon. 'Sorry, Boss. Didn't *really* think you would …'

'Not at all, Lily. I'm glad you're ready to protect your Missus from anyone who makes her scream.' Rick took the fork from her and leant it against the wall. 'Me, included.'

'Sykes?' Mary spoke for the first time. 'That son of a ——'

'Mary! Wash your mouth out!' commanded her sister. 'Where did he go, Boss?'

Rick shook his head. 'You and Mary didn't hear anything on your way down from the cottage?'

'No, Boss.'

'I'll have to go out and look for him. Will you two stay with your Missus?'

'Too right, Boss. Don't you worry, we won't leave her on her own. But you watch out for that fella. He's a *real* snake in the grass.'

'I will.' He glanced at Laura and back to Lily. 'How about you make your Missus some tea and toast?'

'Good idea, Boss,' applauded Lily.

'Only if you and Mary are going to have some with me,' said Laura.

'Rightio, Missus. Don't mind if we do. Bin thirsty work rushin' round this time of night. You stay in the doorway with that shovel, Mary. Whack him with it if he comes back,' she ordered, walking into the kitchen.

'Too right.' Mary gripped the handle like a cricket bat. 'I'll only have to hit him once.'

'That's the spirit,' said Rick. 'You give him what for.'

There was a hurried step on the verandah. Mary raised her shovel, swung it back, farther back—hesitated momentarily— then lowered it with a sigh. 'By cripes, you're lucky, Mr Riley. I dam' near hit you over the head.'

John Riley's startled gaze took in the incongruous figure of gentle, middle-aged Mary in a dressing-gown and hairnet, armed with a garden implement. A muscle quivered in his cheek. 'My God, Mary! You look a dangerous woman with that shovel! I'm glad you didn't let me have it.' He glanced at Rick. 'We've got him. He sneaked down behind the quarters. Mick heard him trip over something and raised the alarm. I'll have to take him to the watch house at the Curry. Can you come to press charges?'

'I can't think of anything I would enjoy more. Well. I can, but …' Rick sent a rueful glance at Laura. 'Will you be right if I go to Cloncurry with John?'

'Yes, I think so.' Laura paused to look back on her way to the kitchen.

'She should be,' said her overseer as Lily came out with a pot of tea and a pile of buttered toast. 'I owe you ladies an apology. I didn't think Laura would be safe in the house with you two so far away in your cottage. But I take my hat off to you: I can see she's got the best set of bodyguards in the country.'

Rick gave a grin. 'Yes, and they don't mind who they hold up, either.'

'Yeah, sorry about that, Boss,' said Lily, not noticeably abashed. 'Little Missus said for you boys to stay and have tea with us.'

Laura brought extra mugs with the milk and sugar. 'Will you stay?'

Rick shared a consultative glance with John. 'No, we must go. We've got a lot to do.'

'Hang on a minute, Boss.' Lily turned back to the kitchen. 'I'll make you a flask of coffee to have on the road. Might be a long night, eh?'

§

'You should try and get some sleep, Little Missus,' said Lily. 'We'll stay here with you.'

'There's only a couple of hours left of the night. I'll be fine if you two want to go home.'

'See how we go. We promised Boss Jamieson we wouldn't leave before morning.'

Unable to move them out of this stance, Laura went off to bed, but tired as she was, could not sleep. When, just before daylight, she felt impelled to get up, she found her guardians dozing in armchairs either side of her bedroom door—their garden implements across their knees. They both jumped awake at the sound of movement.

'Oh, you poor dears! Sitting up to watch over me! Why don't you go home now and have a sleep? It will be daylight soon.'

'Yeah. We better get back before someone sees us lookin' like a couple of frights.' Lily gave Laura a worried look. 'Sure you'll be right on your own, Missus?'

'I'm sure.' Laura hugged them. 'You two are just the most *wonderful* ladies. Thank you for coming to my rescue.'

'Aw, gee,' muttered Mary. 'That's all right, Missus.'

'You didn't need us.' Lily was as truthful as ever. 'You had Boss Jamieson.'

'Yes, I did need you, Lily. I did.' Laura looked at her, then down in confusion. What might have happened if Lily had not arrived when she did? Laura couldn't even go there, let alone try to explain to herself or anyone else what she meant. *I can't think about Rick and what might have been. I dare not!*

'Ah, well,' said Lily after a short silence. 'You know how to call us when you want us. We're always here, aren't we, Mary?' At Mary's smile and nod, she added, 'Come back later in the morning, eh?'

'Yes, and don't hurry. We all need some sleep. I can make coffee and toast if I wake up before you two.'

'Good-o, Missus.' Lily picked up the garden fork and started off. 'Bring that shovel, Mary. We'll keep them at the cottage from now on, just in case.'

They'd gone about halfway along the path before Mary spoke. 'What's up, Lily? You look worried.'

'Boss Jamieson. He's in love with our Missus.'

'He's a dam' fine lookin' man.' Mary sounded thoughtful. 'She might take to him.'

'Not just fine lookin', Mary. He *is* a fine man. Just about good enough for our Missus.' Lily screwed up her face. 'But remember what he said to Boss Neumann one day? That he'd never get married because he wouldn't ask a woman to live out here?'

'Yeah, and I remember what Boss Neumann said to *him*: That one day he'd find someone he didn't have to ask—that was here already because she loved it as much as he did.'

'That's right. And I think he's found her.'

'So, what's the problem?'

'Dunno. But there is one. Missus is scared about something.'

'What? Of him?' scoffed Mary. 'Can't be!'

'You wouldn't think so, but …' Lily took a minute to mull it over. 'Whatever it is, she's scared white.'

'Ah, well … nothin' we can do about that.' Mary shrugged, then gave a chuckle. 'Ain't nothin' can scare us old girls white, eh, Lily?'

'Get away with you, Mary. This ain't no laughing matter.' But Lily was smiling as she leant the garden fork against the wall and opened their cottage door. 'He's a good man, would treat her right. She might see it, yet.'

Chapter Nine

It didn't matter how much Laura told herself that Sykes was safely locked up, every night found her more and more nervous, jumping at sounds she had never noticed before, careful to lock every door and window at dusk. *Houses breathe,* she told herself. *They're always creaking and bumping.* She began to dread the nights, too ashamed to mention it to her protectors and unwilling to inconvenience them on a whim she knew to have no foundation outside of her imagination. *I'll just have to get over it!* she thought in desperation. *I will, in time. I know I will. If only I knew how! If only Bess wasn't so old and deaf.*

The worst part was having to go out on the verandah to use the bathroom. Laura began to regret that she hadn't had the forethought to ask Mr Jenkins to knock through the wall and make an inside door into the bathroom. Of course, that was still a possibility. Laura would just have to get in touch with him and wait her turn.

As for going to stay at Juliana? *It is an option totally beyond consideration*, she thought. *Period.* That was what started her wondering about going out on the mustering camp with her men. It was just as much her right to be there as any other boss. Laura thought she might as well run it past her overseer and use his reaction as a guide. *Anything will be better than how I feel at night in the house.* Part of her mourned the loss of her easy confidence about living on her own; part of her was genuinely interested in the working of a mustering camp.

I must start exercising Ben more regularly, she thought. At fifteen, he was a little old for the rigours of a muster, but if she had him fed and conditioned, she felt that he would stand up to it all right. *And the riding will condition me, too.*

Laura put this plan into action, enjoying her early-morning rides. Her first ride had been much less exciting than she thought. Ben had accepted the saddle and her weight on his back as if it were only yesterday and not a matter of months or perhaps years since he'd last been ridden. He even seemed to look forward to their rides as much as she did, always whinnying and cantering up as soon as he saw her coming.

Soon after, Laura's thoughts were given a different direction by the unexpected arrival of a cattle buyer from the south in his Piper Cherokee. A big, bluff man with greying hair in a crew cut—handsome in a florid style—David Macquarie had been a long-time buyer of her great-uncle's cattle. He had an easy manner that made Laura feel comfortable when she drove to the airstrip and invited him to the homestead for morning tea before John came to get him and show him the cattle.

Laura explained that this year, due to unforeseen circumstances, the muster had been delayed and that, at this point, she only had a few saleable cattle. 'But you're welcome to have a look. Come back for lunch and tell me what you think of them and what's going on in the world.'

But when John brought him back to the homestead, the buyer was no longer smiling. 'I'm sorry to have to tell you this, but your cattle don't seem to have the quality of previous years.' He looked at her closely. 'You know something is wrong, don't you?'

'Yes. But I don't know what—or who.'

'I was sorry to hear about Jonas. He was a great old guy. Everything was shipshape when he was here. Last year was pretty thin, too, now I come to think of it. You might have to look at your management.'

'I've done that. Rather drastically.'

'Good. John has told me there is still about half the place to muster. I hope that when I come back at the end of the season, I can offer you a better price and take many more of your cattle than I can today.'

'Yes.' Laura made a wry face. 'So do I.'

'There's one more thing. I don't know if you're aware of it, but there's a crisis looming in the Top End beef industry. The authorities have started a move to close the meat works at Broome.

'Oh, that's terrible news! No, I wasn't aware of it. When?'

'I only heard it this morning. I've been asked to let all the producers I deal with know about it.'

'What can we do?'

'Some of us are trying to organise an emergency meeting of

all those concerned. I'm not sure where or when just yet, but we should know later today. It would be advisable to go—if you could—make your feelings known.'

'Of course, I will do what I can. Let me know ——' Laura was interrupted by the radio. 'That's Rick now. Do you suppose …?'

'Yes, he knows. He may just have something to tell us. Please …' He gestured for her to answer it.

'Hello, Laura.' Rick's voice dominated the room. 'I wonder if you know about the problem in our beef industry?'

'Yes, I've just been hearing about it.'

'Is Dave still there with you?'

'Yes, he is. Do you want to talk to him?'

'He'll be over here soon. I'll talk to him then. Just tell him the Top End and North Queensland Cattle Breeders Association conference is this weekend at Leonora. There'll be two meetings: one on Friday afternoon, the other on Saturday morning. I'll be going up there in the plane, seeing it is at such short notice. I have room for a passenger, so you can come with me. You're not afraid of flying, are you?'

'No, not at all.'

'That's good, then. I'll pick you up on Friday morning about nine.'

Acutely conscious of listening ears, Laura agreed with as much grace as she could summon and went back to her guest. 'You heard all that?'

'Yes, I'm glad they've got it organised. I'll be staying the night at Juliana, so I can liaise with Rick to let the others know.' He smiled. 'You'll like Leonora. It's a very interesting place.'

§

Laura decided to sort the letters that had been dropped off by the mail plane while she waited for her neighbour to arrive. Riffling through them, she found one from her solicitors and, tearing it open, received an unpleasant surprise. Her trustees had invested a sizeable amount in a new airline called Phoenix, and Mr Phillips had written to inform her, with many apologies, that the airline had collapsed, and because she was not one of the major investors, they had not been able to salvage even a percentage of her funds.

Why does Phoenix have to go bust right now? she wondered. *Right when everything else is so bad? Just what I don't need to hear! Just one more thing,* she thought, as near to despair as she'd been since coming here to her new life in the Gulf. Her trustees had invested fifty thousand dollars on her behalf. *It's not the end of the world,* she told herself, wondering how much it took to be a major investor. *I will be able to manage, even if I have to get a loan from the bank.* It would just make life a little difficult for a while until she could recoup her losses, that was all. Then, she had another thought: As one of her trustees, would Rick have committed her money to this failed investment? Perhaps he had lost money, too? Or if he hadn't invested in the venture himself, what did it say about his trustworthiness towards her? Just one more red flag to get in the way of any future relationship with him.

Jolted out of her unhappy thoughts by the sound of an aeroplane circling to land, Laura picked up her bag and went out to the airstrip.

§

Rick flew the plane as he did everything else: with laid-back competence, and Laura felt safe with him. She looked down with interest on her property as they banked and circled, noting the name painted on the roof of the quarters. From the air, everyone would know it was Polaris.

Rick was silent until he straightened the plane and had gained height, heading west. Then he switched on the autopilot and smiled at his passenger. 'There's a thermos over here somewhere,' he said, rummaging in the basket behind his seat.

A few minutes later, they were sipping coffee and he was pointing out to Laura all the various landmarks and places of interest. She noticed the changes in the landscape as they headed farther west: the way low spinifex-topped hills rose out of the Mitchell and Flinders grass plain here and there; the ironbark and bloodwood giving way to silver box, spinifex gum and gidyea.

'Do you know Leonora?' asked Rick.

'No, I've never been there. I know of it, of course. It was one of the first places up here to really get into the tourist business.'

'Yes. Situated, as it is, where the Barkly Tableland joins the Gulf, its watercourses running seaward have carved some spectacular gorges. We'll fly over them. It is something you should not miss. We'll have plenty of time, I think. We're lucky; it's very smooth flying today. Sometimes, it gets a bit rough up here.'

'Yes, I suppose it does. I haven't been in a light plane for years, but well do I remember the turbulence when I flew as a child from Mount Isa to Polaris. Uncle Jonas asked me if I thought it was St Patrick's Day. And when I asked why, he said I was a rather interesting shade of green!'

'Sounds as if you landed just in time.'

'I think so. I did feel awfully sick.'

'Ah well … No problems today, then?'

'Oh, no. I am enjoying the experience. Except for a slight hitch this morning, that is,' she added on an impulse, just to see his reaction.

'Ah … It wouldn't, by any chance, involve a letter from your solicitors?'

'Yes, how did you know? Let me guess, you got one too?'

'No, but I heard about the Phoenix collapse and knew that some of your funds had been invested that way.'

'So, you didn't invest with them yourself, then?' Laura was careful to employ a disinterested tone.

'No. I was going to, but I was already heavily involved elsewhere in the chopper business.' He glanced at her. 'I had a lucky escape. I am sorry you didn't. I must say, it seemed like a good thing at the time. Lord knows, the country needs another domestic airline. I think it is bad luck rather than bad investment.'

Yes, but do you? thought Laura, biting her lip. *Or are you trying to bring me down?* Just one more thing she dare not ask. He seemed sincere, but how could she tell? She turned her attention to the vista below and found a question she could ask: 'Oh, look at this rough country! Where are we now?'

'Getting close to the gorges.' Rick switched off the autopilot and began to turn the plane. 'I am about to make a detour to show them to you … Here's the first of them, coming up.' Flying low along the length of the gorge, Rick tilted the plane so that Laura could get a better look.

'Oh …' she breathed in awe, experiencing a curious longing to stand at the bottom and look up past its colourful rock walls to the tranquil blue sky above—in another world—safe, protected.

'Amazing, aren't they?' Rick glanced at her rapt expression and repeated the process with successive landforms.

'Incredible! And so unexpected, compared to the rest of the country.'

'I think that is partly what makes them so magnificent. Seen enough now?' At her assent, he made a last sweep and headed the plane north. 'Look. About that other. If you find yourself in difficulties, I can lend you enough to tide you over.'

'Oh, no thanks; I'll be all right.'

'Are you sure? Because ——'

'Of course, I'm sure!' Her vehemence made him quirk his lips. The fact that he seemed to see her independence as a joke annoyed her more than if he had been offended, and the last thing she wanted was to be any more beholden to him than she was already.

'Then, there's no more to be said.' He turned his attention to his controls.

After that, the conversation dried up, and they were silent for the rest of the journey.

§

In a short time, a group of buildings came into view. Across the silver roof of one of the outbuildings the name LEONORA was blazed in two-metre-high black capitals. Laura caught her breath at the size and variety of the buildings and the well-kept lawns and trees. It was more like a small town than an Outback station. On the ground, in rows, glittering in the bright sunlight, a number of light aircraft were moored. It looked as if the meeting would be well attended.

Rick's landing was as smooth and perfect as the trip had been. As they walked together across the concreted area to the motel reception, Laura looked curiously around her at a tourist complex of amazing proportions. Boutiques, a motel, entertainment centre, swimming pool, golf course, and fishing and boating on the huge dam across the river were just a few of the options open to tourists. Leonora was a luxurious resort where no expense was spared for the comfort of its visitors. Kings, queens, big-business people were equally catered for here, as were the four-wheel-drive and caravan tourists who spent time in the well-equipped caravan park and camping ground.

In the circular foyer, luxuriant with tropical plants, Rick glanced at his watch. 'How about we check in to the motel and then grab a bite of lunch? Then we should have some time to look around before the meeting. There's a very good exhibition of Aboriginal art on at the moment. How does that sound?' At her nod and smile, he added, 'I'll meet you back here in, say, ten minutes?'

'Twenty minutes?' She indicated her jeans. 'I'd like to change into something more in keeping with the surroundings.'

He gave her his slow smile. 'I'll look forward to it.'

§

When Laura returned to the foyer, dressed in a smart suit, Rick was standing with a group just now convulsed with delighted laughter. They stopped and looked expectantly at Laura as she walked up to them. *I'd love to know what he said to make them laugh like that,* she thought. *Something outrageous, no doubt!*

Rick stepped back to greet her with a welcoming smile. He put a friendly arm around her to draw her into the group. 'I've found some old friends, Laura. They've come up from the south to add support to our cause. Let me introduce you.'

A tall, handsome man with a quiet manner and an air of reserve and a small, dainty blonde with a sweet face were introduced as Dev and Sarah Mainwaring of Medora Downs. 'My neighbour, Laura Neumann, Jonas's great-niece.' He moved on to a tall, sophisticated honey-blonde with magnificent green eyes; her statuesque figure enhancing the fashionable ensemble she wore. 'Dev's neighbour, Louella Richmond from Emerald Hills and …? I'm sorry, I didn't catch your name.'

'My cousin and husband, Jean-Luc Lemaitre,' drawled Louella with the hint of an American accent. She gave him a teasing glance. 'He came over for a visit from France, but for some *strange* reason or other, I couldn't get him to go home. So, I had to marry him.'

'I fell on my feet, there. Besides, it is a big country,' said the tall, brown-haired Frenchman in his charming accent. He smiled into his wife's eyes. 'There is much to see and learn.'

Laura sensed the chemistry between them and could see that they were in love. She turned to acknowledge the thickset man with reddish-fair hair and twinkling blue eyes that Rick was introducing to her as Jim, Dev's overseer. Laura looked into his good-natured, fun-filled face and warmed to him straightaway.

'It's great to meet you, Laura.' He shook her hand. 'It's a small world: I used to work for Jonas. He was a terrific old bloke. Taught me a lot.'

By the time they went into lunch, Laura felt comfortable with the group, as if, like Rick, she was surrounded by old friends.

They'd just seated themselves at a table in the window, and Rick, ushering Laura into a chair on his right, had handed her the menu when a diminutive brunette in a tropical-print dress swept into the room like a brightly coloured whirlwind. Her hair—a shining black cap cut in a geometric bob—was held back at one side by a clip with a hibiscus flower over her ear. 'Oh, there you are!' she burbled. '*Hello*, everyone!'

'Hullo, here's *trouble*,' said Jim.

Her eyes sparkled with pleasure. 'Jim! It's so long since I've seen you!' She skipped over to sit on his knee and put her arms around him.

'Whoa there, Cass! Take it easy. I'm an old married man, you know.'

'What? Don't tell me you tied the knot at last?'

'He has,' said Dev. 'Believe it or not.'

'Well, where is she?' Cass looked around, quizzing Louella with her brilliant dark eyes. 'Josie, isn't it?'

Louella shook her head. 'Jacqui.'

'Oh, that's right; it's been so long since he announced his engagement, I forgot.' Her glance went back to Jim. 'Well? Why isn't she here?'

'She had to stay with the children ——'

'Children?' shrieked Cass. 'You've got children, already? I'd love to know what your father thinks about *that*?'

'I wouldn't jump to conclusions.' Louella seemed amused. 'She's a *governess*, darling.'

'Only until the new one arrives. Dad has had a fall, and I have to go home, so Dev will be looking for a new overseer, too.'

'Your dad, is he okay?'

'He will be, but he'll have to take it a bit easier from now on.'

'I see. Oh!' Cass dissolved into laughter. 'I've just had a thought: what about Mary?'

'Alas!' he mourned. 'She wouldn't leave Ernie, and he wouldn't leave The Gregory.'

Laura glanced across the table to see Sarah convulsed in silent laughter and raised an enquiring eyebrow.

'Mary runs the North Gregory Hotel in Winton,' explained Sarah, between gasps. 'It's a long-standing joke. Jim's in love with her cooking.'

'And that's another thing ...' said Cass. 'Can she cook, this new wife of yours?'

'So far, so good, but I don't know the full extent yet. Ought I have made it a condition of the marriage, do you think?'

'No, just go and live in Winton.' Cass got up to look around for a fresh victim. 'Then you'll have the best of both worlds!' Her eyes considered the man with his arm resting across the back of Sarah's chair. 'Well … It looks as though Dev's beyond my reach.'

'He always was, darling.' Louella's voice held a hint of spite.

Laura, aware of a peculiar tension, saw that Sarah had begun to look uncomfortable and that her husband's hand momentarily pressed her shoulder.

'Come off it, Lou.' Cass met the warning in the other woman's eyes with a grin and a shrug. 'Oh well, I'll just have to fall back on Rick.'

'Come here, Cass.' Rick pulled out the chair on his left. 'Sit down and behave yourself. You're embarrassing Laura.'

Laura knew she should demur out of courtesy, however mendaciously. But, overwhelmed by the energy and spirit displayed by the tiny brunette, could find nothing to say.

'Laura?' Cass slewed around as she took the chair—her little face vibrant with enquiry. 'Oh, *hi!* I'm sorry; I didn't notice you there. Well, come on, Rick. Introduce us.'

'If he can get a word in edgeways,' muttered Jim.

'You took the words right out of my mouth, old mate.' Rick raised an eyebrow at Cass, who subsided to regard Laura with a hint of mischief, while he made the introduction.

'Cassandra Northing from Rosetta Downs in the Kimberley; Laura Neumann, my neighbour.'

'Oh, so *you're* Jonas's heiress?' Cass eyed her with frank interest. 'Lovely to meet you. The Gulf is so boring compared to the Kimberley. Do you hate it?'

'Oh, no! On the contrary.'

Cass regarded her speculatively. 'Plenty to interest you, in fact?'

'One in the eye for you, Cass.'

'Shut up, Lou.' Her big, dark eyes went to the Frenchman and widened.

'And you can keep your claws out of Jean-Luc. He's already spoken for. How have you not heard?'

'Heard what?'

Louella held up her left hand and wriggled her third finger to show a magnificent set of sapphire-and-diamond rings.

'Where's William?' Sarah made a bid to divert the impending war.

'I left him at home with his nanny. Children under five should be neither seen nor heard in my view. Where's James?'

'Here. I brought Sue to babysit.'

Cass gave Louella a wicked look. 'Now, Lou, you surely don't think your domestic arrangements are going to make a blind bit of difference to me?'

Whew! thought Laura. *There is history here.*

'Rival beauties.' Rick spoke out of the corner of his mouth to Laura. 'Gets a bit tiresome occasionally. Luckily, they live at opposite ends of the Outback and don't meet very often. Thank God my cousin isn't here. It's even worse with the three of them competing. They're all spoilt brats.'

'I *heard* that.' Cass angled a reproachful glance at him.

Rick shrugged. 'It's only the truth.'

'You'll get yours.' Cass raised her voice. 'He's a big boy, Lou. Can't he speak for himself? I can understand French.' Her challenging gaze clashed with Louella's.

'If you're thinking of chancing your arm, darling,' drawled her opponent, 'you know who'll come off worst, don't you?'

'Ladies, please!' Jim gestured to the wine waiter, standing politely in the background. 'This poor man is waiting to see what you want to drink.'

Jean-Luc gave a wry smile and took Louella's hand. 'Come, *ma belle*, pay attention to *le garçon*. Some of us *may* need reviving after that little skirmish.' The words were spoken gently, but they arrested his companion. She bit her lip and fell silent. Dev glanced at him with a flash of admiration but said nothing.

'I think we'd better put the Frenchman in charge of the wine.' Jim pointed him out to the waiter. 'He's probably the only one of us with sufficient *authority* to make the choice. Although, I don't think Cass needs anything.'

'Jim!'

'Well?' He grinned. 'I don't know what you've been on, Cass, but it must be something pretty potent.'

Cass tossed her head. 'It's always the same. As soon as a perfectly good man gets married, he becomes a stuffed shirt!'

Jim gave her back look for look. 'On second thoughts, you'd better have something. If only to shut you up while you're drinking it.'

'How is your dad now, Cass? After his stroke?' asked Rick, diverting her from a pungent reply.

'Recovering. Still in a wheelchair, though. But nothing would stop him coming. He's having lunch in his room.'

'With Daddy,' said Louella. 'Which reminds me: They want you, Dev and Jim to go up after lunch to work on an angle for the meeting. Jean-Luc can squire the rest of us around the exhibition. I want to show him some *real* Australian art.'

Chapter Ten

In an unspoken consensus, Laura and Sarah toured the exhibition together behind Cass and Louella, who walked either side of the charming Frenchman. Laura found Sarah easy to talk to, both having unconcealed admiration for the drama and beauty of the colourful Aboriginal art.

'Did you know that some of these are actually maps?' said Sarah. 'Look, these are hills, grassy plains and so on. Watercourses, too. I got quite a kick when I found out. You can see it if you hold an aerial photo beside it.'

'Incredible!' Laura couldn't take her eyes from the paintings. 'They're a very practical people. I guess they had to be, to survive. I wonder if the animals depicted are what they could expect to find for food in the area?'

'I think so. It would make sense.' Sarah looked across to where Cass was beguiling the Frenchman with her mischievous antics, his wife's eyes darting fire. 'Do you mind if we go this way? I think

I saw a Namatjira on the wall over there when we came in.'

'Oh, yes, Albert Namatjira, over there! I adore his paintings.' Laura followed her in the opposite direction to the other three. Soon, they were absorbed in admiration for the fabulous colours, sensitive and delicate artwork of the Namatjira collection.

The meeting that followed was full of purpose and determination. The federal members for the vast electorates were present, ready to take back their electors' proposals to the government. Finally, the meeting adjourned for dinner, members agreeing to convene next morning with exact strategies and an annual general meeting.

§

Next morning, quite early, Laura came out of her room into the motel corridor to see Cass coming away from Rick's door.

Cass, a hint of devilment in her eyes as they met Laura's, immediately began to adjust her clothing. 'Hi, Laura.' She gave her a cheeky smile. 'Bit of a *hot* night.'

Laura's heart plummeted as she caught her meaning. Dismayed at her reaction, she was swamped by a tide of embarrassment. *I don't know why I care,* she thought, mentally tossing her head. *They're both adults. It's nothing to me what they do in their private lives.*

Cass looked past her—the mischief in her face giving way to a thwarted expression, quickly masked.

Laura followed her gaze to see Rick dressed in a sports coat and moleskins, striding along the corridor towards them. He caught her eye and smiled. 'Morning, Laura. Sleep well? Did you find those notes your father wanted, Cass? No? Give me the key, and I'll get them for you.' He held out his hand, looking back at Laura as he opened the door. 'Don't go away, Laura. I need you.' He saw her expression and grinned. *'Please.* I won't be a moment.'

'Lucky Laura!' Cass eyed her in mock envy. 'What's it feel like to be *needed* by a man like Rick?'

Laura, still in shock from the other's behaviour, had no answer. *Cass wanted me to believe that Rick was in there with her. Why?* She couldn't understand the relief she felt when she'd seen him coming towards them—that he hadn't been with Cass as the other girl had intimated.

Rick came back with an envelope. 'Laura's not used to your nonsense, Cass. She doesn't have the kind of interest in me that you assume. You'd better go. Your dad's waiting.'

'Oh, *doesn't* she just?' Cass gave a derisive hoot as she took the papers and began to walk off.

Rick's hand shot out and grasped her arm. 'Does it ever occur to you, Cass, that some of us prefer peace and quiet to the kind of stirring that your devilish sense of humour leads you into? You've managed to upset both Sarah and Louella, and I'm not letting you do the same to Laura. Get me?'

Cass eyed him with bird-like speculation. 'Spoilsport!' she flung at him—not in the least insulted—and determined to have the last word. She said goodbye to Laura with a rueful grin and whirled away.

'She's all right.' Rick watched her go. 'You just have to be firm with her. Her main problem is that her father owns half the Kimberley, including a diamond mine. And because she's little and cute as well, she's got most of the Top End in love with her and unable to refuse anything she wants. She went away and trained as a nurse, a midwife, I think, which improved her no end, but since she's come home to look after her father, all her nonsense has started again.' He looked more closely at Laura. 'Are you okay?'

'Yes … No.' She gave a wry smile. 'As a matter of fact, I feel as though I've just been run over by a bus!'

'Cass does tend to have that effect on people when they first come across her. You have to learn to take her with a grain of salt. A large one! But I don't think there's any malice there. Come on, breakfast first. Then we'll get on with the next meeting, have lunch and get you home in time for smoko.'

§

Laura saw the utility leave the quarters as they circled to land at Polaris. Rick had been right. Despite delays and friendly offers for them to remain another night, it was still a respectable smoko time.

John Riley was waiting for them to land. 'How did you go?' He took Laura's bag and helped her out of the plane.

'Success,' said Rick. 'We seem to have changed their minds for the time being, at any rate. There's a moratorium on the closure of the meatworks.'

'Very good,' approved the overseer.

'Will you come down to the house with us for smoko?' asked Laura with a little smile. 'Seeing as you got me back in time?'

'I'd love to, but …' Rick patted the joystick. 'I have to put this little baby to bed before dark. I'll come over tomorrow, and we'll go out to the mustering camp.' He gave her his lazy grin. 'I'll have it with you then.'

They watched him take off, circle, salute them and fly away to the north, before turning to the ute.

'I need a word with you, John. Have you got time for a cup of tea?'

'Always.' He opened the door for her. 'You're the boss, Laura.'

I wonder, thought Laura, *if that is what he really thinks?*

At the homestead, Lily greeted them with her beautiful smile. 'Hello, Little Missus. You want your smoko?'

'When you're ready, Lily.'

'Have you got ten minutes, Mr Riley? Whip you up a batch of scones if you like?'

'My word, I have, Lily. I've heard about your scones.'

'John …' said Laura when Lily was busy in the kitchen. She hesitated. 'I'd, um … just like your take on an idea of mine. I've been wanting to stay out on the camp when we muster Miranda, and I was wondering what you thought about it?'

'It's fine by me.' He was silent a moment. 'Do you mind if I ask the men what their feelings are?'

'Not at all.' Laura dropped her gaze to the tablecloth. 'I wanted to find out what you thought before making my decision.'

He looked at her with penetrating eyes. 'You're not feeling vulnerable after your encounter with Sykes?'

'*No!* I …' Laura shrugged.

'I wouldn't blame you if you were. It is a perfectly natural reaction, you know. Most understandable.'

'Well, yes, a little … But I don't want to go away from Polaris.'

He nodded. 'And this would be the perfect solution.'

'Yes.' She hesitated. 'How are the cattle coming in? Are we doing any better?' It was hope against hope.

John shook his head, and Laura saw from his expression that nothing had changed for the better. He was in the middle of a detailed explanation of all that was going on with the muster when Lily returned. 'Ah, Lily,' he said as the cook placed a steaming tea towel wrapped parcel on the table. 'They look and smell perfect.'

When most of the scones had disappeared, and he'd complimented Lily once again on her baking, John took his leave. 'I'm sorry I don't have better news on the numbers, but I really don't foresee a problem with you going out to camp with us. On the contrary. But I will talk to the men tonight and let you know tomorrow when you come out with Rick.'

§

Rick was late. Laura paced back and forth, wondering why he hadn't contacted her on the radio. It wasn't like him not to be in touch if he'd been delayed. He was usually more considerate than that. Or so he had seemed. Laura took nothing for granted, but she did wonder if some accident had befallen him.

Then, the air was filled with a characteristic sound, and Laura ran outside in time to see Rick, grinning all over his face, set down a small Bell helicopter. He beckoned and held out a hand. Laura came over and ducked, holding her hat as she went under the rotors. His fingers closed over hers and swung her up into the cockpit and the seat beside him.

Rick gave her a headset. 'Sorry. I was running late, so I borrowed one of Andy's choppers.' He slanted her a cheeky glance. 'I'm a man of my word. We'll be there in time for smoko.'

Laura, listening to him over the roar of the engine, smiled and nodded. Was this the helicopter business Rick had chosen to invest in over Phoenix?

'I'd better find out exactly where they are, first.' He adjusted knobs and spoke into the transmitter.

John's voice came back clearly: 'Riley. Receiving you.'

'Where are you, John?'

'Down on the double flat near Rocky Creek. At the second spear trap. We're just about to have smoko.'

'Right. Save some for us. We'll be right there.' Rick signed off and turned to Laura. 'Oh, by the way, I had a word with Dyson, one of Andy's chopper pilots, and he said that he and his mates will keep an eye out for those horses of yours.'

'Oh, thank you. That's good of him.' Laura showed puzzlement. 'But who is Andy?'

Rick raised a questioning eyebrow. 'Didn't you ever meet Andy? Mrs Mac's son.'

'No, I don't think so.' She wrinkled her brow, trying to remember. 'No, I'm sure I didn't.'

'Possibly for the same reason you didn't meet me. We were at school together.' He grinned. 'Andy's the good-looking one. Always got all the girls if I remember. He has a chopper mustering business based at Juliana, which is a bit of luck for me. He's a good mate, always has been.' Rick glanced at her, hesitated, then took the bull by the horns. 'I'll warn you now, he'll probably try to get into your pants. He's that kind of guy. He *will* take no for an answer though. At least, he'd *better!* Here we are now,' he added, aware that Laura had stiffened but not waiting for her reaction. 'Look for a clear spot to land downwind of the camp, so we don't blow dust all over them. They won't greet us with joy if we put dirt in their tea.'

Rick set down the helicopter without incident, and they made their way over to the camp. They found the men in sundry attitudes of relaxation, most squatting on their heels—in the time-honoured manner of Australian stockmen—at a short distance from the campfire. They rose as Laura approached and raised their hats to her.

John had been sitting on a log but got up to welcome them and bring a camp chair forward for Laura.

But Laura was looking at the camp cook, a tremulous smile on her lips. 'Is it …? Can it be, Tom?'

'That's right, Missus. Lot of water under the bridge since we last met, eh?'

'That's so true, Tom! Oh, it's lovely to see you again.'

'Same here, Missus. Now, you sit down in that chair that John's holding for you, and I'll bring you some tea and damper.'

'This is the life.' Laura relaxed in her chair, having finished her tin mug of sweet black tea and a large wedge of crusty baking soda loaf, cooked in the camp oven, which was lavishly spread with butter and golden syrup by Tom.

'Too right,' said John. 'It's a great life! That reminds me: one of the boys has a very nice tent he can lend you when we go out to muster Miranda.'

'Oh, perfect! Please, thank him for me.' Laura's heart lightened. Obviously, the men had agreed to her presence. No more fearful nights on her own, waiting for daylight—at least for the three weeks it would take to muster the shared holding. Maybe she would be over it by then.

'What?' Rick looked from one to the other, his voice deceptively quiet.

'It's usual for both owners to be present in these situations, I believe?' Laura lifted an enquiring eyebrow. She spoke coolly, though her heart was hammering. *Don't tell me he's going to cause a scene and try to forbid it? I won't let him!*

'I am sure that you can depend on John to look after your interests if you feel you can't trust me to do the right thing,' he replied in low tones, his brows suddenly drawn together.

'It isn't that.' He sounded so hurt that Laura felt a sudden remorse, but how could she explain? 'It's just that … It's my *right* to be there.'

'You can't rough it out there for three weeks!' His expression told her his views on women doing such things.

Impossible chauvinist! thought Laura, forgetting her remorse and snorting impatiently. 'Of course I can! It won't hurt me!'

'Then, what about all these men? They won't want a woman in their camp. You'll embarrass them.'

Laura stared at him speechless. *I will not! No, I must not—I dare not!—lose my temper!* Her narrowed eyes glittering between their preposterous lashes, she went suddenly white with spots of red on her cheekbones. Lips gripped in a straight line—she was desperate to stay in control—to hold back words that would surely be her downfall.

'It'll be all right, Rick.' The overseer spoke in conciliating tones after one look at Laura's face. 'I talked to the boys last night, and they're all quite happy about it. They'll treat her with respect,' he added, looking dangerous and quite unlike the gentle person he had always seemed to Laura. 'Don't worry. I'll see to that.'

'Was this your idea, then, John?' The voice was soft—the grey eyes cold as the Antarctic. The quietness, the very stillness of him embodied a threat.

The overseer glanced from Rick to Laura and back again. He chose his words deliberately. 'Well … You can't deny that it is a better one than yours.'

There was a moment of tension, then Rick seemed, all at once, to relax. 'No, I suppose you're right there.' He passed a thoughtful hand over his chin. 'At least she took it up. Looks like your invitation was more acceptable than mine.'

'*Rick!*' gasped Laura, fulminating. 'I'll have you know it was *my* idea.'

'And it *does* mean that we can keep her under our eye,' said John, behind his hand.

'There's that,' agreed Rick. 'It could be a better one than I thought.'

'Oh!' Laura closed her lips with herculean effort. Her eyes narrowed again, almost disappearing between their thick lashes. *The beasts!* she thought. *Ganging up on me! How dare they? But I'm not going to bite.*

The look Rick shot at Laura was one of unholy amusement. Whatever had been his problem, he seemed to have well and truly gotten over it, or else decided to take his revenge in some biting humour. 'You'd better be careful, John. You don't want to go upsetting your boss. She might give you the sack. And then where would we be?'

For a few seconds, Laura's temper hung in the balance. Then she saw the funny side. 'Stop it, you two!' she ordered, her lip quivering. 'You don't know what I might do if you keep this up. One of you could even be wearing my tea mug if you're not careful.'

Both men laughed.

'I don't know why you think it's all right to laugh at me.' Laura shot a reproachful glance at her overseer. 'I'd believe anything of Rick, but I wouldn't have thought it of you, John.'

'I beg your pardon, Laura. Rick's a terrible influence.'

'That's right, blame me.' Rick shrugged. 'I've got broad shoulders.'

'*And* a deviant sense of humour, *shocking* timing and you don't care two hoots whether you upset me or not!' declared Laura; hot colour fluctuating in her cheeks.

'Hand on heart, I do.' He made the appropriate action with a disarming twinkle. 'But seriously, we'd better decide on a date to start the muster on Miranda.' He deferred with aplomb: 'Laura?

When would you like to start? The Juliana muster is finished, so any time after the round-up suits me.'

There was so much understanding in his eyes that, in spite of herself, Laura had to smile. Appeased, she looked to her overseer. 'How long before we're finished here, John?'

'A few more days will wrap it up. There's not a lot more to do here. We'll be finished before the round-up. Then we'll probably have to spend another few days looking for stragglers where the fences were down. Might be as well to give us a week or so to get over the round-up, come to think of it. The boys play pretty hard.'

'All right.' Laura looked at Rick who was frowning again.

'How many are coming in?'

'Well, that's the question, isn't it?' John hesitated, his eyes on Laura.

'Tell him what you told me yesterday, John. Unless anything has changed?'

'No, I'm afraid not. Even this morning, things seem to be worse. The farther we go, the fewer saleable cattle there seem to be, only a lot of shelly old cows. There are no decent-sized cleanskins, for example, and only the odd bullock.'

'Was it Sykes, do you think?' asked Rick. 'Or some of his men?'

John shook his head. 'Can't have been, because it's still happening, though we don't know how. Sykes didn't get bail. He'll be doing a long stretch for assault, and all his boys have gone off to the Territory. Sure, he sabotaged the muster, but someone else is responsible for the missing cattle.'

Laura shot another glance at Rick. He sat impassively on the ground, his shoulders propped against the log. He seemed totally immersed in some thoughts of his own, his brows slightly knit, his light eyes unreadable.

Yes, and I'd like to know how much you know about this! The thought that flashed, unbidden, was accompanied by an unexpected stab of pain that shocked her.

As if reading her mind, he turned his head and his light eyes blazed momentarily into hers, but he only said, 'The sooner we get onto it, the better, then. Two weeks after the round-up it is. I'll set my men to work on repairs to the yards and spear traps in the meantime.' He stood up and dusted his jeans. 'We'll go, if you're ready, Laura.'

§

Rick set down the helicopter on the road in front of Laura's gate and cut the engine. He sat back. 'I wouldn't say anything in front of your men, but won't you reconsider, Laura?' He sent her an eloquent glance. His voice was gentle yet becoming louder as the woofing of the blades gradually hushed.

'Reconsider what?' Laura was being deliberately obtuse. So, she hadn't heard the end of it, after all. *I should have known!* she thought, looking down at her hands as she unclipped the seatbelt.

'As if you don't know.' The silence lengthened. 'Your ill-judged decision to go and stay out on the muster.' Rick shrugged. 'Think about it: can't you see that a camp full of ringers is no place for you?'

'No, I can't!' she shot back, heedless of his reasonable tone. 'As you said: They're *my* men. And since I am part-owner of Miranda, I have just as much right to be there as you have!'

'I am not disputing that. Merely, that it is not suitable for a woman of your standing: a woman on her own. Laura, listen to me ——'

'No! *You* listen to me!' The rage that she'd swallowed earlier got the better of her. 'Uncle Jonas may have asked you to look after me, but *I* didn't! You may mean well. I don't know. But I can get along without your interference, and I'll thank you to stay out of my life! I—oh …' Laura stopped, choking on her fury.

He was smiling, eyes glinting with admiration and amusement at her fiery display of temper. 'Did you know that when you're angry, you tilt your chin?' he teased. 'Such a determined little chin …' He stroked it with a thumb and forefinger.

Laura made a little infuriated sound and slapped his hand away. 'Oh, you, *patronising* ——!' She turned to fling herself out of the helicopter.

'Now, just you wait a minute.' Rick forestalling her flight by holding her arm. He spoke as quietly as ever. 'I want to know what you meant by that crack about not knowing if I mean well … Hello, you've got a visitor,' he added in a different voice, releasing her, his attention on a four-wheel-drive pulling up in a cloud of dust at Laura's garden gate. 'I'd better stay with you until we see what he wants.'

Laura, startled out of her fury, turned her head to follow Rick's gaze.

As the dust settled enough for the logo on the vehicle to become visible, he began to laugh. 'Aboriginal Affairs. He's come to review the work conditions of your women and try to talk them into leaving.'

'Has he?'

'That's what they do.'

'Really?' Laura was surprised. 'Well, I doubt if he will succeed.'

'I'm going to leave you with it.' Her tormentor stayed in his seat. 'You will have more patience than I to deal with him. If he gives you any trouble, let your protectors loose on him.' He gestured towards Lily and Mary who had come out onto the verandah. Rick waved to them and the approaching official. 'I'll see you at the round-up.' He laughed as Laura ignored his outstretched hand and jumped out unaided. Then he started up the machine and flew off.

'Good morning.' Laura felt ruffled and unaccountably deserted by Rick as she tried to assess the stranger. 'Or is it afternoon? You'd better come in and have some lunch.'

Having invited him in, she mentally wrote the man down as a desk jockey from the city, completely out of touch with Outback life. 'How can I help you?' she asked when they were seated at the table, and Lily had set out cold roast meat and salad with fresh bread rolls warm from the oven.

'I'm looking into the work conditions of Aboriginal people in the Gulf.' He snorted. 'In most cases it amounts to little more than slavery.'

Laura opened her mouth to speak but closed it again as Lily banged down the teapot. 'No such thing here, Mister! We get a good wage, and we got our own cottage.'

The man looked disparagingly around the homestead. 'I can imagine.' His inference was obvious. Laura could almost hear his thoughts. *If this is the homestead, what must the Aboriginal quarters be like?*

'By cripes, Mister, I've heard enough from you!' Lily ripped off her apron and threw it on a chair. 'You're going to come with me.'

Laura had never seen Lily like this, but she remembered Uncle Jonas telling her once, 'Lily is pretty tolerant, kind and helpful, but when she takes her apron off—watch out!'

She stood back to await developments, bringing up the rear as Lily marched the hapless official down to the cottage, closely followed by Mary, still carrying her dust mop.

Lily opened the door of their modern two-bedroom bungalow and thrust him into the neat and shining interior with its simple but quality furnishings. Her eyes gleamed as she watched him. 'Well, Mister? What you got to say now?'

'Well, uh … Well, I … Very nice. Unexpected.'

'Is it?' said Lily, ominously. 'You white fellas should mind your own business; leave us black people alone.'

'But I'm Aboriginal, like you,' he assured them, looking from one to the other.

Lily rolled her eyes and put her hands on her hips. Her tone was grim. 'Think you're going to pull my leg, eh?'

'By cripes, Mister,' said Mary with her irrepressible twinkle, holding her black velvet arm beside his pallid one. 'Something must have scared *you* white, eh?'

'Yeah.' Lily gave him a look of supreme indignation. 'And he'd be even whiter if I had my way. Wasting our time like that. Now, get outta here! I've got bread and biscuits to bake and the

Missus's supper to get.'

The man stood open-mouthed, plainly stunned by his reception.

'Yeah,' agreed Mary with unusual eloquence. 'And I've got to get on with my dusting.' She fixed him with a serious eye. 'Why don't you go up to Doomadgee and see how them poor blackfellas live up there? Then you might work out they'd be better off living on a station like us. Go on.' She prodded him with her dust mop to wake him out of his trance.

'She's right, you know.' Laura entered the conversation for the first time. 'They came back from Doomadgee of their own free will.' She gave the man a level glance. 'Look, I'd invite you back to finish your lunch, but under the circumstances, I don't think it's wise, do you?

The official's pasty complexion turned even paler as his eyes took in the affronted, unbending attitudes of the two women. He sighed. 'Oh dear, I meant well, but I seem to have upset them … quite a lot.'

He looks aghast, thought Laura. *He didn't expect this.* 'Yes, you have upset them. As a matter of fact, I've never seen them like this.' She made a direct appeal. 'They have lived on this station for most of their lives. *I* think they're happy here. Wouldn't that be a fair statement from what you have seen of them?'

He answered heavily with obvious reluctance: 'It would seem so.'

'I am glad you can admit it.' Laura's smile lit up her face as she ushered him out. 'Can you *seriously* imagine women like that allowing themselves to be used as slave labour?'

Chapter Eleven

Midafternoon on the Thursday of the round-up found Laura rushing to pack a few outfits and essentials. She dressed in a pretty pink-and-white striped shirt, comfortable knickerbocker shorts and joggers, giving last-minute instructions to Lily on the feeding of Ben, and a farewell kiss to Oscar and hug to Bess before she drove off to Juliana. She hadn't wanted to go until Saturday morning, meaning to spend only two nights in Rick's home, but John had relayed a request from her men that she attend the song-and-poetry talent quest always held around the campfire on Thursday night. One of her stockmen, Alan, who, it transpired, had worked for her great-uncle with Tom and Mick, was a talented folk singer and a big favourite to win. They wanted her to come and add her bit to the cheer meter.

'I think he'll win,' had said her overseer. 'But every little helps. And it will be a good thing for you, too.'

'I understand.' It was really a question of loyalty, which would go a long way to acceptance of Laura by her men. *Under the circumstances, I can't refuse,* she thought. But she would have liked to.

A shimmering rooftop, barely visible amidst its surrounding greenery, appeared on the horizon, and her stomach contracted as she drew closer. Through the fence that laned the road on the left were rows of vehicles, caravans and tents. Rick had said it was always a big weekend. He hadn't told her the half of it. *So many people! I'm nervous,* she thought. *I can't believe it! I've never been nervous around people before.* But she had to admit that she was well out of her comfort zone.

Too soon for her peace of mind, Laura drew up before the house. It was as she remembered it: A gracious two-storey building nestling in a park-like setting of lawn and trees. Draped in vivid bougainvillea and bignonia, it stood—a proud monument to human endeavour in a fierce land.

Rick came out to welcome Laura as she opened the door of her Land Cruiser. He reached in and took her bag. 'Is this all your luggage?' He sounded surprised.

'Pretty much.'

'Not like my cousin, then. She would have at least three like this.'

'I'm only staying for a few days.'

'That wouldn't make any difference … Oh no, look who's here!' He raised his voice: 'Cass! Come for the round-up, have you?'

'Hi, Rick. Great to see you! And you, too, Laura. Stealing a march on us, eh?' She turned back to Rick. 'But actually, I've been invited to a twenty-first!'

'Have you? Pete, I suppose?'

'No, by the girl herself: Corinne.'

'Pull the other one, Cass.' Rick laughed. 'I don't believe it! I know how you two get on—or *don't* get on. You've been at each other's throats since you were three-year-olds!'

'I know. Well, she was three; I was about six.' Cass grinned and glanced at Laura. 'United against the enemy.'

Rick drew his brows together. 'I beg your pardon?'

Cass winked at Laura and waited—a wicked little smile on her lips.

'Well, that's the end of our peace and quiet.' Rick shrugged. 'Not funny, Cass! I'll pretend you didn't say that. Does Mrs Mac know you're here?'

'It's all right, Rick. I'm camping with Trish—one of the girls from Brunette. She has a very glam camping trailer with everything that opens and shuts. I wouldn't want to put you or the old lady to any extra trouble on my account.'

'There'll be trouble, all right, if Mrs Mac hears you referring to her in those terms, don't you worry about that. But suit yourself.'

'I always do.'

'Yes, and don't I know it!' commented Rick under his breath, as she blew him a kiss and spun around.

Watching her trim, shorts-clad figure breeze away, Laura felt Rick's expression was one of relief. *What a contrast to the way he objected to my stated intention of doing the same thing,* she thought. Already, there was a little ripple of unhappiness in the air as if

Cass, with her impish energy, had disturbed the peace of their surroundings.

'Come on in,' he invited, as they walked the length of a shady trellis onto the front verandah. He stood aside for her to precede him through the open front door. 'Mrs Mac is waiting for you with afternoon tea.'

'Oh, is she? I am really looking forward to seeing her again. It has been so long.' *I wonder if I will know her? If she is as I remember her?*

'Laura, love!' the voice came from the cool darkness of the hall. 'Still a skinny wee bit of a thing, I see. But, my word, how tall you've grown since we last met.'

'Hello, Mrs Mac.' Laura stooped to receive a kiss on the cheek from the plump little woman bustling towards them. 'Yes, it has been a long while since we met. I'm taller than you this time.'

Mrs Mac's smile widened. 'Everyone is taller than me.'

'I wasn't back then.' Laura was touched by the warmth in the twinkling blue eyes. 'But it's lovely to see that you haven't changed a bit.'

'Have I not? Then I'm happy to hear it.' Mrs Mac shepherded them into the dining room where the table had been set for afternoon tea. 'You'll take a wee bite and a cup of tea, then?' Her voice still held a gentle Scottish burr, despite the many years since she had left her homeland.

'Thank you.' Laura was thinking that there was nothing wee about the loaded plates of delicious-looking cakes, biscuits and sandwiches that flanked the Wedgwood tea service.

While they ate, Mrs Mac asked question after question, not

resented by Laura because she knew they were prompted by a genuinely caring interest.

Soon, Rick stood up. 'Thank you, little Mother. I'd better go out and see how the campers are going. It will be getting dark soon.' He turned to Laura. 'When you've finished chatting to Mrs Mac and have settled into your room, come and join us at the camp site. We're getting ready for the talent quest. There are a lot of entries this year, so we'll have to start early.' He smiled. 'Come down when you're ready. There won't be much doing for an hour or so yet, but there will be a barbecue later.'

'Well, time's getting on.' Mrs Mac rose after a few more minutes of kindly questioning. She began to gather the teacups, refusing Laura's offer of help. 'Come along with me, and I'll show you to your room. I do hope you'll like it. Just along the breezeway here and first left at the top of the stairs. It's my very favourite guest bedroom.' She left Laura at the open door. 'I'm sure you'll be very comfortable, love, but if there is anything you need, let me know. You'll be able to find your way down to the camp, will you not?'

When she could get a word in, Laura answered the questions in the affirmative, thanked her, assured her that the room was gorgeous and that she needed nothing more.

Left to herself in the sudden quiet, Laura glanced around the spacious, welcoming room. Through open, adjoining white doors, she glimpsed a walk-in wardrobe and a tastefully tiled ensuite. There were thick towels, luxurious bathroom products, pampering lotions, scented bath salts: everything a cherished guest could want. She made a moue: there could not be a greater contrast to this beautiful room with its jade-green walls; elegant cornicing and mouldings; soft, thick silver-grey carpet and billowing lace curtains at the casement windows than her own simple bedroom at Polaris with its lovingly polished boards and worn rug—and outside toilet and bathroom.

Seeing that Rick had brought up her bag, Laura took a few moments to hang her clothes in the wardrobe. She shook out her evening dress and inspected it before she placed it with the shirts and pants she'd chosen for the rest of the weekend, then sat on the bed for a moment, smoothing the satin quilt with one hand while she looked out the window, a worried expression in her eyes. Then, realising that the light was fading, she ran a comb through her hair, touched up her lipstick, and made her way down the stairs and out into the sunset.

Laura hurried along the lane to where Rick was leaning on the gate to the camping paddock, talking to Cass and some of the other campers, silhouetted in the setting sun. As she came closer, he turned his head to speak to someone on his right, and she saw him—a cameo against the rosy backdrop. Laura gasped, jerking to a halt. Stopped as if by a brick wall, she stared at him. There it was—the likeness that she could not place: the proud, ruthless profile; the savage beauty of the jawline; the lean, muscular body, relaxed yet powerful.

My dream! she thought. *Rick was the man in my dream? No! He can't be! He can't! I never knew him before. I'd never even seen him! This can't be happening!* Shutting down conscious thought, Laura turned and ran in a blind panic back towards the house. About halfway, she stubbed her toe on a tussock and fell, grazing her knee on the baked earth.

The pain sobered her—how ridiculous to think she could run

away from her thoughts and fears. They would always be with her. An element of shame entered her mind as she got to her feet. How would she explain her stupid flight to those who waited at the gate? *Could I say I'd seen a snake? No, they'd only ask why I hadn't called out to warn them.* She could only hope that they were so busy talking that they had not noticed either her approach or intemperate departure.

Taking stock of her injury, she realised she had no choice but to go back to the house to clean and dress the wound and change her torn and bloodstained knickerbockers for a fresh pair of jeans. *Lucky I brought that pair of cargo pants,* she mused. *The legs will be loose enough to hide a bandage.* If she found Mrs Mac, maybe she would supply Laura with some dressings and a bowl, so that she could clean and bandage her wound and go back to the campfire. And start again.

Intent on her purpose, she drew back in blank surprise when a handsome blond man barred her passage in the hall.

'Aha, a damsel in distress! I've always wanted to meet one of those! Come along with me.' Taking advantage of her uncertainty, he put an arm around her shoulders and ushered her into a huge kitchen. 'Are you there, Mum? Better get me a bowl of water and antiseptics and stuff. We've got a casualty here.' He smiled down at Laura. 'I'm Andy, by the way.'

So, this is Andy; the owner of the helicopters, thought Laura, but before she could reply, Mrs Mac came out of the pantry, her kindly face all concern.

'Oh, Laura: What's happened to you, love? Oh, dear, dear! That's a nasty graze. Hang on a minute, and I'll get something to clean it up.'

'Here.' Andy picked up Laura as if she had been a feather and sat her on the benchtop. 'You'd better sit up on this. I don't bend very well.'

The housekeeper returned with a bowl and some bottles and dressings. 'Now, look, Andrew, you'd better let me ——'

'Not on your life, Mum! This is my best chance to get my hands on a pretty woman, and I'm taking it!'

'Andrew!' reproved his mother, but she smiled, set down the equipment and spoke to Laura. 'You look a bit pale, love. In a bit of shock, by the look of you. Are you in a lot of pain?'

'No, it isn't too bad. It will be better once it's dressed.'

'Would you like some Panadol?'

Laura shook her head. 'No, thanks.'

'What about a nice cup of tea—black and sweet?'

'No, thank you.' Laura smiled her gratitude. 'Really, I will be all right.'

'It's just that you look so pale, like you've had a shock.'

I have, but it's not what you think. And I can't tell you or anyone.

'She'll survive, Mum. Now, hop out of the way so I can get on with my first aid.'

'But there's nothing wrong with my hands,' objected Laura. 'And I've done a first-aid course. I can clean it up myself.'

'Uh, uh. No buts. Believe me, I know all about dressing wounds.'

There was a slightly bitter tinge to the words, and Laura, seeing fine scars on his forehead and neck, had already noticed that he moved with a slight limp. None of this, however, diminished his charm or his looks. And the deft way he cleaned her wound and began to dress it showed that he told the truth.

Mrs Mac came over to examine his work. 'That's looking better already, love. Do you think you'll be up to going down to the camp when Andrew's finished? I know they're waiting on you. That sounds like someone looking for you now,' she added, moving out into the hall.

Laura listened to her voice while Andy finished covering the wound with a neat gauze bandage. She sensed that he was listening, too, as a slight smile touched his well-moulded lips. Although, his attention did seem to be completely on his task.

'Ah, Cassandra! To what do we owe the pleasure …?' said the housekeeper in friendly tones.

'Hey, Mrs Mac, how are you?' trilled Cass. 'I've come for the birthday bash, of course. Wild horses wouldn't drag me away.'

'Of course!' Mrs Mac chuckled. 'No doubt, you'll be the life and soul of the party.'

'I like to enjoy myself.'

'And why not? It's safe to say that there will be plenty to enjoy.'

Cass pouted. 'Not as much as last time.'

'Ah well, that's up to you, love.'

'Where's Laura?' Rick stepped through the doorway behind her. 'One of the men said he saw her run, then fall …'

'In here, love.' Mrs Mac preceded them into the kitchen. 'Andrew is looking after her.'

'All finished.' Andy straightened. 'How does the knee feel

now?'

'Fine.' Laura tried to take refuge in humour. 'You're not such a bad nurse, after all.'

'I'm glad you think so.' He lifted her down from the bench, letting his hands linger on her waist just a moment longer than was necessary. 'How about a little reward? You're really something, you know.'

Laura began to feel uncomfortable as he bent his head closer to hers. She tried to avoid him by backing away and found herself pressed hard up against the bench. She was just wondering how best to escape his questing lips when the others walked in.

'Well!' Cass looked them up and down. 'This *is* a cosy little scene, isn't it? What do you think, Rick?'

Rick didn't seem to hear Cass. 'Are you all right, Laura?'

'Yes, thank you.' Laura's most pressing reaction was annoyance with herself for feeling hot and ruffled.

Andy moved away from Laura and spoke easily. 'How are you, Cass? Rick? Now, what have you two been up to?'

'We could ask you the same question.' The tiny brunette had a challenging light in her dark eyes.

'I've been ministering to a lady in distress.' Andy opened his arms wide. 'Behold, Sir Galahad!'

'Sir Get-ahead, you mean!' quipped Cass. 'You can always find the right moment.'

'I don't know what you mean.' He pretended to be hurt. 'The right moment to help someone is when they need it, wouldn't you say?'

His tormentor disregarded the question. 'What do you think I mean?'

He shrugged. 'You're full of it, Cass. You tell me.'

'I'll put it another way: you never miss an opportunity, do you?' Her eyes mocked.

Andy returned no answer. His glance flicked over her before he turned to Rick with unimpaired humour. 'You're a cunning old fox. You've been keeping Laura hidden away from me, haven't you? Why have you never told me about her, eh?'

'I can see it has been a serious oversight,' drawled Rick. 'But you seem to have been making up for lost time.'

Laura, catching the gleam in his eye and remembering his warning to her in the helicopter, could not tell whether it denoted amusement, cynicism or a spark of hidden anger.

'You boys behave yourselves!' Mrs Mac became aware of her guest's suddenly heightened colour. 'I'll not have nonsense of that sort in my kitchen. Look how you've embarrassed Laura. Think shame to yourselves! You go up to your room and change, love. And don't worry about a thing.' She took Laura by the arm to point her in the direction of the stairs. 'Never mind, love. They're a rowdy bunch. Take some getting used to. But their hearts are in the right place.'

As soon as Mrs Mac left her, Cass ran after Laura. 'Laura, you have to stop this. You're taking all our men. Now Andy's fallen under your spell.'

'Don't talk rubbish, Cass.' Laura was thoroughly fed up with the other girl's odd behaviour. 'In any case, you're welcome to him,' she added, keeping her back to her and hobbling as fast as she could up the stairs.

'I bet you won't say that about Rick!' Cass called after her.

What is the matter with her? wondered Laura in frustration as she reached her room and shut the door with relief.

Cass's elfin laughter followed her all the way to her ensuite.

Mrs Mac came back into the hall to frown at Cass. 'You should leave Laura alone. I know your naughty ways. Trouble starts with a capital C when you're around, my girl!'

'Think so?' Cass followed her back into the kitchen, meeting the reproof in her eyes with a wicked sparkle. 'Well, you ain't seen nothin' yet!'

'And I hope I never do! Get away with you, boasting like that!' The housekeeper flapped her apron. 'Go on, the three of you, out of my kitchen. I want to tidy up in here before I go down to the talent quest, which is where you all should be!'

'Okay, Mum. Don't get your knickers in a twist. We're going. Coming, Cass?'

'I'm waiting for Rick.'

'You and Andy go on ahead, Cass.' Rick strolled with them onto the verandah. 'I'll wait here for Laura and Mrs Mac.'

Cass sent him a speculative glance under her lashes then, seeming to think better of her chances of winning an argument, took Andy by the arm and started off.

Chapter Twelve

They found Cass and Andy standing with the crowd in front of the board showing the competitors' names and approximate performance times.

'How come you're not in this, Rick? I suppose it's a rude question?' Cass, bird-like, tilted her head.

'You're right. It is.' Rick gave his lazy smile. 'Why don't you ask Andy?'

'Now, Rick. You know I can't hold a tune,' protested the blond man, mildly.

'I know that,' said Cass with a grin. 'That's why I didn't ask him. But you're a different story.'

'Didn't I just tell you …?'

'But, why? You're good—very good.'

'Haven't we got enough contestants?'

'I suppose. But quantity is not the same as quality.'

'What about Alan? Plenty of quality there, wouldn't you say? Not to mention Bob here and Johnno. And your guitar solos have been known to send the audience wild on more than one occasion. Besides, it would hardly look good if I were to set up in competition with my own men.'

'Dunno about that. Don't think anyone would mind,' offered Bob, one of the Juliana stockmen, standing with Andy.

'I think it would … look good, I mean. Joining in with your team.' Cass placed a beguiling hand on his arm.

'Read my lips, Cass. It's not going to happen.'

'Oh, go on!'

'I have guests to take care of. I'll leave it up to you to entertain us.'

'Okay, you're the boss.' Bob moved away with a smile.

But Cass wouldn't take no for an answer. 'Oh, go on, Rick! I'll play for you.'

'That's a magnanimous offer, almost too good to refuse. But, sadly, I must. You go and play the guitar for Alan, Cass. Now, I'd better find a spot where we can hear you. And we'd better hurry up. Looks like we're about to start. This way, ladies.' Rick moved as he spoke, taking Laura and his housekeeper by an elbow each. They made slow progress as Rick and Mrs Mac stopped to greet old friends and introduce Laura in the dim light.

Responding to the friendly reception, Laura was sure that she would never be able to recognise them in daylight, even if she did manage to remember all the names.

'Comfortable enough? How is your knee?'

Laura looked up to see Rick smiling down at her as he steered her and Mrs Mac towards a likely looking log near the campfire.

'Yes, it's fine now, thank you.' Laura returned his smile, seating beside Mrs Mac who'd plumped down with a satisfied sigh. 'Oh, here's Alan, ready to sing now. We're just in time.'

'We'd better pay attention, then.' He murmured his thanks, settling down between them as the housekeeper made room for him, patting the log. 'It's not often you hear a singer of his quality outside an opera house. The way he's going, it won't be long before he's discovered and signed by a record company. He wouldn't be the first from up here.'

'Oh, I know, perhaps he'll be another James Blundell?'

'I feel sure you're right,' agreed Mrs Mac.

Rick nodded. 'Yes, despite his humility, Alan is at least as good.'

Laura detected admiration in his voice and agreed, but what she was feeling had little to do with admiration, despite the wonderful voice that was due for better things, and a song that she knew in her heart was destined to be a hit. The camp was still as they listened.

Seated so close to her disturbing neighbour, Laura acknowledged to herself that her main sensation was fear. Rick's large presence was protective, kind and comforting, so why did she feel so close to panic? As if she were suffocating with tension? It was all she could do not to get up and run. *Insult poor Alan? And make a fool of myself again?* she thought. *Don't be so stupid!* But it took all her resolution to sit there and involve herself in the music, to subdue her irrational desire to flee.

Laura's evening passed slowly, despite the great entertainment and the fact that Alan easily won the talent quest. Her white rigidity was inevitably noticed and commented on by both her neighbour and his housekeeper.

'Is your knee hurting, Laura?' Rick's solicitous tones upset her more than ever.

'You look in pain to me, love,' added Mrs Mac, before Laura could voice her denial.

Thankfully, grasping the straw held out to her, Laura said that her knee had started to worry her a little and that if nobody minded, she might sneak away and go to bed. Glad the darkness hid her sudden flush from an unaccustomed lie, Laura turned her head and began to rise.

'I'll take you back.' Rick's tone brooked no argument.

Laura said nothing, desperate to escape from overwhelming emotions and find refuge in the quiet sanctuary of her room.

'Yes, love, you go with Rick,' said Mrs Mac. 'There are painkillers in the first-aid cabinet in the pantry. Rick will get them for you.' She smiled and sat back down. 'I will come and see how you are going after the prize-giving. Someone has to show an interest.'

'That's all right, Little Mother. You're about the best ambassador Juliana's got. No-one's going to miss me for five minutes. They'll probably wonder what's happened to Laura, but she has an excuse.' He watched Laura take a first limping step. 'Can you walk, or will I carry you?'

'Of course I can walk! I'm not a cripple. My knee's hurting, that's all. It's probably just stiffened up from sitting too long.'

'Probably. Take my arm, then, and stop being so damned independent.' He folded her arm through his and held her hand to keep it there. 'This way.'

All the way to the house, Laura was panicking about what would happen when they arrived there, but Rick was the soul of courtesy, making her tea and toast to have with her painkillers and wishing her goodnight at her door. Conscious of both the power of his presence and a sense of anticlimax—and still unable to sleep—Laura decided that she must be the most contrary woman on earth.

§

Next morning at the large horse complex and stockyards, round one of the campdraft was in progress, and Laura was an interested spectator after she'd protested to Rick that her knee was fine.

'There's a doctor here today.'

'I don't need a doctor. For heaven's sake, it's just a graze, Rick. I'm not even limping this morning.'

'All right, I'll say no more. This looks like a good spot to watch the campdraft.' He made a place for her on a handy log bench.

There was little between the competitors other than the luck of the draw. Sometimes, with top competitors, the difference between winning and losing was only in the nature and agility of the beast they had chosen to show off their horse's skill.

Laura noted that all the men from Juliana and Polaris were amongst the avid competitors lining up to take a shot at the championship. 'Wouldn't you think that they'd have had enough of this with the muster?'

'They can never get enough of it. When it is your life …'

'I suppose so.'

'You don't sound sure?'

'Yes, yes, I do understand. It is like this country. It grabs you. Oh look, here's Cass on Alan's best horse.'

'Yes, he's given her the ride and is competing on his young horse. Devotion, indeed.'

Laura watched the graceful way Cass cut her cow out from the mob in the camp and guided it around the course. 'She's doing pretty well, though, isn't she?'

'Not bad.' Rick afforded Cass some critical attention. 'She can give most of these ringers a run for their money.'

There was a spontaneous round of applause as Cass retired with one of the better scores of the competition.

'Come and sit up on the fence.' Rick leapt onto the top rail beside John and some of her men and held out his hand as the campdraft gave way to the wild horse riding. 'We'll have some entertainment now.'

Laura didn't, at all, approve of this sport as a way to educate a horse, but she knew that these horses had already been spoilt in the past and, as old campaigners, were more than ready to pit their skills against anyone trying to master them. She watched intently as each of her men approached the horse they had drawn. *Because,* she thought, *you can learn a lot by the way a man approaches a horse.* In the main, she was pleased by what she saw. Each of her men was ready to give the horse a chance to come up to him and settle down before using the rope as a last resort.

Some riders were more skilled than others. A few were dumped unceremoniously, but most gave a good account of themselves on horses with one ambition: to rid themselves of an annoying burden, as they had done so many times before.

In the middle of the arena as the dust cleared, they could see a small figure seeming to argue with the ringer that had just parted company with a particularly mean chestnut with laid-back ears and a hat full of tricks. A horse, Rick told Laura, that many were keen to draw because no-one had ever managed to stay on his back long enough to claim they'd ridden him. 'They call him the Terminator because he puts paid to everyone's dream of being a top buckjump rider.'

'It's Cass!' whispered Laura. 'What is she doing?'

'I don't know.' Rick called to someone who shouted something back. 'What?' He listened again. 'Well, I'll be …' He turned to Laura. 'Cass has taken a bet that she will be the one to ride him.'

Genuinely horrified, Laura put a hand on his arm. 'Don't let her, Rick. She'll get hurt. I know it.'

Rick looked at her askance. 'A lot of notice she would take. And she wouldn't thank me, either. I'm not going to start a brawl out there. And that's what it would be if anyone tried to stop her, believe you me! One thing you'll find out if you have much more to do with Cass: she might look little and fragile, but she can look after herself.'

Laura said no more, but her sense of danger for the small woman was working overtime. *Why must Cass do these things?* she wondered. *Is she a poor little rich girl that wants more from life than her daddy's money can buy her?* It did seem that she courted notoriety—that the things she said and did were designed to shock—or perhaps she got her kicks from doing things that other girls would not.

Cass had apparently prevailed over the ringer. It was true that most of the men could not bring themselves to refuse her anything she wanted, especially when she was in a persuasive and beguiling mood.

Two men took charge of the horse: one at his head, the other holding up a foreleg to keep him still. Laura's heart jumped into her mouth as a third threw Cass up into the saddle where she settled before giving the signal that she was ready. The ringer holding up the horse's leg released it and stepped back at the same time as the other took his hand off the bit and jumped clear.

There was a curious hiatus; a tiny moment of silence and stillness as if the universe was waiting. Then all hell seemed to break loose. The horse gave a bad-tempered squeal and flew into the air, kicking out viciously before setting into his devastating routine. Cass seemed glued to the saddle: a series of punishing bucks could not dislodge the tiny figure. The crowd gasped as the horse screamed in fury and threw himself over backwards. His poll almost hit Cass in the face, but she stepped off to the side before he landed and leapt back into the saddle as he was getting up. It was a graceful and athletic feat of raw courage, and the crowd cheered in admiration.

The Terminator began another series of back-breaking bucks, but Cass clung to him like a burr. Then as Laura watched, the tiny figure seemed to slump a little. Cass coughed and a red stain blossomed on her lips, joined a trickle from her nose and flowed down her chin.

'Make her stop, Rick! Her nose is bleeding.'

'Not her nose. The little fool has taken such punishment that she is bleeding from the stomach. Time to call a halt.' Rick swung down off the fence into the yard. 'Doc, hey, Doc, where are you? John, get the Flying Doctor; he's here somewhere.'

Alan and another man with the same idea followed, waving their hats to baulk the horse and herd him into the corner as Rick leapt for his head.

Laura almost fainted with fear as she saw Rick amongst the flying hooves just for a moment, before he disappeared in the dust. One practised hand found the soft velvet either side of the cartilage above the horse's nostrils, the other grasped the reins below the bit. The Terminator threw up his head once, taking his determined burden with him, then lowered it and stood still—his revolt at an end. He knew from his vast experience that it was the only way he would be allowed to breathe again. Rick moved his hand to stroke the horse's forehead, and the Terminator thankfully filled his lungs, rubbing his head on Rick's chest. 'Yes, and that'll be enough, you old devil. Can you come here, Al?'

'Sure.' The ringer stepped forward to take hold of the bridle.

'I think he'll be all right now but cut off his wind if you have to. It's the only way with this fellow.' Rick gave place to Alan and reached up to the rider. 'Come on, Cass. Get off while you can. You've had enough, and he's not going to stand quiet for much longer.'

'Get lost, Rick! I was winning. I had him beaten. How dare you!' gasped Cass between short, sobbing breaths. 'I can't stop now.'

'You have to. Look at you—you're bleeding all over the place.'

'Violet Skuthorpe used to bleed, but she always rode her horse.' Stubbornly, Cass clung to the saddle.

'You're not Violet Skuthorpe,' said Rick through his teeth. He unbuckled the girth, pulling the girl and the saddle from the horse in one sweep. 'And you've finished your ride.'

He picked her up and began to carry her to the fence.

Laura jumped down into the yard to bring a towel someone handed her, as Cass pummelled Rick's chest. 'Let me go, you brute. You have no right! Oh …' She slumped against him.

'Hand her to me,' said the doctor. 'We've got the ambulance right here. I think she's just fainted, but …' He took the small burden tenderly in his arms. 'What have you done to yourself, this time, eh, little one?' he murmured. 'Bitten off more than you can chew, as usual.'

And we can add the doctor to the ranks of the besotted, thought Laura, watching him hand Cass gently to the waiting paramedic and begin a preliminary check of vital signs. She turned to Rick who was looking after them, tight-lipped. 'You have to admire her courage.'

'Courage? I could find a better word for it!' He spoke with a suppressed passion that effectively silenced Laura and made her look at him closely.

Could it be that he wasn't as immune to the charms of the feisty beauty as he claimed? *Can we put him in the same category as the doctor and most of the male population of the Territory and Gulf?* The thought made Laura feel suddenly ill.

'Take her up to the house, Jack, if she doesn't need to go to hospital,' said Rick. 'The convalescent unit is ready and waiting.'

The doctor gave him a thumbs up and returned to his examination.

Laura had heard his story. Dr John 'Jack' Moore: A tall, fair man in his early thirties, grew up on a cattle station in the Kimberley. After witnessing one of his father's ringers speared on the horns of a wild bullock and the arrival of the Flying Doctor to save him, Jack grew up with one ambition, to become a Flying Doctor himself and devote his life to the people of the Outback. He completed his medical degree, obtained his pilot's licence at around the same time and headed back to his territory. A lifelong friend of Rick's, he usually took his annual leave to coincide with the Juliana round-up.

'The convalescent unit?' asked Laura. 'Is there such a thing?'

'Yes, we set it up for Andy when he had his accident. He was a long time in rehab, so we brought him home to make it easier for him.' Rick smiled. 'And his mother. It was a very worrying time. He almost didn't make it. You've probably noticed his limp?'

Laura nodded. 'And his scars. Was it one of his helicopters?'

'No, a car accident on a lonely road about ten years ago. We were lucky to find him in time. We always keep the unit ready, furnished with simple hospital equipment, just in case someone needs it. A bit like a bush hospital, except it has no staff. We fly them in when they are needed.'

'That's a great idea.' Laura looked up to see a small plane coming in to land. 'Oh look, you have some more visitors coming.'

'So, I have. We'd better go over to the house. I want to introduce you to them.'

Chapter Thirteen

In the convalescent unit, the doctor was sitting by his sleeping patient. She stirred and opened her eyes, looking around as if she didn't know where she was. 'Oh, Jack …' Cass frowned in concentration. 'What am I doing here?'

'Now, that is the question, isn't it?' He picked up her wrist to check her pulse. 'You're looking much better. How are you feeling?'

'Like a fraud. I'm fine. I need to get up.'

'No.' He shook his head and wound a cuff around her upper arm. 'I'm going to take your blood pressure now, and I'll be keeping you here under observation today and tonight. Then, if I'm satisfied there will be no more bleeding, you can get up.'

'Aren't you being a bit heavy-handed, Doc? Ordering me about like that? I mean, where is your famous bedside manner?'

Jack smiled, released her from the monitor and smoothed her silky hair back from her forehead. 'If I thought it would work …'

He shook his head and began again: 'Look, I know why you do these things, Cass ——'

'You don't! Not even I know why I do them.'

'I've seen you do a lot of dangerous things, but this is the worst yet. If you keep on this road, you know you're going to kill yourself, don't you?'

Cass shrugged.

'Why don't you let me tell you why you do them? Then, you can tell me if I'm right.'

'So, now you're a shrink? Go on, then.' Her eyes began to sparkle. 'How do you know that I'll tell the truth?'

'I'll know.'

Cass was silent. Of all the men she knew, liked and pretended to chase, this one had depths she had no idea how to plumb. She met his gaze expectantly.

'One: You're bored. That's why all the mischief.'

Cass laughed.

'Two: You need to prove yourself as a person in your own right. Not just as the daughter of a very rich man.'

Cass's laughter died. Her eyes clung to his.

'Three: You need a challenge worthy of your strength and courage. Something meaningful that fulfils you—makes you know that you've earned your place in life—so that you no longer feel lost and worthless. Because, deep inside, you do feel like that, don't you?'

Eyes cast down, Cass played with the edge of the crisp white bedcover. Her lips trembled. 'Yes.' She raised her head. 'And what's your prescription, Doc?'

'A challenge,' he said, admiring her bravery, her innate honesty. 'But not just any challenge. One that will satisfy your spirit and courage.' He took her hand. 'Go to Adelaide, enrol in a refresher emergency-resuscitation course. And when you've finished, come and work with me in the Flying Doctor Service. Is that enough of a challenge for you?'

'I expect it would be enough for anyone!'

'Will you do it?'

'Will you help me?'

'Of course I will. In any way I can. You know that. But it must be your decision. Your venture.'

'I know.'

'Well? Are you up for it?'

Cass threw up her head, eyes sparkling. 'What do you think, Doc?'

'I think you are a sweetheart,' he said a little unsteadily, his professional mask slipping.

Her lips curved upward. She gave him her other hand. 'Strange, how we think alike. Perhaps we'll work together quite well.'

'I am certain that we will.' He squeezed her hands momentarily then released them with a pat and resumed his professional manner. 'Now, rest for you until teatime.' He took her blood pressure once more, said 'good' and left her alone.

Cass pulled a face as the tall figure walked away but was content to do as she was bid. For the first time in her life, she was free of the restless energy that drove her so relentlessly to so many extremes.

§

'Come and meet my family, Laura.' Rick led her on to the terrace where a small group of people were gathering around the barbecue. 'We'd better give them some lunch before we go much further.' He waved a hand. 'Hello, you lot. Did you have a good trip?'

'Hello, Rick. Yes, we did, thank you. Isn't this country magnificent? You don't really appreciate it until you see it from the air.' A tall grey-haired man strode forward to shake his hand.

Rick introduced him as his cousin Iain. 'They're all my cousins. How does it go, Iain? Our great-great grandfathers were brothers. Or is there an extra great? I forget.'

'Something like that.' Iain smiled at Laura. 'As far as I know, Rick's my closest relative. We're very sparse on the earth, and Rick hasn't done anything to improve things.'

'Steady on, old mate. Laura doesn't want to hear family grievances. Especially not before lunch. Where's Sandra gone? Oh, there you are.' Rick called over a slim blonde woman carrying a large salad platter. 'Put that down and come and meet Laura.'

Sandra's greeting was warm and welcoming, and Laura soon found out that she and Iain had two children in their twenties: Peter, who came over from the barbecue armed with a set of tongs to greet her with an engaging grin, and Corinne, who was nowhere to be seen.

'Where's the birthday girl?' Rick looked around.

'She went to visit Cass in the sick room,' said Peter. 'She should be back soon. Ten minutes in each other's company is usually enough to set them brawling.'

'Peter, please …' protested his mother.

'What? It's only the truth. Could be a pretty lively party if Cass was feeling more the thing.' He met Rick's amused glance with a wry grin and beckoned another man in his early twenties. 'Jason, come and meet Laura; Rick's neighbour.' After explaining that Jason was a friend, not a cousin, he ambled back to the barbecue and began plying his tongs. 'See? I told you,' he said as a delicately lovely blonde girl ran onto the terrace straight into Rick's arms. 'Not even ten minutes!'

'Oh, shut it, Peter,' she snapped, her tone breaking the spell of her doll-like beauty. 'Jack wouldn't let me in. He said Cass has to rest, and if she's going all right, she can come down to afternoon tea, and I can see her then.' She turned wide blue eyes to Laura as Rick made the introductions. 'Old Mr Neumann's place? Did he leave it to you? Really? Wow! I wish someone would leave me a fortune!'

'Don't we all!' This time, Peter's comment was ignored by his sister.

'Seriously, Laura, I do so envy you inheriting a huge property like that!' Corinne surveyed her with an air of innocence and candour. 'It must be worth a fortune!'

'Oh, I don't know about that,' murmured Laura, a little taken aback.

'I didn't know you wanted to be a landholder, Corinne,'

interrupted Rick with an ironic smile. 'I must keep it in mind.'

'Do you mean you're going to leave me Juliana?' She stared at him, round-eyed.

'I might … if you go about it the right way.'

'Oh, you're always pulling my leg!' Corinne stamped her foot. 'But seriously, who are you going to leave it to?'

'I might tell you one day, but I don't think it's something we need to discuss right now. Not when you're in the process of meeting people.'

'No.' Her laughter tinkled. 'Sorry, Laura. What did you do before you inherited your property and came here?'

'I worked in a delivery business in Adelaide, helping out some friends. It got pretty hectic at times. What about you? Studying, perhaps?'

'How did you know? You're good. Oh, Rick told you?'

'No.' Rick shook his head. 'I thought I would leave that to you. Go on.'

'Well …' Corinne looked from one to the other. 'I've just finished an arts degree at Brisbane University, majoring in journalism. I've always wanted to be a journalist—freelance, you know—handing in stories to magazines lining up for me …' she broke off, lips parted, eyes shining, departing into a dream that only she could see.

'That would mean you would have to work, my pet,' said Rick, bringing her back to earth.

'Now, don't be mean, Rick. Of course I am going to work. I have this brilliant idea of doing a series of articles on life in the

Outback. That's why I am staying here when everyone goes back.'

'Well, that's news to me. Wouldn't it be polite to ask?'

'I did ask when I phoned. You just didn't listen. Besides, how can I do my story on you if I don't? Oh, you're pulling my leg again!' Corinne turned her back on him. 'So far, I am doing three stories, Laura. One on Rick, one on Andy and one on Cass. Can I do one on you, too? Oh, please, *please*, say yes!' Her hands clasped together; she looked like a sweet little girl begging for a treat.

§

After lunch, Sandra and Laura prevailed upon Mrs Mac to rest while they washed up the lunch dishes.

'You might have gathered that while we're quite distantly related in some ways, we're a very close family?' Sandra was giving Laura a run-down on the Jamieson family history while they worked.

'Yes, I can see you get on very well.'

'Rick is Corinne's special hero. She's idolised him all her life—since a toddler basically.

Laura smiled. 'More of a big brother, perhaps?'

'Well, no, actually. Peter's her big brother, and they don't get on in anywhere near the same way. She has always said she wants to marry Rick when she grows up. And if she's not grown up at twenty-one, when would she be?'

When, indeed? 'She's very pretty.' Laura was hoping to change a subject she was finding increasingly discomfiting.

But Sandra was not to be deterred. 'Rick's Dad and I often talked about them getting together when she grew up. We used to watch her following him around when she was little. Rick was so patient with her. I don't think a thirteen-year age gap is too much, do you?'

'Not if they love each other.'

'Oh, I knew you'd understand! Just between us, I have high hopes this weekend. Rick is giving her a special birthday gift. She doesn't know what it is yet. But *I* do. Cross your fingers.' Sandra winked and moved away, leaving Laura to wipe down the benchtops.

Well, is that to tell me to keep my hands off him? wondered Laura. *She has no need to worry!* But if that were the case, why had Sandra's words disturbed her so much?

When Laura went back out onto the terrace, Peter introduced her to Trish—the friend Cass was camping with. She had an open, friendly face with long, light-brown hair in a ponytail.

'You will be lonely without Cass,' commented Laura.

'Yes, but only for tonight as Rick has offered me a room in the house. When they heard what happened to Cass, my olds decided to come for the ball. And to make sure I get home all right. Over-protective.' She tucked her hand in Peter's and smiled at him. 'They should know I would be fine here with Rick's family.'

§

At afternoon tea, Laura noticed that Cass and Corinne had

their heads together. *I wonder what those two little cats are hatching?* she thought, watching their expressions. *They're up to something, that's for sure.*

Suddenly, Cass looked up. The mischief left her eyes, and Laura saw something strangely vulnerable there. She turned her head to see the doctor standing in the doorway, looking at Cass. For a moment, it seemed that no-one else existed for them. Then he stepped into the room.

'Hullo, everyone. Am I too late for a cuppa?'

'Of course not! There'll always be a cuppa for you, Jack.' The housekeeper gave him a smile.

'Thank you, Mrs M. You're a treasure.' He moved to where Cass was sitting. 'And how is my patient? Not getting too excited?'

'Only to see you,' retorted Cass, her buoyancy restored. 'Don't you know better than to sneak up on your patients? You might have caused me a heart attack!'

The doctor only smiled, accepted a cup from Mrs Mac with thanks and turned to speak to Rick. 'Where's Andy? I didn't see him about this morning.'

'Mustering down south. He double booked by mistake, and since it was his mistake and none of his men wanted to miss the round-up, he had to go himself.'

'Oh, too bad.'

'Yes, he likes a party.'

'Don't we all. This one especially.'

Laura glanced at Cass, whose eyes were still on the doctor. *The girl's in love with him,* she thought, turning her attention to Rick who was responding with friendly ease to the doctor's remark. She looked back to find Cass studying her with an expression of mischievous speculation. *She might be in love, but she's still Cass,* mused Laura, mentally shrugging.

At dinner, Laura found herself in the spotlight in a way she found particularly embarrassing—worse because there was nothing she could do about it. Laura noticed Cass and Corinne looking at each other as if some kind of message passed between them. When they saw Laura watching, they both looked down at their plates. Remembering their heads together at afternoon tea, Laura began to feel uncomfortable.

In the middle of an animated discussion with Iain, Sandra and Rick, Laura suddenly noticed Corinne staring at her as if she were hanging on every word. Cass, talking quietly to Jack, seemed to have forgotten her, but Corinne gave her all her attention.

'Doesn't Laura have lovely eyelashes?' she cooed, suspending the conversation. 'You must show me later how you fix them on.'

'I beg your pardon?' Laura looked and sounded bewildered.

'If you're interrupting a perfectly good dinner conversation to talk inanities, Corinne, then you'd be better off to listen instead,' said Rick, dryly, but with a hint of amused indulgence.

'But I'm interested! Surely, you've noticed them, Rick.' She turned to Laura. 'Your eyelashes: they're false, aren't they?'

'No.' Laura was aware of eyes on her. 'Of course not.'

'Here, Corinne, pass me the slaw,' growled her brother. 'Can't you ever think of anything besides your appearance?'

Silently blessing Peter, continuing his criticism in an undervoice, Laura resumed her conversation and, looking across at Cass, saw that she was concentrating on placing some salad on her fork, a mischievous quirk to her lips.

The evening dragged a little after this, with Corinne's childish utterances seeming to gag every conversation.

She might be decorative, thought Laura. *But she's as dumb as they come. Or is she? Maybe she's smart enough to be doing this on purpose to break up the conversation. But why? To keep the attention on herself?* she wondered, becoming increasingly frustrated.

'It might be as well to have an early night tonight.' Rick looked around the table and summed up the situation. 'We've got a big day tomorrow.'

'My birthday!' announced Corinne, unnecessarily.

'I haven't forgotten,' said Rick. 'But ——'

'No, none of us have been allowed to forget!' Peter grinned and was instantly told by Corinne to shut up.

That seems to be the sum of her conversation with her brother, thought Laura. *Oh, for an excuse to leave the table.*

'But …' Rick ignored the interjections. 'We have a lot to do to get ready for the ball. Some of us have to set up the outdoor dancefloor and decorate the verandah and terrace.'

'Mrs Mac and I have got the decorating covered,' said Sandra.

'Can I help?' asked Laura.

'And we'll organise the dancefloor—me and Jason—if you like?' offered Peter.

'I'll take all the help I can get.' Rick laughed, jumping up as Mrs Mac came in with the tea tray. 'Thank you, Little Mother.' He took the tray and set it down on the table. 'Pour the tea, please, Corinne, if you feel up to it; otherwise, I'll do it.'

'Of course, I'll do it, Rick.' Corinne, rushing to obey, tripped over a chair, neatly tipping the contents of the milk jug into Laura's lap. 'Oh Laura, I'm so sorry! I just can't help being clumsy sometimes. Here, let me help you.'

'It's fine.' Laura mopped up with the tea towel Mrs Mac handed her before going back to the kitchen for more milk and a magnificent Victoria sponge cake. 'No, really, it's fine,' she assured Corinne who was fussing around her, exaggeratedly apologising.

'Shut up, Rinnie, and cut me a piece of cake. How many times does Laura need to hear it?'

'Don't call me that, Peter. I've told you a million times! Cut the cake yourself if you want it!'

'Children, children …' Rick picked up the knife and deftly sectioned the sponge. 'Don't let your manners get in the way of a good party, will you? Can I get you a cup of tea and a piece of this, Laura?'

Laura gave a rueful smile; she'd been given her perfect excuse. 'No thank you, although it looks scrumptious. If nobody minds, I think I'll take myself off to bed. It's been quite a day, one way and another, and I really do need to shower and change.' She wished everyone a good night and shut herself in her room, stripping off her wet, sticky clothing and stepping into the shower with a sigh of relief.

Just as she was wondering whether to try and wash her jeans and shirt in the handbasin so the milk wouldn't stain them, a knock fell on her door.

'Can I come in, love?' called Mrs Mac.

'Of course.' Laura, clad in her dressing-gown, opened the door.

'Give me your clothes, and I'll rinse them out for you and put them in the drying room. They'll be dry by morning.'

'You're an angel, Mrs Mac. I was just about to try and wash them in my handbasin. Are you sure?'

'Of course. It's no trouble. I have some other things to do as well, and we can't let them stain.' She took the garments from Laura and cast anxious eyes over them. 'Ah, she's a worry, that wee girl.'

'You mean, her clumsiness?'

'Aye, that's what I mean. Clumsiness—in more ways than one.'

Chapter Fourteen

Drifting in and out of troubled sleep, Laura awoke early to the noise of running footsteps and what sounded like muffled sobs. Curious, she pulled on her dressing-gown and put her head around the door to investigate.

Mrs Mac was just coming away from a door farther down the hall. When she saw Laura, she stopped and put the handkerchief she had been holding to her mouth in her apron pocket. 'Morning, love. You're up early.' The ravaged face belied the jaunty tone.

'So are you, Mrs Mac. Is something wrong? Or can't you tell me?'

The handkerchief was whisked out of the pocket, as tears sprang into the older woman's eyes. 'Oh, love, I'm sorry. It's Andrew. I had a call this morning. He didn't come in from the muster last night. Each camp thought he was with the other, and it wasn't until the camps stirred this morning that they found

173

out. They called to see if he had come back here, but he hasn't. His room is empty. The bed hasn't been slept in, so he hasn't come and gone again.'

'Oh, Mrs Mac, I'm so sorry. Have you told Rick?'

She nodded. 'He's coming now.'

Laura's head snapped up as a tall, vital figure strode down the hall and put his arms around the weeping woman. His voice was gently comforting.

'Hang in there, Little Mother. There's no point in thinking the worst just yet. Andy's a very experienced pilot. He may have had to ditch her and damaged his radio. I'll call his crew and find out where he was last seen. You go down to the kitchen with Laura and have some tea. I'll leave at first light.' He took the stairs three at a time, vanishing into the office.

'I'll be right down, Mrs Mac.' Laura dived back into her room. She dressed swiftly in jeans and a long-sleeved shirt before running down the stairs, but Rick was before her. In the kitchen, she found him making toast. Rick looked up as Laura entered, then significantly towards Mrs Mac, sitting, pleating her handkerchief.

'The kettle's boiled, Laura. Can you make the tea?' He glanced at her over his shoulder.

Laura did so, pouring them each a cup just as Rick came to the table with a pile of buttered toast.

'Come on, Little Mother, drink your tea. Try to eat something.' His voice was gentle. 'I'll keep in touch by radio. Laura, can you keep an eye on her?'

'Of course.'

'No, Rick!' Mrs Mac tugged urgently at his sleeve. 'Take Laura with you. Please!'

'I don't think that's a good idea.'

'No, please, Rick! She's had first-aid experience.'

He turned an arrested gaze on Laura. 'Is this true?'

'I've done a course in first aid for accident victims.'

'Please, Rick. It would make all the difference to how I feel.'

Unable to stand the anguish in the housekeeper's pleading eyes, Laura hoped that Rick would agree for Mrs Mac's sake. For herself, her heart lurched at the idea of being alone with Rick, and her stomach churned sickeningly at another thought—that of what they might find. However unpleasant she had found Andy's overtures, he was someone's beloved son, and she would not wish such a fate on him. Or anyone.

'We'd better make some sandwiches and a thermos of coffee to take with us.' Rick began rummaging in the refrigerator.

'I'll do that,' offered Laura.

'Thanks. I'll go and get some blankets and spare clothing for Andy. The first-aid kit is already in the chopper.'

In the helicopter, Rick explained what was happening, 'We're searching in a grid formation. Jack is taking a line to the east of us, and Dyson is on our west. Ours is an area south of Polaris in approximately a straight line from here. Keep a good eye out for anything unusual, won't you?'

'Well, I'll do my best, but everything looks different from up here.' She found the glare so trying; as early as it was, she had to put on sunglasses.

'A downed aircraft can be surprisingly hard to spot from the air, particularly if it went down amongst trees or on the wrong side of a rocky outcrop or hill.' His eyes narrowed in concentration. 'So, if you see anything unusual, we'll take a closer look, even though he is not supposed to be anywhere near here.'

Laura nodded—his words emphasising the reality of the situation. Andy had not come in from his mustering flight. There had to be a reason. At best, it was an emergency landing, at worst … She forced herself to focus on the terrain below as they approached the river where Rick had saved her from the crocodile.

'There's our yards. They look quite extensive from the air, don't they? Let's just check this flat over here … No, nothing. So, if he's made an emergency landing, it's not here.' He glanced at Laura. 'Recognise that place?'

'Yes.'

'You don't know how close you were, do you?'

'Oh, I do, I do. It's just that —— And I never thanked you! I'm sorry.'

'I don't want your thanks. Don't you know that? If anything had happened to you … Laura, you know what I want.'

'Do I?' Laura's hands began to tremble. She clenched them in her lap.

'If you're not blind, deaf and … Look, now is not the time, but I think we need to have a conversation.'

Unable to answer, her heart thumping in her throat, Laura turned her attention to her property, trying to pick out familiar landmarks, when a brilliant flash of light almost blinded her. She pinpointed a second shaft. 'Rick! There's something way over there, look. Between the rocks and the ti-tree scrub.'

'On Miranda? Shouldn't be …' Another ray of light speared around the perspex bubble of the cabin. 'That's a signal!' He swung the machine around to investigate. Hope sounded in his voice, and for the first time, Laura realised what it must have meant for him to go out on this search. From what she'd seen, he seemed to regard Andy more like a brother than a friend. He even called Mrs Mac Little Mother, treating her the same way, so there was definitely a closeness there. And he was right about keeping a lookout from the beginning. Andy was in a place no-one would have expected to find him.

They landed on a claypan a short distance from the disabled helicopter. When the dust cleared, a grinning Andy came out from behind his craft, pocketing a small, compact mirror. His shirt was torn and dirty, and there was blood on his face, but other than that, he seemed fine. 'Good old Rick,' he said after greeting Laura. 'Always coming to the rescue. I was hoping you'd see me. Thought you could have been a bit far away, though.'

'Don't thank me. You were lucky Laura saw the sun flash off something over here. I might have gone right past without noticing. We can be grateful you're in better shape than you were the last time I found you.'

'Yeah.' Andy patted his pocket. 'I've carried this little mirror since Boy Scout days, but that's the first time I've had to use it.' He glanced around. 'The chopper's a bit of a mess, eh? Beggared my radio, too.'

Rick ran an appraising eye over the wreck. 'It'll be an insurance job by the look of it. What happened?'

Andy shrugged. 'Dunno, mate. She just lost power suddenly. I tried to make it to that claypan over there, but she just couldn't do it.'

'What were you doing over here on Miranda? Everyone thought you were well south of Polaris. Even your own men.'

'Well … I was coming home. There was a bit of daylight left, so I thought I might join the party, socialise a bit and go back in the morning.'

'But you were down south of Conroy's, weren't you? What direction were you coming from to end up over here?'

'I thought I'd do a sweep over Polaris and Miranda, just to make sure there's no *unauthorised* activity going on while everyone's at the round-up. Check how good a job the boys had done with their mustering, keep an eye out for Laura's horses, that sort of thing—you know, like I do for you.'

'That's very kind.' Laura instantly forgave him for his amorous attitude the last time they'd met. 'Thank you. I'm only sorry it has caused you so much trouble.'

'Ah well …' Rick left the subject. 'You've had a bit of an uncomfortable night, but it could have been worse. Better let Laura dress that cut on your face while I get the thermos, and we'll give you some breakfast before we go.'

'Too right. I could do with a feed. My backbone's rubbing on my belt buckle.'

Rick handed Laura the first-aid kit, water bottle and turned to the radio. 'I'd better let the others know you've been found.' He picked up the transmitter with a grin. 'I know one little lady who is going to be made very, very happy in the next few minutes.'

'Turning the tables, eh, Laura?' Andy's smile of bravado did not quite reach his eyes. Other than that, he was the same charming, carefree person she had met the day before yesterday.

Laura cleaned and dressed his wound in amicable silence, pleased that Andy had acknowledged the possibility of stock theft and was doing his bit to prevent it.

'Well?' he joked. 'Will I live?'

'Yes.' She smiled. 'You'll live. I don't think there will even be much of a scar to remember it by. You were lucky.'

'I always have the devil's own luck, don't I, Rick?' He accepted the steaming mug and sandwich the other was handing him.

'More lives than a cat.' Rick smiled at Laura. 'But I wouldn't push it if I were you.'

At the sight of coffee and sandwiches, Laura realised she was famished.

The return journey was accomplished quickly, and in no time at all, it seemed to Laura, they were back in the hangar.

'Are you going to give your patient an arm, Laura?' Andy leant on her shoulder as he got out of the chopper.

'If you need it.'

'He doesn't. Don't you think you'd better go and find your mother, instead of fooling around?'

Andy grinned. 'Straying onto your patch, am I? But you're right. I'd better go and show myself to Mum so that she can see I'm still in one piece,' he agreed, sauntering away.

Laura turned to take some of the gear out of the chopper, but Rick's hand on her arm held her back.

'Let's talk now, Laura, while we have some peace and quiet. I'll never get a word in edgewise when we go up to the house.'

'Rick! Rick!' Corinne erupted through the door of the hangar—her face a study in petulant fury. 'Is it true what Andy just said? You went without me! Why? Why didn't you take me? I wouldn't have minded getting up early.'

'Damn!' He let his hand fall from Laura's arm and turned to face his stormy cousin. 'It wasn't exactly a joy ride, you know. *And* it has had a much better ending than it might have done.'

Corinne almost stamped her foot. 'But you took Laura! Why not me?'

'Laura has first-aid experience.'

'Oh, do you?' Her mood changed, chameleon-like, to one of interest.

Laura nodded and Corinne seemed satisfied. She turned to push in between them.

'But, Rick, it's my birthday and you promised me a special gift,' she said, hanging off his arm. 'You haven't forgotten?'

'So I did. And, no, I haven't forgotten. It is just that a lot has been going on this morning. But we'd better check in with Mrs Mac first.' Rick cast up his eyes and shot Laura a rueful glance. 'We'll talk later, Laura. That's another promise.'

Watching them walk away together—Corinne looking up at Rick and chattering, listening to his indulgent replies—Laura felt that she'd been given a breathing space. *If I'm not grateful to that brat, I should be,* she thought, following slowly. There was no question in her mind that Corinne had been spoilt all her life and that Rick had had as much of a hand in it as anybody.

In the kitchen, Mrs Mac was ecstatic, arms around her son's shoulders where he sat at the table. She straightened as they entered, hugging and thanking both Rick and Laura. Back to her kindly, bustling self, she had an array of dishes in the warming oven. 'You didn't get time for a proper breakfast, so sit down, both of you.'

Rick laughed, his eyes meeting Laura's with an amused message: *We'll have to humour her,* they said.

Laura responded with a smile, feeling warm and happy to be at one with him. Surprisingly, she found that she was hungry again.

Corinne, sinking into a chair beside Andy, told him pettishly that he had ruined her day.

'Sorry about that, didn't do it on purpose. Besides, there's plenty of it left—the day, I mean. Anyway, happy birthday.'

'Thanks,' she said shortly, turning away.

'Don't go anywhere, Corinne,' said Rick. 'Have a cup of coffee while we eat. Then I might be able to find something for you that will put a smile back on that pretty little face.'

Corinne danced to his side like a child, her humour magically restored. 'Ooh, my special present! Oh, Rick, I can't wait! What is it? What have you got for me?'

'You'll see, in a while.' He cut into a crisp rasher of bacon. 'And I hope it makes you a bit easier to live with.'

Cass came in, looked them over with mocking eyes, declined Mrs Mac's invitation to eat, made a flippant comment to Andy and turned her mischievous attention to Laura. 'And how's the Girl Scout today?'

'Don't answer that, Laura,' said Andy. 'Cass is just jealous that she wasn't there to take care of me.'

Cass gave a hoot. 'Unless you needed an out-of-practise midwife, I probably wouldn't have been any more use to you than Laura.' She accepted a cup of coffee and sat down next to Andy to chaff him about his carelessness.

Chapter Fifteen

Laura and the others spent most of the day decorating the outdoor dancefloor that Jason and Peter had erected in the garden adjoining the verandah, with Rick and Jack kept busy rigging up the sound system for the evening's celebration.

'For those of us who want to dance under the stars.' Sandra gave a romantic sigh and broad smile as she wound fairy lights around a potted shrub she'd dragged to a strategic spot near the musician's dais the men had placed on the verandah. 'My daughter loves dancing.'

Hanging streamers, balloons and mirror balls to best advantage, Laura worked as quickly as she could under the able direction of Mrs Mac, who passed everything up to her as required. Verandah posts were decorated with greenery and flowers with long tendrils of coloured lights hung on several close growing shrubs.

'Aye, and doesn't it look, for all the world, like fairyland?' Mrs

Mac had a happy lilt in her voice.

'Yes,' agreed Laura. 'Just think how beautiful it will be tonight!'

By this time, everyone was exhausted, so Mrs Mac's suggestion that they have a quick sandwich and go away to rest for the remainder of the afternoon was well received.

'Cass,' whispered Corinne from the door of the convalescent unit. 'Are you awake? Can I come in?'

'Yes, come in. Just don't tell Jack. I'm supposed to be sleeping.'

Corinne extended her right hand. 'Look what I got for my birthday!'

'Wow! That's some rock you've got there, girl!' Cass took in the huge diamond. 'And I'm an expert! Is this the special present Rick had for you?' She noted the setting. 'Did it belong to his mother?'

'Yes, Rick's Dad left it in his will to be given to me on my twenty-first.'

'Oh, man! That's some special gift. Lucky girl!'

'I know.'

'Hey!' Cass's lips curved into a secret smile. 'Why don't we play a little joke on Laura?'

'I like the idea.' Corinne looked at her expectantly. 'Go on.'

'Put that ring on your other hand.'

'What?' Corinne gave a nervous giggle. 'But what will Rick say?'

'It doesn't matter. He won't know anything about it if you're subtle. Here's how we do it.' Cass elaborated in a whisper. 'Ready?'

'Ready!' Corinne put her head around the door. 'The coast's clear. Will we do it now?'

'Come in,' said Laura in answer to a tap on the door and a whispered request, looking up to see the two girls in the opening. 'Cass, Corinne: is there something you need?'

'Not really.' Cass's eyes were sparkling. 'Corinne is just a teeny bit excited. She has something she wants to show you. Naturally, it has to be a secret for the present. We can trust you, can't we, Laura?'

'Well, of course, but ——'

'Look what Rick has just given me!' Corinne thrust out her left hand. She waggled the third finger, watching Laura closely for her reaction.

Laura found herself gazing at a magnificent diamond in a heavy, old-fashioned setting, glowing with a pure inner fire. 'Oh …'

'Well? What do you think?'

'It's gorgeous!' Laura spoke in a hollow voice, aware that both girls were subjecting her to intense scrutiny. 'Congratulations. But I don't understand. Why does it have to be a secret?'

'Rick's a bit old-fashioned.'

Like the ring, thought Laura.

'He doesn't want to announce anything just yet, while I'm so young. You see, he's been waiting for me to grow up.'

Hmm … That could take a while.

'And he wants to be sure I won't change my mind. I mean, of course, I'm sure, but he says it is not to be announced until my next birthday. So, you won't say anything will you? You'll respect my confidence?'

'Of course.'

'Thanks, Laura. I knew you'd be pleased for me.'

'Of course!' Laura smiled. *And why is Cass grinning like the Cheshire cat?* she wondered as the girls said goodbye and whisked themselves out of the room on a shared giggle.

What business of mine is it if Rick wants to tie himself up to an empty-headed child? And why should I care, anyway? There's something wrong with all this, she thought. *It just doesn't sound like Rick—any of it.* Although her earlier conversation with Sandra did add some credence to the story. Was this what Rick had been wanting to talk to her about? Surely not! Not by his body language, at any rate. Or had his obvious attraction to Laura got in the way of his future plans with someone else? Again, she wouldn't have thought it. But whichever way she looked at it, she had to admit that her rest was at an end, with no logical explanation for the hollow, empty feeling inside her.

§

Laura spent more time than usual on her make-up, swept her hair up into a chignon with little jewelled combs and sat on at the dressing table, biting her lip, reluctant to face Rick after Corinne's disclosure. Finally, she stepped into her narrow-strapped aqua chiffon evening gown with its fitted bodice and heart neckline and zipped it up, standing back to view the effect in the mirror. The skirt fell in soft folds from a low waist to mid-calf, swirling gently as she placed her feet in delicate silver sandals and took a last doubtful look at herself. *My jewellery!* she thought, encircling her throat with a little collar of pearls and placing pearl-and-diamond drops in her ears. *Now I'm as ready as I'll ever be,* she mused, her eyes luminous between their thick fringe of lashes, subtle use of the blusher concealing her pallor and highlighting the sculptured planes of her face: none of which she noticed.

Descending the stairs, head high, she had no idea of the effect she had on those observing. Rick, looking up, stopped what he was saying and moved to the stairs; Corinne glanced at Cass with a downward turn of her mouth; Sandra drew in a sharp breath, troubled eyes on Rick; and Mrs Mac turned to view her son's predictable reaction.

'You look … breathtaking!' Rick held out a hand as Laura paused on the bottom stair, her eyes locked to his. She could have said the same of him, handsome in his perfectly fitting black dinner suit, except that she found his effect on her senses far too overpowering to speak.

Andy went down on one knee beside Rick, extending his arms theatrically. 'My queen, my rescuer! How thy light shines forth!'

'Get up, Andy, you ass!' hissed Corinne. 'This is supposed to be *my* night, not hers!'

'But of course it is, poppet.' Andy rose to his feet, apparently feeling no chagrin at having his extravagant gesture unnoticed by Laura. 'You don't like to share, do you?' But he wasn't looking at Corinne. Then he shrugged, met her stormy eyes. 'Come on.' He hustled her away. 'We'll have this dance. I won't mention names, but some people are off with the pixies already. Without even having one drink!' He heaved a comical sigh and gave her his charming smile. 'It's a sad state of affairs, little one. You and I must console each other.'

Corinne went with him without demur, but she didn't smile at his antics. Both of them could see that something was going on between Rick and Laura that no-one else could have any part in.

'Dance with me,' invited Rick. Or was it a command? Everything she thought she would say to him in the light of her new knowledge went out the window. Like an automaton, Laura reached out to place her hand in his.

They danced without speaking for the most part. The time flew past as dance after dance went by with Laura savouring the feel of Rick's arms around her. It was as if she was meant to be there and knew it was the same for him. After a while, she became aware of his eyes upon her—intense, searching—as if there was something about her he was taking in. It made her feel strange: she didn't know whether to bask in it or turn and run. In the end, she couldn't help but ask, 'Why are you looking at me like that?'

'Like what?'

'I don't know.' She shrugged. 'As if you've never seen me before?'

He smiled and held her closer. 'Can't you guess?'

I'm afraid to, she thought and shook her head. 'No.'

'I've just realised something I thought I knew.'

Laura drew in her breath, not daring to ask him what, knowing he was going to tell her anyway.

'Do you know how beautiful you are?'

'Rick! What kind of question is that?'

His answer took her breath away. 'A rhetorical one, of course, because you don't, do you? You don't even care about things like that. It is one of the things I love most about you. That and your independent spirit. But that wasn't it. There is something more—something most important …' He bent his head towards her as he spoke, so close that she was certain he was going to kiss her right there on the dancefloor. Her heart beginning to beat wildly, Laura melted towards him.

A swift movement beside them distracted her. 'Oh, there you are, Rick!' Sandra, Corinne and Andy magically appeared on their other side. 'I've been looking all over for you. We need you for some family photos.' She turned to Laura. 'You don't mind, do you? Andy will look after you.'

'Sorry, Laura. Duty calls.' Laura watched Rick shrug his shoulders and allow his cousins to lead him away—one on each arm.

'Now, don't tell me!' Andy observed her with an engaging grin. 'The last thing you need is looking after, but we may as well humour them. *Force majeure*,' he murmured, beginning to dance with her. 'Are you sure you want to take them on?'

'I beg your pardon?'

'Nothing.' He eyed her impishly. 'Just a figure of speech.'

They danced for a while, with Andy giving a humorous run-down on everyone around them, then he said, 'I might have the golden hair, but Rick's the golden boy, all right.'

Laura hadn't been paying attention to his nonsense, but this statement, coming out of the blue the way it did, puzzled her. 'What are you talking about?'

'Nothing much. Dancing with you has given me an appetite. Let's go in to supper. The Little Princess has to cut her cake. And—whoopy-doo!—we all get to eat it.'

Laura could not help feeling that there was more behind these words than his usual insouciance and tried to shake off the vague sense of disquiet that had settled on her. They clapped and cheered with the others, sang *Happy Birthday* when Corinne, looking like a beautiful porcelain doll, played her ceremonial role. Laura felt a pang when she saw how sweet and innocent she looked. *She really is beautiful,* she thought. *And it is obvious that Rick, like the rest of her family, dotes on her.* The diamond, this time on her right hand, flashed a warning as Corinne sliced her cake into portions.

'Have this, Laura.' She looked up to find that Rick, having done his duty with the photos and speeches, was handing her a plate with a piece of cake. 'It's good.' He put both plates he was carrying on the table, pulled out a chair for her and sat down beside her.

'Thank you. It looks delicious.' She tried a morsel. 'Mmm, it tastes heavenly.'

The cake, a beautiful blackforest torte, was a testament to Mrs Mac's culinary art, as Rick wasted no time in pointing out. He was regarding her quizzically. 'Can she upstage Lily, do you think?'

'Wash your mouth out!' said Laura in Lily's best style with a cheeky grin. 'Lily has never made me a chocolate cake, so we'd better give her the benefit of the doubt. But in this instance, perhaps. It really is a magnificent cake.'

'And very rich. Ready to dance off the calories?'

She looked into his eyes and what she saw there sent her pulse rocketing. 'I think we'd better.' She forgot that Corinne wore a big diamond ring and that she had meant to refuse.

'It's about time I got you to myself again. I've had enough interruptions. Now, where were we?' Rick danced her into the shadow of a tree and drew her towards him. Laura shut her mind to all her fears and leant into him. This time, there was no interruption, no guardians to save her. Her arms, of their own volition, crept around his neck—her lips raised themselves to his in a heart-searing kiss that neither was prepared for. When eventually he lifted his head, he held her fiercely for endless moments: his eyes searching her moon-drenched face; the deep pools of her eyes, though his own were in shadow, unreadable.

'Oh, Laura, Laura,' he murmured against her hair. 'You don't know what you do to me.'

Likewise, thought Laura, *except that I think you know very well what you do to me!*

'You must know that I love you.' Rick felt her go rigid in his arms. 'Laura?'

Shocked out of her trance, Laura suddenly remembered his cousin's claim. 'Isn't there someone else to consider?'

'What do you mean, "someone else to consider"?'

'Corinne?'

'Corinne? What about Corinne?'

'Are you saying you have no commitment there?'

'Well, of course not! Only ——'

'Did you give her a ring or didn't you?'

'Yes, I did, but … Laura!'

Not waiting to hear any more, Laura wrenched herself out of his arms, ran into the house and up to her room, turning the key in the lock. Rick followed, tapped on her door, calling to her in a concerned voice, but when she refused to answer, went away.

Hardly knowing what she was doing and sobbing her heart out, she packed her things, left a note for Mrs Mac and crept down the stairs and out of the house, drawing back into the shadows as she heard voices.

Suddenly, there was a scuffle.

'Get out of it, Peter!' whispered a determined little voice.

'Aw, c'mon, Trish. You know how I feel about you.'

'No, I said! You know the rules.'

'Okay, okay! Take it easy.'

Peter and the girl from Brunette Downs! Laura shrank back against a vine-covered trellis post and wished that she was anywhere but here. But if she didn't want to be noticed, she would just have to stay put until they went far enough away not to hear her leave.

There was a short silence, then: 'Hey, Pete?'

'Mmm?'

'Did you see that big diamond ring your sister was wearing? She's going around looking all mysterious and saying Rick gave it to her. And making out that it's something more than a birthday gift!'

Peter gave a derisive snort. 'She would!'

'Well? Did he?'

'In a manner of speaking he did, and then again, he didn't.'

'Oh, come on, Pete! Why don't you say what you mean?'

Laura, by now standing bolt upright, almost shouted, 'Hear, hear!'

'Well, it was Rick's mother's ring, and Rick's dad left it in his will that it was to be given to Corinne on her twenty-first birthday. So, Rick, being the executor, or some such thing, gave it to her. Satisfied?'

'I don't understand. Why would she pretend?'

'Well, that's her all over, isn't it?'

'I guess …' Trish sounded troubled. 'Fantasising again. I don't know where she gets these ideas.'

'Well, I know where she got this one—Cass!'

'That'd be right! If ever I saw a stirrer! Don't get me wrong, I love Cass, but sometimes she goes way over the top.'

'Yeah, she overdid it this weekend, that's for sure.'

'Maybe the doc will take her in hand?'

'Looks that way. I don't envy him the job.'

'Don't you?' she mocked. 'Plenty will! She's not Daddy's little girl for nothing, you know.'

'Money's not everything. Now, shut up and come here.'

Laura slowly let out her breath. So, it was just a made-up story, after all. *Cass and Corinne,* she thought, remembering the sly looks and giggles. *Why am I not surprised?* But that didn't make it any better.

Laura dare not think about her own vulnerability where Rick was concerned. Aside from all her demons, he was her trustee. Why had he done nothing about what was going on with her cattle? He had to know. He had to! Yet he hadn't even tried to address it. Pain screwed up her face. She waited until the others went inside, crept to her Land Cruiser and, turning the key in the ignition, eased out onto the road.

A short time later, Cass, saying goodnight to everyone at the inexorable command of her doctor, heard what Trish had to say about the ring and made a moue. 'Corinne,' she whispered as the other came off the dancefloor. 'Come here.'

'Going up to bed already are you, Cass?'

'Yes, Jack's a hard taskmaster. Come up with me. I want to talk to you.' Cass took her arm and pulled her towards the door. Once inside her room, she let her exasperation show. 'Listen, you silly muggins, why are you going around telling everyone what we told Laura? She'll find out the truth, and you'll ruin the joke.'

'Joke? What joke?' Corinne turned limpid blue eyes on her companion. 'You might be joking, but I'm deadly serious.'

Cass stared, dumbfounded. 'But what about when Rick finds out?'

'Rick loves me. What is there to find out?' Corinne tossed her head and walked to the door. 'Anyway, Laura's gone home. Andy saw her drive away. Goodnight.'

'Oh, my Lord, what have I done?' Cass collapsed onto the bed and buried her face in the pillow. For the first time in her life, she began to consider the consequences of her actions and to regret a mischievous impulse.

Chapter Sixteen

When Laura returned to Polaris, the house was dark and silent: a strident echo of her loneliness without Rick. *Without Rick!* She stifled a sob. *Whatever I want, whatever he makes me feel, this is how it has to be.* The moon was bright, bathing the landscape in a silvery glow, dramatically dividing light from shadow. She made coffee and sat on the verandah with Bess at her feet, lost in her thoughts until stiff and sore; she realised with a start that dawn was breaking. Making fresh coffee, she watched the sun come up as she had aeons ago before any of this had ever happened.

Restless, she rose, moving around the house, tidying already immaculate rooms, turning on a few sprinklers in the garden, before going down to catch Ben for his morning exercise. Her mood was reckless enough to cope with whatever he dished out, which, since she had instructed Lily to feed him oats every day, might be a little more than she bargained for. But Ben was the perfect gentleman, allowing her to enjoy her ride so that, for just a little while, she forgot despair.

Lily and Mary made no comment about Laura's early return from the round-up, both going about their chores with their usual matter-of-fact thoroughness. It was only when Rick made a surprise visit to the homestead that Lily rolled her eyes at her sister, and they both unaccountably disappeared, leaving Laura to face him alone.

'Hello, Laura.' He loomed in her doorway.

'Rick, I …' Laura swallowed, resisting an overwhelming urge to turn and run. 'Come in.'

'Thanks.' He looked around. 'Where are your staff?'

'I don't know. I …' Laura moistened dry lips. 'They … they were here earlier, but now they seem to have just … vanished.'

'They are very sensitive to atmosphere. Probably giving us some privacy. I've been worrying about you. Do you feel you can tell me why you ran away from me last night? Just when we seemed to be getting on so well?' He paused, noting the colour rise in her cheeks. 'Because if it is about Corinne ——?'

'It isn't … I mean, not entirely.' She hung her head. 'I heard the others talking later and realised that it was a made-up story.'

'Cass …' He rubbed his jaw. 'I warned you about her and Corinne, well … Don't get me wrong, I love Corinne. She is the little sister I never had. But that doesn't mean I am blind to her faults. She tends to live in a fantasy world that has no bearing on reality. And her mother encourages her. Somehow, that worries me more than anything.'

'I suppose there is nothing wrong with dreaming big.'

'Well, that depends on the dream, doesn't it?'

'Yes, you're right. It does.'

'I've warned her about making up stories about the ring she inherited, so there shouldn't be any more of it.'

'That's good.'

'So, if it isn't that: what is it?'

Laura shook her head and turned away.

'Laura, come here.' He moved towards her. 'Whatever is bothering you, we can work it out.'

'Don't touch me, Rick!' She stepped back. 'I'm sorry, but I can't … I just can't!'

'You know, Laura, Jonas always said that most of life's problems can be thrashed out over a billy of tea in the bush.' Rick spoke in gentle tones, obviously aware of her plight. 'But if you never stop to talk to me—always run away—how can I understand what's going on with you?'

Laura shrugged but could find no answer, tears welling at the mention of her great-uncle. Rick's soft, reasonable tones were nearly too much for her because she remembered Uncle Jonas saying exactly those words to her.

'So, in the absence of Lily, why don't I brew us a pot of tea, and we can sit down and make a start?'

Laura sat at the table, chewing her lip, listening to Rick's quiet footsteps moving about her kitchen as he boiled the kettle, made tea and found some of Lily's baking. He seemed just as much at home here as he had at Juliana, and perhaps, he was. Who could guess how many pots of tea he had brewed for her great-uncle over the years? Stifling a sigh, Laura knew she had to talk to him this time. She owed it to the man, after all. But how could she tell him her fears and suspicions? Until she knew beyond doubt that

Rick wasn't the one robbing her, there was nothing she could say.

Then, he was setting out cups, pouring her tea just as she liked it, placing a plate of Anzac biscuits within reach. He put his hand over hers. 'I know this won't be easy, but I'll make a start. If it is because of the hard time you had with your late husband ——'

Laura gasped, all her colour receding to leave her starkly white. She snatched her hand away. 'What makes you say that?'

'It's the way you begin to respond and then freeze as if you're expecting something to hurt you. It puzzled me until … Look, Jack has friends in Adelaide: Sally Winter's family. He knows something of your tragedy. No, he didn't gossip, that's not Jack's way; he just told me the bare facts and to treat you gently—that you might have more to deal with than anybody knows.' He saw the anguish in her face. 'Real love isn't like that, Laura. Whatever he did to hurt you, we can overcome it together.'

You couldn't begin to know the half of it, thought Laura, wringing her hands. *Oh, if that were all!* Dimly, she could begin to see that Rick was right—if only she could trust him.

'Laura, these things can be addressed with patience, love and understanding. Why don't we take it as it comes? I won't rush you, do anything you don't like. What we need is time; time to build some trust between us.' Again, he read her expression. 'Laura, what is it? What is it that stands between us? Tell me.'

Her mouth twisted. *How can I?* 'Rick, no! I can't go there! Please, I … just go!'

'Don't you see? You won't begin to heal until you do. I'm not leaving until I find out why you don't trust me: what this is all about.'

Are you the one stealing my stock? I don't think so, but I have to be sure. No, I can't ask it! She was saved from having to answer by the sound of a helicopter descending to hover at her front gate. They both moved to the doorway in time to see Corinne jump down, reach up for a briefcase and come running across to the verandah.

'Yoo-hoo, Laura! Can I come in? Oh, good, Rick's here with you.'

'What are you doing here, my pet? I thought you were interviewing Andy.'

'I was, but he had to go, so I told him to drop me here on his way, and I could make a start with Laura's interview. He was going to come back for me later, but I saw your vehicle and said I'd go home with you. You don't mind?'

'It would be all the same if I did! I suppose it didn't cross your mind that I might have something of my own to discuss with Laura?'

'But what could you possibly have to discuss that I couldn't hear?'

'That would be telling, wouldn't it?' said Rick with gentle irony. 'And another thing, young lady, wouldn't it have been manners to have asked Laura first?'

'I did when I first requested an interview, and she said to come any time. Isn't that right, Laura?'

'Yes, that's right. I did say that.'

'Well, is it okay?' Corinne looked expectantly from one to the other.

'Yes, of course.' Laura spoke with an effort. 'Come in, we're just having a cup of tea.'

Rick drained his cup, rose and picked up his hat. 'Thanks for the tea, Laura. I'll leave you to your interview. I need to talk to John about your muster.' His eyes went to his cousin. 'You'd better get on with your interview if Laura is agreeable. I'll come back in one hour. Be ready.'

'Will you stay for lunch? I don't know what we'll have if Lily doesn't come back, but there must be something we can use to make sandwiches.'

'No, it's okay, thanks. I'm a bit pressed for time just now.' He put on his hat and walked to the door. 'I'll be in touch. One hour, Corinne. Don't keep me waiting.'

'Ooh, I love a man to be the boss, don't you?' sighed Corinne as he drove away.

'Not particularly.' Laura leant back and indicated the chair opposite. 'Now, what did you want to ask me?'

'I've got to have a riveting title. How about: *Rags to Riches Story for Outback Heiress?*'

'Oh, that's a bit over the top!' Laura laughed, thinking to herself, *The way things are going, it will be the other way: more like riches to rags!*

'Well, at least I've made you smile. You and Rick both had the longest faces when I came.' Corinne sat down and busied herself setting out pad and pens. 'I've done my research on you.'

'Oh, have you?'

'Yes, and before we start, I want to remind you that Rick is mine.'

'Right.' Laura raised her eyebrows. 'Next item?'

'Why are you looking like that? Don't you believe me?'

'I think we both know it isn't true.'

'Yes, it is! It *is!*'

'Look, I heard about that little stunt you pulled with the ring.'

'It wasn't a stunt.' Corinne tossed her head. 'You'll find out! Rick loves *me*. Besides, I know all about you.'

'No-one knows *all* about anyone.'

'Well, try this for size.' Suddenly, Corinne went off at a tangent, the same way she had during conversations at Juliana. 'Oh, who is that handsome man?' She pointed to the photo on the mantelpiece, sidetracking her victim.

'Uncle Jonas when he was young,' said Laura, bewildered by this change of tack.

'Oh, really? I thought it might be your husband. His name was Stephen, wasn't it?'

'Yes, but I don't see what this has to do with ——'

'Good journalists: they do their homework,' purred Corinne. 'Find out the background to their story. One that could be very interesting—or not.' She sat back, eyeing Laura with limpid malice.

'What are you talking about?'

'Sally Winters.' Corinne spoke with relish. 'Your husband, he ran off with her, didn't he? They were into something you didn't like. I won't go into specifics.' She pursed her lips. 'It's not *nice*.'

Shocked, Laura stared at her tormentor. There was a moment's silence while she tried to deal with this body blow. *She can't be this terrible*, thought Laura. *She doesn't know what she's doing… Oh, doesn't she?* scoffed her inner voice. Finally, she found words to reply: 'Corinne, please, I think we'd better define some boundaries for this interview.'

'Of course. I'm sorry, Laura. It must be so painful for you. What would you like to talk about?'

That's a good question, thought Laura. *I'd like you to go, you little monster.* She shrugged. 'What it is like to live in the Gulf? But first, I would like to know something.'

'Yes?'

'Where did you hear about Sally?'

'She was your best friend, wasn't she? She and your husband died together in a car accident. Laura, I am so, so sorry.' The words oozed false sweetness, like poisoned honey. 'It must have been just too dreadful for you.'

'Where,' repeated Laura with deadly calm, 'did you get your information?'

'I told you: research …All right, Cass overheard Rick and Jack talking privately in the unit. They didn't realise she was there.'

'But that's a privileged conversation. Cass had no right ——'

'Oh, nothing's sacred to Cass. Anyway, you know the old saying, "All's fair ——"'

'I'm going to terminate this interview because I've had enough of you.' Laura took a deep breath, wondering how she was going to keep her temper. 'Rick is down at the overseer's cottage. Why don't you go down there and wait for him? It's the grey one on the left, next to the men's quarters.'

'All right, I will! But first I need the bathroom.'

'You'll find it on your way.' Laura pointed. 'Out that door. Back verandah, on your right.'

Laura had just flung herself down, shaking with suppressed fury and distress, when a piercing scream rent the air.

'What's the matter, Corinne?' Laura raced out onto the verandah to stand in front of the bathroom. 'Open the door.' She had to repeat herself several times as scream followed scream. Finally, she was rewarded with an answer.

'I can't! You open it! Oh, please hurry!'

'Is it a snake?' Laura looked around for the hoe.

'No. Oh, hurry, hurry!'

Laura pushed open the door and stood back, dissolving into helpless laughter as a large and extremely indignant goanna exited the room, flicked an outraged tongue at Laura and vanished under the house. 'It was only a goanna, Corinne,' she pointed out when she could stop laughing. 'You're all right.'

Corinne, standing on the edge of the bathtub and clinging to the shower-curtain rail, wore a look every bit as outraged as the goanna. 'Don't you laugh, you beast! I know you put it in here to frighten me. Beast! Vile beast!'

'Yes, I trained him specifically to protect me from nosy journalists! Of course I didn't put him in here! They live under the house. I must have left the door open this morning. They're only lizards: they don't hurt you, you know, unless you try to harm them.' Laura's rage dissolved in the humour of the situation. 'Look at it this way, it's an Outback experience for you to write about.'

'Oh, you ——!' Sobbing, Corinne pushed past her and ran down the path towards the overseer's cottage.

Karma, thought Laura, feeling avenged as she went back inside the house. *I must remember to give that goanna an extra lump of mince next time I see him. I would have felt sorry for her if she hadn't been such a spiteful little madam. I wonder what explanation she'll give when she gets down to the cottage?*

Rick looked up as his cousin reached the cottage verandah. 'What? Finished your interview already? That didn't take long.'

'Come in, Corinne,' invited John. 'Like a drink?'

Their visitor took a deep breath. 'No, I didn't finish my interview! And yes, after what I've been through, I *do* need a drink.' She took another breath. 'Laura can get mad, can't she? She just told me to go away and not come back! Then, when I was in the bathroom, she set her pet goanna onto me!'

The men's eyes met in silent laughter as Rick said, 'Did she, my pet? You must have upset her. Were you a little too probing in your interview? Laura is a very private person.'

'And feisty,' added John.

'That, too.'

'Oh!' Corinne surveyed their teasing expressions. 'You're just the limit, both of you! No wonder Laura is like she is!' She slammed down her glass and left the room, pacing up and down the verandah, stormy eyed, until Rick came out.

'Over your tantrum, are you? We'd better go home, then.'

'Rick, I've been thinking.'

'Have you?' He glanced at her as they drove away. 'That's a

prospect. What about?'

'I'm sick of trying to write articles on people who won't take me seriously, and I've just had another idea.'

'And?'

'I want you to let me work for you, so that I can write an article on what it is like to work in the Outback.'

'Work for me?' repeated Rick. 'What will you do? You can't help Mrs Mac. Your hit-or-miss housekeeping techniques would drive her to distraction in the first three minutes, and your bush skills are non-existent, as far as I know.'

'I could be your station secretary and bookkeeper. You know, like in the old days.'

'Oh my God!' Rick slapped his hands down on the steering wheel. 'Will the office ever recover? All right, I'll give you two weeks' probation, and if you don't measure up, I'll send you home. Deal?'

'Deal! Thanks, Rick.'

'And tread carefully with Laura. She's more vulnerable than you might think.'

'Yes, Rick. Of course, I will. I'm so sorry I upset her.'

Rick nodded, satisfied with her answer and the docile tone. Watching the road, he didn't catch the malicious gleam in his cousin's innocent blue eyes.

§

Laura picked up the receiver of her new colour-coded

touchphone, which had just been installed along with its satellite tower and solar batteries, to answer her first call in the house.

'Hello, Laura.'

'Corinne,' said Laura, wondering what she wanted.

'I must apologise, Laura, for any misunderstanding the other day. I really didn't mean to upset you.' Corinne watched Rick close the office door with an approving smile as he left. 'I don't seem to have made a good journalist.' She pre-empted Laura's reply. 'So, Rick has given me the job of station secretary until we, um, get married. Look, the main reason I'm ringing is to pass on an urgent message from Rick. He needs you to meet him as soon as you can on your Miranda boundary.'

'The Miranda boundary? But why?'

'I'm not sure. Something has come up about the muster, and he stressed it is urgent.'

'All right. Where on the Miranda boundary?'

'Um, the bore.'

'Which one? There are two.'

'Oh, I've forgotten. Say the names for me, would you? … Yes, that one, the second one.'

Laura put down the receiver, nonplussed. *Why would Rick want to meet me way out there at Manson's bore?* she wondered as she caught up her handheld radio and went out to the station ute. *Unless he's found the cattle or the horses? Maybe the horses?* The thought made her hurry into the vehicle, preoccupied by what such an odd message might mean. Then, realising she should take a flask of coffee and some food, she went back inside, calling to Lily to help her. 'Why would he want me to meet him out at

Manson's bore, Lily?'

'Dunno, Missus. But if it's Boss Jamieson, he'll have a good reason. Didn't he say?'

'No, the message was relayed by his cousin. She's his secretary now. Something urgent, she said.'

'Ah. Well, no matter. He'll tell you when you get there.'

'I wish I had your faith in him, Lily.'

'I wish you did, too, Missus. No reason why you shouldn't. Here you are: sandwiches, cake and biscuits. And your flask.'

Laura thanked her and rushed out to the ute, dropped the basket on the seat and took off, driving as fast as she dared. *At least I've got the handheld,* she thought, fretting at the time the long winding drive was taking over the rough track. *He won't be able to accuse me of not having a radio.*

Three-quarters of the way out there, the engine coughed and cut out; her vehicle rolling to a halt. With disbelief, she stared at the fuel gauge. Empty. Why hadn't she thought to check it before she left, instead of dwelling on maybes and possibilities? Annoyed with herself, she took up the handheld radio to call Rick and tell him what had happened, but John Riley answered.

'Rick must be out of range. I'm not far away. Can I help? Pass a message on?'

When Laura explained her problem, he told her that he would go back and get a drum of fuel and be along as soon as he could.

Laura sat fuming, furious with herself for not checking something as fundamental as her fuel level. *At least I remembered to bring some smoko,* she thought, trying to make the best of it. *I wonder why Rick isn't answering? If he's at Manson's, he shouldn't be out of range. Maybe he's forgotten his radio?* The thought made her smile. Rick would not forget any essentials; she was sure of that.

It seemed to take forever before she saw a dust cloud coming her way. *Oh, good, here's John coming now. I hope there's still time for me to meet Rick unless he's gotten sick of waiting.* For the hundredth time, she wondered why he wanted to meet her way out here.

The vehicle pulled up, and she saw with relief and surprise that it was Rick. *Perhaps he did hear the call, so that's good. He's not sitting out there waiting.* She'd just begun to wonder why he was coming from the direction of Polaris when she saw his set face, compressed lips, and unbending attitude as he got out and strode towards her.

'You make it very clear, Laura.' His eyes were hurt and angry. 'Very clear.'

'I'm sorry; I don't understand. I thought you wanted to meet me.'

'I send a message to tell you I'll see you at your house, and you come all the way out here without even checking to make sure you have enough fuel, so anxious you seem to be to avoid me!'

Now was Laura's chance to tell him that Corinne had given her a false message, but somehow, she couldn't. *Let him think it,* she thought. *At least it will stop me having to answer the impossible.* She bowed her head.

'You know how I feel about you, but I'm done beating my head against a brick wall. Maybe one day you'll want to talk. If that day arrives, come to me, and we can start afresh. But until you do, there can be nothing between us.' He looked up at the sound of another vehicle. 'Here's John with your fuel. You'll be all right with him.' And he walked away, driving off without a backward glance.

Chapter Seventeen

It was with relief that Laura finally went out to the cattle camp on the shared holding with Mick in the truck, carrying the horses for the muster. Driving through the open woodland with its tall, thick grasses, she suddenly shed all her worries and was a teenager again. How she had loved camping out when she had come to visit Uncle Jonas: a freedom that was balm to her spirit.

At the camp, she was touched to find that, beside the modern blue-and-white tent—with its gauze front and windows, completely enclosed against snakes, goannas and biting insects—there was a hessian shower cubicle set up under a tree limb. Strung by a rope with a set of pulleys from the branch was a twenty-litre bucket with a tap and shower rose soldered to the bottom: a luxury bush shower, easily pulled up to the proper height when filled with water because of the pulleys.

When Laura tried to thank Mick, knowing it was his work, he turned a deep red and hurried away, mumbling something about having to unload the horses. She went to help him, and quite soon, the camp was a bustle of activity. Men were checking their gear, bringing wood for the campfire and the branding fires, a water tank was brought up on the back of a truck and a road train pulled in. Laura knew that, as well as his other off-farm investments, Rick owned a fleet of road trains, something that if she thought too hard about, added to her unease.

The Juliana horses were on the road train, sleek and well-muscled, obviously well-bred. Jim, their groom, seemed to be a good mate of Mick's, and they went about their duties together amicably while the other Juliana men checked and repaired the bronco and holding yards.

The two cooks, Tom and Jack, were chatting as they assembled their pots, cauldrons, trivets and camp ovens, supervising the placement of wood for the campfire. Laura, catching snatches of wry laughter here and there, saw that they seemed to be old friends.

She wandered over to where Mick and Jim were hobbling and belling the horses and caught Ben to lead him out onto the grass for a while, then gave him a generous dipper of oats in a nosebag, before turning him out with the other horses. There seemed to be no sign of the boss of Juliana, for which she was thankful. How would he treat her after their latest contretemps? *I suppose he will be polite in front of his men,* she reasoned. *And he said I would have to come to him. So, if I don't, he should leave me alone, and I will be safe.* She wondered why the thought gave her so little comfort.

The evening around the campfire was a comradely affair, and Laura enjoyed it hugely—to begin with. They had grilled steak and beef ribs, apparently a stockman's favourite meal, though Laura could never understand their predilection for them—

though tasty, they were often tough and stringy. *Be that as it may!* she thought with a little inward smile, knowing that the ringers must never be deprived of their beef ribs roasted over the coals whenever there was fresh meat. Potatoes baked in the ashes and damper with golden syrup completed a meal that kept Laura locked in the memories of her childhood.

Later in the camp, they would all be too tired to do more than turn into their swags after they had eaten, but tonight the men were fresh, and when they had washed their tin plates and pannikins in the bucket of hot water provided by the cooks, they called on Alan to sing for them.

'No can do.' Alan shook his head. 'My throat's a bit sore. Sorry.'

Waiting for the clamour of protest to die down, he apologised again. 'Why don't you ask Bob? Or how about getting Johnno to recite *The Man from Snowy River*? That'd be the go. I can listen as well. Rest my throat.' He gave a grin. 'No lubrication out here!'

Laura smiled at his reference to the absence of alcohol. All the mustering camps on Polaris and Juliana were known as 'dry camps'.

The camp cooks provided a bit of light relief by devising a tall-tales contest with themselves the only entrants, everyone agreeing that no-one could come near them for imaginative interpretation.

Bob agreed to recite *The Man from Snowy River* if Johnno would add his repertoire of Banjo Patterson favourites, taking turns with him. Somewhere between *Clancy of the Overflow* and *The Man from Ironbark*, Rick arrived, and once again, Laura saw firsthand how his men admired him, greeting him with acclaim and making room for him on one of the logs around the fire. He acknowledged Laura and her team with a gesture and a smile and turned back to his men.

'I'm sorry I'm late. Some paperwork to finish before I came out here. You know how it is.'

'Yeah, we know,' they chaffed. 'Always some excuse.'

'You ought to be pleased I take that kind of thing seriously.' Rick grinned. 'Otherwise, you blokes won't be getting paid. And we can't have that. Missed supper, have I?'

'It's all right, Boss. I saved you some scraps.' The Juliana cook handed him a plate piled with succulent ribs. 'At great risk to myself, I might add, fighting off these greedy beggars. Enjoy.'

Laura seated between her overseer and Mick, on the other side of the campfire, thought he seemed perfectly in his element as he tucked into his meal.

Johnno, pleading exhaustion, declared that he would have to leave further entertainment to Bob, who took his guitar and led them in a few popular bush ballads. Laura enjoyed singing along with him as much as the men appeared to. And Rick, having finished his meal, was sitting back, relaxed and listening, a mug of tea in hand.

'Hey, Bob,' whispered the ringer seated next to him. 'Why don't you see if you can get the boss to give us a song?'

'Righto. I'll give it a go, but I think you've got Buckley's, mate. You know the boss; he don't usually …'

'Aw, come on, Bob! He'll take it better from you. You're the one that's been doing all the singing.'

'All right, Charlie. I said I'd give it a go,' came the faintly irritable reply. 'Just don't get your hopes up, that's all.' Bob uncurled his long frame and went over to where Rick was sitting. 'How about it, Boss?' He held out the guitar with a deprecating grin.

'You've been doing a pretty good job, yourself, Bob. You don't need me. I thought you and Alan and Johnno would've had it covered pretty well.'

'Yeah, normally we would, but it's too soon after the round-up for us. We've all been going it a bit hard. I'm getting a sore throat, and Alan's already got one.'

'Come on, Boss, give us a song?' added Johnno. 'You're the only one of us that hasn't strained your voice.'

'Okay, okay, I get the picture.' Rick held up his hands. 'All right, just one. Then you unruly lot had better roll into your swags.' He smiled as he took the guitar.

'Yeah, yeah, we know. Early start. We've all done this before, you know.'

Amidst the general laughter, Rick said something Laura didn't catch and turned his attention to the instrument.

'Now you'll hear something, Miss Neumann.' The Juliana cook had left his chores to come and listen. 'The Boss don't often sing, but when he does, no-one forgets it in a hurry.'

'Laura, please, Jack.'

'Thanks, Miss Neumann, but if it's all the same with you, I'll call you Missus, same as Tom does. Then we'll all be on the same page. It's true enough, anyway.'

For a startled moment, Laura wondered what he meant. Then she realised that all the men would know that she was part owner of Miranda. 'Of course. Whatever you like.' She braced herself for the old joke about not being called late for dinner, but he only asked her if she had heard the Boss sing.

'No, I've never heard him. Is he as good as Alan?'

'Dunno, Missus.' The cook stroked his chin. 'There's some say he's better than Alan because he has a greater range. But all in all, I think he's about as good. Just different, that's all. You'll hear him now, and you can decide for yourself. But enjoy it because it don't happen very often …' He fell silent because Rick had begun to strum softly, tuning the guitar.

Laura was caught up in the current of silent anticipation that flowed almost tangibly through the still figures seated in the glow of the campfire.

The song took Laura by surprise. It was the haunting ballad, *Annie's Song*, written and made famous by John Denver; the kind of song that is loved by bush people and touches hearts the world over. But Rick's voice surprised her even more. It was a pure, rich baritone—a subtle mix of clarity and velvet that was indescribably beautiful, and the impact on the audience was such that a megastar might have envied. Laura felt an actual physical pain in her chest and throat while the magical voice caressed the poignant lyrics of the song, rose in triumphant volume and gently faded away. She was held captive by the silken web of that voice, as were all the others.

There was a deep silence, broken only by the incongruous chirping of a cricket somewhere in the night and the small sounds of the dying fire. Jack had been right: she, for one, would never forget. *Alan is good, really good,* she thought. *But Rick's voice is truly something else.* Adding to the sudden applause and appreciation, Laura became aware that Rick was looking at her across the embers. His eyes were dark and secret, the planes of his face grim in the dull firelight, and he held her gaze as effortlessly as he had held her in his arms the first day she had ever seen him. The pain in her chest grew worse, and she had the odd sensation that her heart was being drawn out of her body. Her hands were clenched so tightly that the nails bit into her palms. She felt as a moth must feel when it beat its wings so desperately against a lamp glass, only to be destroyed when it reached the source of its obsession.

No! I can't—I must not!—fall in love with him! she thought in panic. *What will I do?* Inwardly, she writhed, but outwardly, Laura looked calm, serene, with the firelight gleaming red off her hair and throwing into relief her delicate features. Then, Rick's attention was caught by one of the ringers, and he released her from his spell.

Laura moved restlessly and looked up at the starry sky. Without knowing why, she began to tremble and, sick and shaken, went away to her tent.

Sleep evaded her until the early morning hours. Over and over, she thought of Rick saying that she would have to come to him. How easy—and how impossible! She dare not think of that blazing kiss they shared at the ball. Before she slept, Laura was determined on one thing: she could not—would not—fall in love with a man she didn't know if she could trust. She had loved and trusted once before, and it had brought her years of heartache that had culminated in a final, shattering blow. She had not clawed her way out of the dark abyss that followed, just to fall right back again.

Staring with pain-filled eyes into the darkness, Laura thought back to her decision to make a new life here. She had been sure that managing the vast enterprise she'd inherited would keep her too busy to worry about the ghosts that haunted her consciousness. She recalled how she had yearned with a great longing for Uncle Jonas's shabby old home and the majestic solitude of his lonely lands. And now? What had it brought her? Tears squeezed out from under her lashes, soaking her pillow before she slept.

Laura was up before dawn, pale and silent, to join the ringers for breakfast. Bacon sizzled in a great pan on the fire, and they ate it with damper, washed down by hot black tea. Normally, Laura would have revelled in it, but she could not recapture the mood that had carried her through yesterday. She went, as did the others, to saddle her horse. As soon as it was daylight, the chopper would be here spotting cattle and sending them out of the scrub, and they must all be ready.

'Let me do that for you, Miss Neumann.' The friendly face of Ned, the young Juliana jackaroo, appeared before her. With an ease born of long practise, he swung the heavy stock saddle up on her horse's back, pulling up the front of the saddlecloth into the gullet to create an air channel, tightening the girth and surcingle. He coiled her stockwhip, placing it over the kneepad. 'Now you're right to go.'

'Thank you, Ned.' Laura smiled at him, and he flushed under his fine skin, not yet weathered like the other men's.

'S'all right, Miss Neumann. Glad to be of help.'

'This is your first muster, isn't it, Ned?'

'In a manner of speaking, Miss Neumann. This is my first time up here in the Gulf. But I used to help my old man in the holidays. We come from the falls country near Grafton on the New South Wales North Coast.'

'You'll notice the difference, then. Are you enjoying it here?'

'Too right, Miss Neumann, I ——'

'I'll finish here for you, Ned,' said Rick, coming up unnoticed. 'Better go and hop on your horse. The chopper's coming.' He checked the girth. 'You too, Laura. Are you right to go?'

'Don't you think I know how to saddle a horse?' Laura twitched the reins over Ben's head and swung gracefully into the saddle.

'Now, don't be like that. I hope you didn't say that to Ned. You would've hurt his feelings. I expect my jackaroos to behave like gentlemen.'

'Well, of course I didn't. I thought it was very kind of him.'

'It was,' he agreed, straight-faced but with a twinkle. Rick was his old, genial self. Their previous encounter might never have been.

'Well, I'd better move.' She began to turn her horse as the ringers filed past.

'Hold on a minute!' A bronzed hand shot out and grasped her nearside rein. 'Is that old Ben you've got there?'

'Yes, he's looking good for an old boy, isn't he?' Laura ran a hand along the silken curve of his neck. 'Rick? Are you going to let him go so I can get going?'

Rick shook his head, maintaining his hold on the rein. 'He is looking well, very well,' he conceded, meeting her eyes. 'But you can't ride him, Laura.'

'Of course I can! Why not?'

'You know why not.'

'I know he's not a spring chicken any more, but I've got him well-conditioned, and I'll take care of him.'

'Take care of him? If you get stuck in a rough place with a rough beast, you're going to need him to take care of you! It wouldn't matter in the softer country, but up here, even ten years can be too old, and he must be, what? Fifteen or sixteen?'

'Fifteen,' she admitted.

'Too risky. Now, get off him, and I'll give you one of mine.'

'Don't tell me what to do!' Agitated, she tried to turn Ben and ride away, but Rick caught both reins and stopped him.

'You'd better get off him.' He didn't raise his voice, but there was no mistaking the purpose behind his words, and Laura felt the hair rise on the nape of her neck.

'He's a good horse. We'll be all right.'

'He *was* a good horse. He's past it now.'

Laura made a little sound of frustration as the last of the ringers rode by, hiding their smiles. 'You're making a fool of me in front of my men!' she hissed. 'Now, let me go!' Her emotion communicated itself to the horse, and he sidled and threw up his head.

'You're the one behaving like a fool.' Rick took one hand off the reins to rub the horse's face and soothe him. 'The old man admired your spirit, and so do I, but this is just plain wilful pig-headedness. Now will you get off, or do I get you off?'

It was no idle threat. Laura's memories of Cass in the cattle yard told her that he was more than capable. Fury rose in her, blinding her to everything except her refusal to be bent to his will. Her eye fell on her stockwhip, and without thinking, she snatched it up and brought the handle down hard across the back of the hand holding her reins.

'You little ——' he gasped, pain widening his eyes.

The temporary paralysis of his hand, combined with Ben's violent reaction to a blow aimed so close to his head was enough to free her, and pressing home her advantage, she drove her heels into her horse's ribs. 'I'm sorry, Ben, but needs must …' she murmured as he bucked in disapproval of this unaccustomed rough handling, relieved that she managed to stay on until he settled down and cantered away to join the others.

Laura didn't dare look back. Part of her exulted that she had beaten her adversary, and part of her, filled with guilt and regret, realised it had diminished her to have resorted to violence and hit him like that. Why had she done such a thing? Laura shrugged. Just another stupid act to add to the long list of things she owed Rick apologies for. She couldn't understand herself— the fury he was able to engender in her. But to lash out physically? Even to her, it was beyond the pale.

In all the pain, both mental and physical, Stephen had caused her during the four years of their marriage, she had never once reacted like she had just done, had never lost control enough to use physical violence. And at someone who was right in what he said, who was really, at the end of the day, only trying to help her.

Closing her mind to conscience, Laura took her place on the wing of a small mob of cattle that the chopper had just sent out of the scrub and started guiding them back to the yards. But her concentration was not what it should be, and several times, Ben almost left her behind when he saw a beast break out of the mob before she did and went after it. 'Nothing wrong with you, is there, Ben? You're still a good horse, no matter what Rick says.'

Laura didn't know what she could say to Rick, so it was as well that he was nowhere in sight. *Probably herding up another mob*, she thought, resolutely putting him out of her mind.

After the first full day, Laura was tired and went away to her tent as soon as she had eaten. Weary, but satisfied, she went to sleep without being prey to thoughts and worries that normally had her tossing and turning.

This was the pattern for the next few days. Rick, busy with his own horses and men, seemed to have forgotten her existence, for which she was grateful, because she couldn't look at him without being galled by the memory of her shameful conduct towards him. In her heart, she was beginning to deepen the realisation that Rick had been right, and this made her feel even more guilty. Loath, though, she was to admit it, each day Ben was tiring more and more quickly, much earlier than the younger horses, and she had to nurse him along to get him back to the camp in good shape.

One day, mainly to rest him, Laura stayed behind to watch the men in the bronco yard branding and marking the cattle that were coming into the holding yards. She marvelled at the grace and skill of the horseman roping the cattle and the ease with which his heavily built horse kept the rope taut, steadily dragging it up the sloping rail of the bronco fence until it dropped into a slot in the centre, holding the beast to be branded up against the fence with the horse on the other side out of harm's way.

The next day, Laura rode out to muster again, and they were bringing a good-sized mob back to the yards, when disaster struck.

All morning, Laura had been heading off a determined heifer that was attempting time and time again to break back to the scrub. On each occasion, Ben had galloped out and successfully shouldered her back into the mob. Occasionally, Laura glanced at Rick, riding easily on the other wing and quickly averted her gaze. He was still not noticing her existence. *And that suits me fine!* she thought, making a wry mouth.

They were passing a thick patch of ti-tree scrub, and Laura was keeping a good eye on the heifer, thinking that it was a likely spot for her to break away again, when she heard Rick shout from somewhere near the tail of the mob: 'Look out, Laura! Behind you!'

Turning, she gave a gasp of sheer horror and wrenched her horse around to avoid the charge of a wild 'micky' bull. Ben leapt clear of its horns just in time, but came down on some stones, slipped and fell, throwing Laura cleanly out of the saddle. He heaved himself to his feet and stood, trembling and snorting but, mercifully, uninjured.

The bull, salivating and issuing a rumbling bellow, turned and charged again, straight for Laura, who lay dazed on the ground. She tried to get up and move out of the way, but somehow, she couldn't. She was conscious of a loud drumming in her ears. *The hooves of the bull,* she thought, hazily. She saw the wickedly gleaming eyes, the distended blood-red nostrils, the deadly razors that were its horns and tried to brace herself for what was to come.

The drumming grew louder, and suddenly she saw Rick range his horse alongside the feral bull, galloping neck and neck. In one fluid, graceful move, he leant down, picked up the bull's tail and swung it up and forward along the beast's back as the horse passed him. With a bellow of rage, the bull went down, and Rick dived off his horse and, in an instant, had the bull on his back with the tail pulled well forward between his hind legs, completely immobilised. One hand went to his hips to unbuckle his belt, and Laura was stricken with shame and remorse when she saw the livid bruise on the back of it. Working swiftly, he tied the beast's hind legs together and stepped back. It was all over. A man who had flung himself off his horse to come to his aid stood still.

The men were silent, and it was a silence filled with respect. It was a thing any one of them could have done—had done, many times—with cows, bullocks and calves, but this was the most treacherous of all cattle, and the slightest error of judgement could have resulted in tragedy. Only his skill as a cattleman and his split-second timing had saved Laura from horrifying injuries, perhaps even death—and they all knew it.

Painfully, Laura picked herself up and dusted her jeans. The movement brought his light eyes to her face. She read in them a cold anger.

'Are you hurt?'

'No.' She met his gaze. 'Thank you.'

'Then get back on your horse and stay with your men. I won't say I told you so. I'd just be wasting my breath. Didn't I tell you this was no place for you?' He shook his head, seemed to bite off his words and turned away to his horse.

Laura, flushing at the sting of his words and summary dismissal, forced her trembling legs to carry her to where her horse stood waiting, out of range of the furiously struggling bull, which, although able to stand, would fall down again when it attempted to charge. But, to her shame, she was unable to mount, so she stood leaning against Ben's shoulder for support and comfort while she listened to Rick issuing orders concerning the feral bull.

'Johnno. Get a few old coachers out of the mob, wait until we get away a bit and let that micky up when you've got him surrounded. If he tries anything, don't take any risks: shoot him.'

'Righto, Boss.' His head stockman passed on the instructions to his men, and a bunch of quiet old cows, indispensable for leading wild cattle to the yards, were soon ambling towards the enraged bull.

'All right, Laura?'

Laura turned her head to meet the sympathetic eyes of her overseer and achieved a smile that wrung his heart. 'A bit shaky,' she admitted. 'I can't even get on.'

'Here, I'll give you a leg up.' He grasped her left boot and threw her up on the horse. As she settled herself in the saddle, a tear sparkled on the end of her lashes and fell to the pommel. He pretended not to notice, mounting his own horse and riding up beside her. 'Come on. What you need is a cup of tea. It's not far to camp, and these blokes can look after things here. The cattle are moving along well, and Rick's there taking charge. Lucky he was with us, eh?'

'He said …' Laura's voice suspended on a hastily camouflaged sob. She took a deep breath. 'He said Ben was too old. It was my fault. I should have listened to him, taken one of his horses.'

'Never mind,' soothed John. 'It could have happened to any one of us, you know. We all live with the possibility of coming off our horses and being at the mercy of a beast: It is just a part of the job. I only hope that when it happens to me, there'll be a man like Rick around.'

Amen to that! thought Laura. 'Yes, indeed. Ben *is* tired, though. It is too much for him to go out day after day. I should have realised …' She shrugged as they rode into camp.

'Hey, Tom!' yelled John. 'Where are you?'

The cook's head appeared over the yard rail. 'Over here, John. What do you want?'

'The Missus's horse fell with her. She's in a bit of shock. Needs a nice cup of tea.'

'Aw, did he? That's no good! Be there in a couple of shakes, Missus.'

John helped Laura off her horse, promising to look after him for her, as Tom bustled about, and in no time at all, she was seated on the back of the cook's wagon, drinking hot, sweet tea and feeling much better for it. She briefly answered all his solicitous enquiries, and when she told him how Rick had thrown the bull when it was almost upon her, he exclaimed, 'Fair dinkum! He's a man and a half, ain't he? That's why we all call him Boss, even though, strictly speaking, he ain't our boss. You are, Missus.' He tipped his hat. 'Not that I mean ——'

'I know.' Laura made a little gesture of understanding.

Watching her out of the corner of his eye, he added, 'He's a man like your great-uncle, Missus: A Big Country man. His men'll work theirselves to the bone for him, 'cause they know he don't ask 'em to do nothin' he can't do better himself.'

'And I do,' murmured Laura.

'Now, Missus, don't beat yerself up about it. No-one don't expect a woman to do what a man can do. And we're loyal to you because, well, you've got guts, and that's something everyone don't have, man or woman. And it's what you've gotta have to do what you do up here in this country, taking on a big station and running it yourself. All of us admire you for that.'

'Thanks, Tom.' Laura was touched by his words.

'You and Boss Jamieson, you're two of a kind. You know …' He hesitated, peering at her even more obliquely. 'Your great-uncle always hoped you and him would get together one day.'

For some reason, maybe due to the shock she had suffered or the innate kindness of the cook, Laura did not stiffen at this blatant probing, but she was taken aback at what were obviously the expectations of the men who had known and worked with Uncle Jonas.

There was a short silence, then Laura smiled wryly and rose. 'I don't think there's much chance of that, Tom. Thanks for the tea. I might go and rest for a while.'

'That's the ticket. You'll be right as rain in no time.'

'I'm okay.' She turned to walk away.

'Look, Missus,' he called after her. 'I know it ain't my business, but you can trust Boss Jamieson.'

Yes, but can I? That is the whole matter in a nutshell! Laura looked back to give him a troubled glance before going off to her tent. In spite of her protests to the contrary, she had discovered that she was really very sore.

The next morning, Laura ached all over, and it was with a real effort that she dressed and presented herself for the muster, discovering to her dismay that she was late. Tom had saved some bacon for her and, while he cooked her an egg and made her some fresh tea, tried to convince her to stay in camp, but to every argument, she shook her head. Already saddled with her gear was an athletic young black horse, so after checking that Ben had indeed received no hurt, she mounted him and rode off in the wake of the ringers.

Taking a little time to get used to her new mount, Laura found him a lovely ride. Obviously well-trained, he was calm yet sensitive to her lightest aid. She also found he didn't tire as easily as Ben. Consequently, she was not so tired at the end of the day. Laura could only be thankful that for the rest of the camp, the muster proceeded smoothly, and no more untoward incidents occurred.

From time to time, though she did her best to avoid him, Laura's gaze encountered Rick's, and the condemnation she thought she read there left her feeling shattered. It told her that he had neither forgotten nor forgiven the injustice of the blow she had dealt him, nor the many times she had taken his kindness and thrown it in his face. He had saved her from certain death on one occasion and serious injury or death at least twice more. And what had been her response? Here, another thought left her gasping for breath: What if he *was* all he seemed? Innocent of her darkest suspicions? The kind of man that comes once in a lifetime if you're lucky. Would he be offended beyond all chance of forgiveness?

Suddenly, she saw herself as Rick must see her: ungrateful, intemperate, irrational, not only brushing off his attempts to help but reacting with unjustified anger and violence. Guilt and remorse hit her squarely between the eyes. Sooner or later, there would be a reckoning between them, and she would have to answer for her treatment of him. How could she do that when she had no answers for herself?

Chapter Eighteen

At the end of the muster, Rick's men trucked his share of the sale cattle out, the respective breeding herds were returned to their run on the shared holding and the two teams said goodbye to each other. Most importantly for Laura, she had a paddock full of saleable cattle and a chance of recouping some of her losses, even though she grieved that there had been no sign of her stud stock.

It seemed that the thieves, whoever they were, had left Miranda strictly alone. Was that one more finger to point squarely at her neighbour? Laura didn't want to believe it. How many times had the man saved her life? But until she knew beyond doubt, all evidence must be considered. *But what if the person doing it wants me to think it is Rick?* The idea stopped her in her tracks, but before she could mull it over, her overseer came up to speak to her, taking her mind off this novel train of thought.

'Well, Laura, this is just about it.'

'Yes, I'm so thankful to have finally found some decent cattle.'

'It is a relief; I must say.'

'But I seem to have lost my last hope of finding the thoroughbreds and the stud Brahmans.'

'Yes, I'm sorry. It looks like it.'

'I'd better inform the Stock Squad. I was just waiting to see — —'

'They already know that there's something going on in this part of the world. Rick let them know the numbers were down last year.'

'Oh … But it hasn't stopped the thieves, whoever they are.'

'That's true, sadly. They must know that the Stock Squad have been nosing around, but it hasn't deterred them.' He frowned. 'More front than The Queen Mary!'

'Yes.' Laura gasped. 'John? I've just had a terrible thought! What if these cattle go missing before I can sell them?'

'Now, don't worry. We'll stay till the end of the month, see your cattle safe until they are sold. Then, we must go. You will need some men—a skeleton staff to help year-round, you know.'

'Yes, I've been worrying about that, too: wondering if some of your men might stay?'

'I think I have the perfect solution for you, Laura. Mick, Tom and Alan have expressed a wish to stay, if you would like them to?'

'The ones who used to work for Uncle Jonas!' Laura's brow cleared miraculously.

'The very same.'

'You're right.' Her smile dazzled. 'It is the perfect solution.'

§

At dawn, two days after the muster had finished, Laura sat up, wrenched out of a deep sleep. At first, she didn't know what had woken her, then she heard knocking and the voice of her overseer calling to her.

Pulling on her dressing-gown, she rushed to the door. 'John! Is something wrong?'

'No. I'm sorry to have woken you at this hour, but my team and I have to leave right away.'

'But I thought you were going to stay until the cattle are sold?'

'So did I, but I've had an urgent call from my usual employer. I can't really refuse.'

'No, of course not. I understand. What about your cheques?'

'Here's a forwarding address.' He handed over a card. 'You can send them if you don't mind? It really is urgent.'

'Of course. It's no trouble.'

'I've told your men who are staying to put your sale cattle in the best fattening paddock—the one closest to Miranda—for the buyer to inspect when he comes at the end of the month. They're doing that today. And Mick has faithfully promised that he will do all your firebreaks with the grader before the storm season begins. Your men are old hands; you can trust them to do a good job. Your great-uncle trained them well.'

'Oh, yes, I'm sure I can.'

'On the card I gave you is a phone number. If you ever need help, don't hesitate to call it day or night. If I'm not actually there, someone will give me the message so that I can contact you.' His eyes were serious. 'Promise me, if you ever need anything, you'll call?'

'Oh, John.' She was touched. 'Thank you. Yes, I promise.'

He smiled and held out his hand. 'Well, all the best, Laura.'

'You, too, John. Thank you. And thanks for everything.' Laura, watching him drive away in his Land Rover, felt as though she had lost her best friend.

§

'Hello, Lily. This is a surprise.' Rick looked up from where he was mending a fence near a bore in a picturesque part of Miranda.

'Mornin' Boss. Thought I'd find you here.'

'Did you?' Arrested, he put down his pliers and straightened. 'Why is that, then?'

Because Jackson told me I would. 'Oh, well, you and our boss used to meet out here often. Every Wednesday, if I remember right.' She looked around. 'It's a pretty spot.'

'Yes, it was his favourite place.' A shade of anxiety entered his voice. 'Why have you come? Is everything all right, Lily?'

'Yeah, Boss, all right. Just got somethin' to tell you that I think you ought to know.' Lily pursed her lips. 'Someone who should have told you ain't goin' to. I know that much. And the kind of thing that's been goin' on … Well, you need to know about it so you can put a stop to it before someone gets properly hurt.'

'As bad as that, is it?'

'Too right, Boss. I think so, or else I wouldn't say nothin' about it.'

'Okay, Lily. Fire away.'

Rick listened to what Lily had to say, in silence. At first, she twisted her hands in her apron. 'Don't like to carry tales, Boss.' But at his encouraging gesture, went on concisely with her story. At the end, he put his hand on her shoulder.

'I'm deeply indebted to you, Lily. Thank you. Rest assured, it will all be taken care of. Can I give you a lift home?'

'Nah, Boss. The walk will do me good.' Lily, treading swiftly, felt a great weight lift from her shoulders. She'd felt guilty that she hadn't tried to call Boss Jamieson back the day he'd spun around and walked out when she'd told him Laura had gone to Manson's bore. Still, he had taken her disclosures today better than she thought he would. He hadn't seemed angry. On the contrary, it was as if he'd glimpsed a ray of light.

§

Mrs Mac, passing the office door, stopped in amazement to listen to Rick laying down the law to his cousin. *I canna believe it!* she thought. *He's finally decided to stop spoiling that wee brat and give her what she deserves—her comeuppance!* Smiling a little, she went on her way.

'Now, look.' Rick spoke in the sternest voice Corinne had ever heard from him. 'As I've explained to you *four* times already, I am sending you home because your behaviour was stupid and irresponsible. You can't send someone on a wild-goose chase out here. People can *die* if they break down or run out of fuel miles from anywhere. That's what I can't seem to get through to you.' The phone rang, and he turned away to answer it. His reply was brief. Then he turned back to his cousin. 'I have to go out now. Tell Mrs Mac I am not sure when I will be back.'

'Rick? Can't I come with you? Please?'

'No. Now, you go and pack. Because I'm serious! Right?'

Corinne stood silent—her big blue eyes holding his.

He grasped her arm, for once unmoved by their entreating expression. 'Right?'

'Right,' she agreed in a small voice, and he let her go and strode away, leaving her biting her lip, tears flowing down her cheeks—her dreams finally shattered. After a while, she dried her tears and lapsed into thought. Then, her brows drew together; a calculating expression gleamed in the baby-blue eyes as she glanced around the office and went off to follow her cousin's orders. As far as she was willing to.

§

Laura sat alone on a log that had, long ago, been placed carefully in a secluded corner of her garden, fighting her conscience. She *had* to go and talk to Rick. The more she thought about it, the more she knew he couldn't be the one stealing her cattle. Apart from the idea being ludicrous, wouldn't he have taken some of his own, as well, to make himself look innocent? *He's not stupid,* she thought. *No, it's someone trying to make it look like it's him, and I've fallen for it all the way!* Her brow wrinkled.

But who? Maybe this was something she *could* talk over with him.

A great relief came over her and, with it, an overwhelming remorse. Thinking about Rick's kindness—his generous and forgiving nature—all the rude, ungrateful behaviour and insults he'd put up with from her loomed so large as to overshadow the relief. He'd told her she would have to come to him, and she knew he was a man of his word. Not only that, it was essential for her own self-worth that she thank him for all the times he'd saved her life, apologise for her execrable behaviour and try to explain her reasons.

For both their sakes, Laura knew that she had to get everything straight in her head before she went to him, knew she would have to address issues too painful for her to open the door on. Because until she did, she couldn't give him the explanations he deserved—couldn't move on to the loving relationship he'd offered—that she could finally admit she so desperately craved. How could she begin a new relationship weighed down by the pain of the old one? That's why she'd come down here to Uncle Jonas's thinking log; the place he'd always sent her to meditate on a problem before they discussed it together over a billy of tea. A place she hadn't thought of for so long.

As she pushed her mind deeper and deeper into her motives— the drivers of her behaviour—tears began to trickle down her cheeks. Laura made no attempt to stop them; they had to flow to cleanse her soul. Worried, Bess came to push her nose under her hand, and Laura stroked her absently, a little comforted, but undiverted from her purpose. Laura acknowledged that she'd let Rick think she was put off by his relationship with Corinne, but wasn't it only a mask for her real fears? In the same way, she'd fooled herself that she was worried about Rick being a stock thief, when in her heart, she knew he couldn't be. But what was really wrong, she hadn't been able to face. *But now I must,* she thought. *Whatever it costs me.*

Slowly, painfully, she forced herself to visit and acknowledge every degrading and humiliating moment of her four-year marriage, and at the end, felt drained of all emotion. She went back inside the house, touched to find that Lily had left her favourite chicken casserole in the warming oven and that Mary had given the floors an extra polish to leave them even more gleaming than usual. *As sensitive to atmosphere as always,* thought Laura, grateful that they had left her to herself.

Tomorrow, she thought as she finally drifted off to sleep, too drained to care about the settling noises of the house. *Tomorrow, I will find Rick and tell him everything.*

Chapter Nineteen

'We're a little bit worried, Missus,' said Tom, arriving on her doorstep early the next morning. 'We can't find your sale cattle.'

'Don't tell me they've been stolen, too! Already?' Laura showed her despair.

'No need to worry too much yet. Alan is still out looking for them. We think they may have got back into Miranda. It might be an idea to tell Boss Jamieson, get him to send some men over to give us a hand.'

'All right, wait until Alan has a good look, and if there is still no sign, you can do that.'

'Righto, Missus. I'll go back and see how he's getting on.'

Laura stood in deep thought after Tom left her. She had a terrible feeling that these cattle were gone in the same direction as all the rest. The thought made her defer her resolve to seek out Rick and try to set things right between them. Making a quick impatient movement with her hands, she sped down to Jackson's *gunyah*, where she found him seated cross-legged before his tiny fire. His bright eyes searched her face.

'More cattle missing, eh, Missus?'

'It looks like it. The men think they may have got back into Miranda. What do you think, Jackson?'

'Dunno, Missus. Could be gone, orright.'

'If someone has stolen them, where would they take them to truck them out?'

He screwed up his eyes, staring into his fire whilst he mulled over her question. Laura waited patiently while he stirred and prodded the coals with a stick. At last, he lifted his head, and she saw that his eyes were glazed as if he were drugged. He blinked and they cleared to a brightness that belied his age. 'Better you not go, Little Missus. Better you leave it to Boss Jamieson.'

'Where, Jackson?' she urged.

'Set of yards near the old ford. Might be fell down by now. Might be fixed up, too.'

'So, you think if I went there, I might see some sign of the cattleduffers?'

'Might be.' He raised his eyes to Laura's so that she saw a warning flash in them. 'Better you not go. Better you leave it to Boss Jamieson.'

Laura thanked him, paying little heed to his stricture. Curiosity and an overwhelming urge to bring to justice the person responsible for all her difficulties got the better of her. She disregarded the danger to herself.

Dressing quickly in a khaki shirt and trousers, her feet shod in sturdy workboots, she packed herself a picnic lunch while Lily was busy kneading some bread and hurried out the door, relieved that Lily was too occupied to ask where she was going. Taking the work ute, she drove to within walking distance of the old river crossing to Juliana—well to the east, and out of sight and sound of the new one. It had been long disused, but she might as well be careful, just in case Jackson was right.

Creeping soundlessly through the scrub along the river, Laura kept a wary eye out for signs of life, both animal and human— her heart leaping into her throat as a rustle in the bushes was followed by a small plop and splash in the river. *A crocodile? Or just a harmless goanna or waterbird?* She moved away from the river into sparser scrub and went on. Peace reigned for some time, and then she stopped dead, her mouth dry, for vaguely, through the trees on the other side of the river, loomed the massive bulk of a road train.

Laura saw him before he was aware of her presence, drawing back into the scrub with a little audible gasp that made him turn quickly: a dangerous expression on his face. For a moment, they stared at each other, she in sick horror, he in irritation and disbelief. Laura could not have uttered a word to save her life.

'Go back, Laura. I can't allow you to ruin our plans this time.'

'But ——' Laura stood, immobilised in shock. John Riley stealing her cattle? He couldn't be! The one person she *had* trusted.

'Go on, Laura! All hell's going to break loose here, shortly. Now, get out of here. Hurry!' He turned away to speak rapidly into a handheld radio. Laura only heard the concluding part of his speech and suffered such a dreadful jolt that her legs refused to obey her. '… and get her out of here, Rick, before she blows the lid off the whole thing!' He strode away without so much as a backward glance at her and vanished into a patch of scrub.

Laura reeled and clutched at the trunk of a tree for support— a great bitterness rising in her throat, threatening to choke her. *Rick! Not Rick! Both of them. In collusion: Together! No!* She bent double with the pain of her grief. All her suspicions about Rick had been right after all, and her heart, once again, had been wrong. So terribly, terribly wrong.

Stumbling through the scrub, Laura flinched away from the tall figure striding towards her.

'This way, Laura,' he commanded in a low, urgent voice. 'Quickly!'

'Don't come near me!' She spun away.

'Quiet!' He grabbed her by the arm, silencing her with a hand over her mouth, half-dragging, half-carrying her through the thicket. 'I'm sorry for the roughhouse treatment,' he whispered. 'But it's too dangerous to make a noise here.'

After what seemed an aeon of brushing through the scrub, Rick opened the passenger-side door of his Land Cruiser and let her go free. 'Please, Laura, get in and come with me now. There's someone who might need our support and, quite possibly, the comfort of another woman.'

Laura stared, too shocked to take in the import of his words. 'What are you talking about?'

'I'll explain later. I'm a little nonplussed, myself. Please, just trust me?'

'Trust you?' *How can I? After what I've just seen?*

'Look, it's a long story, but we're close to the end. I hope it's not true.' He shook his head, his face grey and distressed. 'But if it is, it has ramifications for all of us.'

He's looking just as shocked and upset as I feel, thought Laura. *It can't be him. It can't be! My God! Just what is going on here?* She climbed in without another word, sitting in troubled silence as Rick pushed his vehicle to its limits, bouncing over rough areas but always in control. Laura could have admired his driving skills if she hadn't been so distressed herself.

'Come in.' He pulled up before his front verandah and jumped out. 'I don't know what we'll find …'

Mrs Mac met them at the door. Uncannily, her face bore the same shocked, grief-stricken expression as had Laura's. 'Rick! It's Andrew! He …' She could hardly speak in her agitation.

'I know, Little Mother. I know. I'm sorry,' soothed Rick, taking her in his arms and casting an appealing glance at Laura over her head. 'I was hoping it wasn't true. I can't believe it, myself.'

'But, Rick, he's gone! He … he left a wee while ago. He told me what he'd done—admitted everything—said you'd never find him.' She twisted trembling hands in her apron.

'Don't worry, Little Mother. If it helps, at all, Laura won't press charges.' Again, the look of appeal to which Laura nodded agreement. 'I'll recompense her for the cattle she's lost. Andy will be all right. He can't be arrested since he's not with the others, and it's only someone's word against his. He'll probably do a bit of island hopping until the heat dies down.'

'I can't understand why he'd do such a thing? I brought him up to be honest,' she grieved.

'I know you did. You mustn't blame yourself.'

'But, Rick, there's something else! You won't like it. Your wee cousin, she went with him.'

Rick swore and turned to leave—a thunderous expression replacing the distress—but was stopped in his tracks by the older woman's urgent tone.

'No, Rick! Let her go. She's jealous and devious and trouble. Can't you see that they're two of a kind? I hate to say this about my own son, but it is true enough. They belong together. She said to tell you she's over twenty-one, and there is nothing you can do about it.'

'Oh, isn't there, just!'

The housekeeper put a hand on his arm. 'You could chase them all over the country. And I know you would if it was the right thing. But it's not. It will be better for you and Laura to leave things as they are. Please, Rick?'

'All right.' Rick glanced at Laura, but she wasn't paying attention, her mind grappling with all she had seen and heard, trying to put the pieces of the puzzle into place. *So, it was Andy,* she thought. *I stumbled into a trap to catch the thieves and almost sprang it. No wonder John and Rick spoke to me as they did.* It all made sense now: The reason Andy couldn't be caught was simply because he knew all their moves and could make sure he was nowhere about whenever someone got too close. Whatever may have applied to make her suspicious of Rick could also apply to him. He had his own helicopters he didn't have to account for and an intimate knowledge of the country he mustered. Who could be better equipped? *Poor Mrs Mac—poor darling—she's beside herself, having to face truths like that,* thought Laura, watching her with compassion.

John came in and took the housekeeper's hands. 'I'm really sorry, Mrs Mac. I know you're a good woman, and this is a terrible blow for you. I'll try and make it as easy on you as I can.'

'Thank you, John,' she replied, her voice muffled. 'I'll go and rest for a wee bit while you talk. I don't think I can stand to hear any more.'

'Let me take you to your room, Mrs Mac.' Laura's heart went out to this poor grieving mother. 'Is there anything I can get you?'

'No, thank you. I'll just rest for a wee while. Laura, I'm so sorry. My son ——'

'None of this is your fault, Mrs Mac. Andy made his own decisions, and I know they are not the kind that you would have made. Rest now and try not to worry.' Underneath her natural concern for the troubles of another, Laura was aware of a little spark of joy tugging at her heart. Rick *was* the beautiful person her heart had told her. When all this was over, she might be able to look forward to a wonderful future with him. Together, battling the elements in their own wild kingdom, just as Uncle Jonas had wished for them.

§

'I'm sorry, Laura,' said John with a wry twist to his mouth. 'I have been guilty of deceiving you.'

Laura raised her eyebrows. 'An urgent summons from your usual employer?'

'No. Funnily enough, that bit was true.'

'Explain it to her, John. Tell her who your employer is,' urged Rick. 'Oh, perhaps it will make it easier if I introduce you. Laura, meet Detective Sergeant John Riley of the Stock Squad Division of the Queensland Police.'

'Oh.' Laura nodded. 'Now I begin to understand.'

'You've given me a lot of trouble, Laura, one way and another.' John shook his head, but with a twinkle in his eye. 'Did you know that we were all set up for this sting a few months ago and you turned up and sacked all your men the day before? So, we had to start again. The fact that you needed a new mustering team was a way in for us to track down the thieves at the coalface, so to speak. The reason I had to leave early yesterday was because we got word that another theft of your cattle was about to take place, and we needed to be where we could catch them in the act. Then, lo and behold, there you were again today, right in the middle of it! At the crucial moment! I couldn't believe it.'

'Neither could I. I thought for a minute that it was you and Rick. And that was just too … Why didn't you tell me?'

Both men looked at her with raised brows.

Laura put up her hands. 'Okay, I get it—need to know! I'm sorry for getting in your way.'

'No matter. We got them all, except for the leader, of course. But it will quieten him down for a bit. At least we caught them before they vanished with this last lot of cattle. They are being returned to your paddock as we speak. You will, of course, be reimbursed for the salaries of those of us who are policemen.' He turned to Rick. 'Oh yeah, you know that question we used to ask ourselves? We rounded up three of Sykes' men with the gang.'

'So, Sykes and co could have been involved? I thought you

said they went to the Territory?'

'They did, but apparently these three sneaked back under aliases. I think that's it. Thanks for your help, Rick.'

'Well, we had to do something. I never saw so much onslaught on one property. I wonder why he made it so willing?'

John raised an eyebrow. 'Can't you guess?'

To implicate Rick. Laura could see it all now. *He set me up to accuse Rick, and I didn't do it, even though I thought it. But it poisoned our relationship.* What was it his mother had said about Corinne? Jealous, devious, that they were two of a kind. Both beautiful, charming people, hiding their real selves behind an impenetrable façade; both looking so innocent and well-meaning that no-one could believe it. By implication, that meant Andy had done this purely because he was jealous of Rick.

John said nothing. Raising both eyebrows, he looked steadily at Rick.

'How can it be Andy?' Rick shook his head. 'All this time? We grew up together, as close as brothers as you could get, and you're saying he set me up?'

John moved his head in assent.

'And you, Laura? Is that what you thought? That I was a stock thief? So that's what all this has been about! Well, I'll be damned! A trustee? Jonas's friend? You've cast some serious aspersions on my character, haven't you?'

'Oh, Rick …' Laura's eyes were brimming.

'Not now.' He put up a warding hand. 'I need some time to get all this straight in my head. Take Laura home, John. I'll get my accountant to talk to her about recompensing her for the value of her stolen stock.'

'I don't want your money! I don't want *anything* ——' Laura stopped and spun around at a gasp behind her, eyes widening. 'Mrs Mac!'

'Rick …' The housekeeper stumbled into the room, ashen-faced, one hand clutching her chest, her mouth twisted in pain. Rick got there just before she fell, supporting her to the sofa and laying her down gently. 'What is it, Little Mother?'

'I think it is her heart.' Laura arranged cushions behind her head and felt for her pulse. 'See the bluish tinge around her mouth?'

'I'll call the Flying Doctor,' said John, disappearing into Rick's office for a short time. 'He's on his way,' he told them as he came back into the room. 'He said to give her an aspirin if she's conscious and keep her lying down.'

'Hang in there, Little Mother,' said Rick, after Laura had brought her an aspirin. 'Jack will be here shortly. How's the pain now?'

'It's eased a bit; not so bad now. Jack won't be happy if I've got him here on false pretences.'

Laura noted that her colour was still bad. 'I don't think he'll see it quite like that. Try to rest until he comes.'

Rick stayed with Mrs Mac, holding her hand. 'Don't you leave me, too, Little Mother. What would I do without you?'

It seemed to take forever for the welcome drone of the plane, but soon, Jack's capable presence was in the room, soothing his patient, greeting his friends, working amicably with his nurse, who was none other than Cass. For a time, both were busily treating their patient, and Laura saw a serious, professional side to Cass that she'd never witnessed before.

Laura went with them to the plane, while Rick went off to pack, having decided, after a low-voiced conversation with the doctor, to go with Mrs Mac. She waited outside while doctor and nurse made some further adjustments to their patient's treatment.

After a time, Cass stepped down from the aircraft and went to where Laura was standing. 'We've got her stabilised,' she said in answer to Laura's anxious glance. 'I think she'll make it, but it might be touch and go. We'll have to take her to Adelaide. Jack says he thinks it is going to mean open-heart surgery. We're hoping not, but ——'

'Oh, no!' said Laura. 'Poor darling. But can you wonder when she's had such a dreadful shock?'

'Yes, it's been a shock to us all.' Cass's big, dark eyes were serious. 'Andy was our friend. Rick's been knocked sideways. He thought a lot of him, even financed him into his helicopter business. It's like being stabbed in the back by your best buddy and your only brother, combined. He's going to need a lot of TLC to get over it. But I'm sure you'll step up to the plate, Laura.'

'I don't think ——'

'Jack's just given me a minute to speak to you because I want to apologise for my past behaviour … with Corinne. Look, both of us could see that Rick was in love with you. It was mischief on my part, spite on Corinne's. I had no idea she would do what she did, and I am sorry: so very, very sorry. I hope you can find it in your heart to forgive me?'

Laura shook her head and smiled. 'There's nothing to forgive.'

'It's like you to be generous and say that, so thank you.' Cass beamed. 'Listen, Jack and I are getting married in early October, and we want you to be there. Will you come?'

'Yes, of course, thank you. And congratulations!' Laura found it hard to believe that this warm, sincere, professional creature was Cass. 'It is good to see you so happy and content. I've never ——'

'Seen me like that? That's because I've never been like that: A feeling of doing what I was meant to do. It is fulfilling, invigorating.' A hint of the old mischief shone in her eyes. 'You should try it.'

'Flying Nurse? I don't think ——'

'Now, Laura, you know I don't mean nursing! I mean teaming up with the man of your dreams.' Cass gave her a quick hug and kiss. 'Bye, Laura. Take care. I have to get back to my patient now.' She ran back to the plane as Jack appeared briefly in the doorway, waved and moved to the pilot's seat.

Laura saw Rick hurrying back with his overnight bag and knew she had to try and begin to apologise for misjudging him. 'Rick, please. Before you go …'

Rick looked down at her, his eyes bitter. A travesty of his ironic smile just touched his lips. 'Congratulations, Laura, I think you finally found it.'

Laura stared blankly. 'Found it? Found what?'

'The straw that broke the camel's back. As Jonas said, "It's no use trying to make something broken work, unless you can fix it first." And believe me, I've tried. But too much is broken. You don't know how hard I've tried to reach you, knock down that barrier. But what is there—what can there be—without trust?'

Love, thought Laura. *As I've found out too late.* But she couldn't find the words because the despair in his voice hurt her so much more than she could have imagined.

'I apologise for being so slow to get your message, but I've got it now.' He shook his head. 'I won't be bothering you again. If you need anything in future, tell Tom to talk to Johnno.' He threw his bag up into the plane and stepped through the open hatch without looking back. 'Goodbye, Laura.'

§

'Come on, Laura. I'll run you home,' said John out of the silence, after they'd watched the plane circle and vanish over the horizon. He held the door open on his Land Rover. 'Don't worry. Mrs Mac is in good hands.'

'Yes, everyone has done all they can.' Laura was surprised at how normal she sounded. 'Can you take me to my ute? I'd forgotten all about it.'

'A couple of my men have taken it home for you. They're waiting there for me to pick them up.'

Laura thanked him and the conversation lapsed. John seemed to be concentrating on the road, and Laura might have sounded normal, but she was feeling far from it. She sat mulling over the events of the day, and it wasn't until they were close to her home that she voiced some of her thoughts.

'John, can I ask you something? Did you suspect Andy?'

'Well, only in the way of who it could possibly be. But he

always seemed such a good bloke, so loyal to Rick ...'

'So, how did you find out it was him?'

'One of his former henchmen grassed him up—had some sort of grudge against him—to do with a woman, I think. He is a bit of a lady's man. But he has been seen in some funny places, even though he's always produced a perfectly legitimate reason for being there. Don't forget where you found him when his chopper crashed.'

'Yes, and I believed his answer to that, too!' Laura thought of how she'd been fooled by Andy's apparent sincerity. 'I even thanked him.'

John tapped the steering wheel with his fingertips. 'He's a smooth operator; I'll give him that. More or less the perfect con man.'

'True, and now he has Corinne to help him.'

'As pretty as a picture,' he mused. 'Those innocent blue eyes. I shudder to think ...'

'Look at what they've done already!' Laura clenched her hands. 'I don't think Rick will ever forgive me for suspecting him.'

'Laura, Rick's a good bloke.' John pulled up to let her out. 'But he's sustained more than one severe shock today. I think by the time he comes back, he'll have settled down and be ready to talk.'

'Thanks, John.' Laura watched him drive away. But, remembering the finality of Rick's words and his bleak expression as he boarded the plane, she didn't think so.

Chapter Twenty

Laura got as far as the front verandah before she collapsed in tears. Lily came out to meet her, concern in her eyes. 'What's up, Little Missus? You sick or somethin'?'

'I'm sorry, Lily. I …'

'It's all right, Missus.' Lily supported her into the house. 'You eaten today?'

'No, I don't think so. It's been such a —— Have you heard what happened?'

'Yeah, Johnno told Tom they caught the thieves. It's that chopper fella, eh? Poor Mrs Mac, gave her a bad turn.'

'Yes, her heart. Rick went with her to Adelaide. I don't know when they'll be back.'

'Well, she like a mother to him.' Lily brought her to the table. 'Lucky she got him. Her own son not much chop. Make you some coffee. Got a nice carrot cake. Boss Neumann always liked my carrot cake.'

'Thanks, Lily.' Laura fell into a chair. 'I don't know if I can eat anything.'

'Well, you just try. That's all I ask. Boss pretty upset, eh?'

'Oh, Lily, he won't even talk to me. Won't let me apologise for misjudging him. You were right about him. I should have listened. And now, it's all …'

'Never mind, Missus. You and Boss talk when he gets back, eh?'

'No, Lily. He said … that if I want anything in future to tell Tom to ask Johnno.'

'Oh … That bad, eh? You must've upset him properly.'

'Oh, Lily.' Laura lay her head down on the table and burst into fresh sobs. 'I have!'

'That smarmy chopper fella. I never liked him. Drink your coffee, Missus, and eat somethin'. You feel better then.'

No, I won't, thought Laura with conviction. *Nothing will ever be right again.* How could it: without a big, kind, tolerant man whose love she had trodden into the ground?

§

There were only two rays of light in the bleakness of the weeks that followed. The first was that Mrs Mac had not needed open-heart surgery and was doing well on medication. The second was a message from Johnno, relayed as always by Tom—now Laura's head stockman due to seniority—but first he had his usual round with his household rival. 'I'm a good cook, Lily, but, by jingo, I can't match you.'

'If you want a cuppa, Tom, just ask the Missus.'

'He doesn't have to ask, Lily. Give him some of your carrot cake and make him properly jealous.'

'Righto, Missus. Won't make you scones, Tom. That's somethin' you can do pretty good yourself.'

'True, but cakes are another matter.'

'Yeah, they burn in the coals. You better sit down, Tom, and tell us all the gossip.'

'Now, Lily, you know I don't gossip.'

'Course, you do. Men are worse gossips than women, ain't they?' scoffed Lily. 'If you want to know somethin', ask a man.'

'Well?' Laura smiled at their skirmish.

Tom grinned and took an appreciative mouthful of cake, followed by a swig of tea. 'It's good news for a change, Missus. They found your horses.'

'No! Did they? Where?'

'Do you remember old Percy Brown, the racehorse trainer in Cloncurry?'

'Yes. He used to train Uncle Jonas's racehorses, didn't he?'

'That's right, Missus. Well, he used to train your stallion when he was a youngster, too. Anyway, to cut a long story short, he was down the street yesterday morning, and he saw old Starry Way on a dog truck parked at the servo.'

'No!' Laura was truly horrified. 'What … what happened? Is he …?'

Lily raised her voice. 'Come in here, Mary, and listen to this. Cuppa-tea time.'

Tom greeted Mary, waited until they were all hanging on his words and went on: 'He said the old fella recognised him and whinnied from the truck, otherwise he never would have noticed him.

'Now, old Percy's no fool, and he'd heard about your stolen stock, so he held the truck up while he checked with the Stock Squad.' Tom ate another piece of cake, enjoying his moment. 'And—would you believe—when they unloaded the truck, there were all your mares and foals as well. All twenty of them!'

'Oh, that's good news, Missus,' said Lily. 'Best news I've heard in a dam' long time.'

'Yes. Oh, yes! Oh, thank goodness Percy recognised him!'

'Don't you mean, Missus,' Mary spoke for the first time, 'thank goodness he recognised Percy?'

'Yes.' Laura joined in the laughter. 'I guess I do mean that. Starry was always so special, and Uncle Jonas was so fond of him.' She blinked back sudden tears: 'A dog truck! Uncle Jonas would never have heard of his beloved horses meeting such a fate.'

'We know, Missus,' said Lily. 'We know. But why did Percy ring Johnno, Tom and not our Missus?'

Laura turned to Tom. 'Yes, why?'

'Percy hasn't got the new number—you know, since the phones were changed—but Boss Jamieson apparently gave him his number a little while back and told him to ring if he heard anything, so when he rang with Boss away, he got Johnno.' He grinned at Lily. 'Satisfied?'

'It's not me you should be askin'.' Lily turned to her employer. 'What you think, Missus?'

Laura shrugged. 'Sounds reasonable to me.'

'Yeah,' said Mary. 'Good news is good news, however you hear it.'

'I won't disagree.' Laura's eyes went to her new overseer. 'So, what happens now, Tom? How do we get them home?'

'Percy said to tell you that he's got them in his spelling yards, and he's more than happy to look after them for you as long as you need. He was great mates with yer great-uncle, and he says he's tickled pink to have old Starry Way back in his stables again. Just like old times, he reckons.' He poured himself another cup of tea. 'Says there's a likely looking yearling he'd like to train for you if you'd let him.'

'I'll give him the colt for finding Starry.'

'That's a pretty good offer, Missus. But he wouldn't take it—might offend him.'

'Oh, right. Well, of course he can train him, if he wants. It is the least I can do. But what about the rest?'

'Johnno tells me that, in about a fortnight, one of Boss Jamieson's road trains is coming back through the Curry from the south with two drivers, says he'll get them to bring your horses home.'

Some of the joy went out of Laura's day. More and more she owed to Rick, and she wouldn't be able to repay or thank him. But there was no other way. If she wanted her horses back, she had to accept.

Tom, sitting smiling at her, so pleased with the news he'd brought, had no idea what was going on behind her outwardly happy expression. But Lily saw and her heart sank.

§

When Tom brought the news of Rick and Mrs Mac's imminent return, Lily told Laura she had a big favour to ask.

'Certainly. What is it, Lily?'

'If you can spare us, Missus, me and Mary think we should do two days a week at Juliana. Give Mrs Mac a hand. Boss Jamieson helped us with Boss Neumann when he got sick. Now our turn to help him, eh?'

'I don't see a problem. That's very kind of you to think of it.'

'Thanks, Missus. Thought we might go tomorrow, have a good clean-up before she gets home. Do a bit of baking for her.'

'All right. Mrs Mac will need as much help as she can get. How are you going to get there?'

'Haven't thought.' Lily shrugged. 'Johnno might send someone over to pick us up.'

'You'd better take the ute. Then you can come and go as you please.'

'Gee, thanks, Missus, that'll be a big help.'

'And Lily? If Mrs Mac needs you more than two days a week, it is okay. I can manage.'

'Two days be enough, Missus. Only her and Boss Jamieson now.'

§

Later, on the way back to their cottage, Mary confided to Lily that she'd seen Laura crying, more than once. 'Seen her down on that log in the garden. You know, the one Boss put in for her when she was a little girl, just sittin' there cryin' her eyes out. Little Missus dam' upset.'

'Well, it's Boss Jamieson, ain't it? Boss try to talk—she don't want to. Now she want to talk—Boss won't talk to her. Got the pips about somethin' properly, he has.'

'Can't blame him.' Mary pursed her lips. 'He took a lot of crap before he gave up. Anyway, we don't know what happened.'

'Yeah, we do! That smarmy chopper fella done the dirty on Boss Jamieson. Set it up to look like Boss was stealin' Missus's cattle, and she believed it. I tried to tell her, Jackson tried to tell her, Tom tried to tell her. But she don't listen. Now Boss has got his back up, and you know what that means.'

'I know—up on his high horse and won't get down for nobody. But what can *we* do?'

'Dunno what we can do, but someone better do somethin' 'cause I never seen two such stubborn people.'

'Yeah, stubborn as hell, I know.'

'That's what I'm sayin', Mary. They're both stubborn as hell, and I don't know what we can do about it.'

'Talk to Jackson?' offered Mary.

'All right, I'll see what he says when I take him his dinner.' Lily lapsed into deep thought. 'He might come up with somethin'. You know, Mary, Boss Jamieson and Mrs Mac are prob'ly gunna need our help for quite a while.'

'Yeah, she gotta rest but she won't.'

'She will if the work's done for her.'

'Yeah, good idea. You better talk to Missus, like we said.'

'Already have, Mary. We start tomorrow. Missus is lending us the ute.'

Chapter Twenty-One

The days passed strangely—a surreal movie in which Laura went through the motions of living like an automaton. She lost her appetite, could not hold a train of thought and was unable to escape the feeling that life had nothing left to offer her. It hurt too much to think about Rick: how he had always looked at her, how he'd made no secret of his love, the safe harbour of his arms, the sweet fire of his kisses. Andy and Corinne's plans may have ultimately gone awry, but the result was the same: a fragile, beautiful thing had been destroyed, and Laura could see no way that the shattered pieces could ever be brought together.

The horses came home, renewing her thoughts of her neighbour with hurtful clarity. Percy Brown wrote to her, lauding the ability of the colt he was training. The phone rang occasionally. More often than not, it was Mrs Mac checking to see how she was. Of Rick, she saw and heard nothing.

Rick's accountants sent her a cheque for the estimated value of the stolen cattle. Laura tore it up. She sent a cheque to the accountants for her estimate of the delivery charge for the return of her horses: The accountants sent it back, accompanied by a polite note. With tears of frustration blinding her eyes, Laura tore that up, too. Still, she had no contact with Rick.

Lily and Mary went about their duties quietly, occasionally casting worried glances at Laura and then at each other. Even Bess and Oscar seemed to sense her grief.

Though she tried, nothing Laura did could lift her spirits. She'd stopped riding, ostensibly because Ben needed a spell, but really because she couldn't find the energy. With the help of Alan and Mick, she put the geldings in another paddock and ensconced old Starry Way and his band of mares in the horse paddock where she could see them every day.

One day, after one of these visits, Laura stopped, as always, to speak to Jackson. She thought he looked a little frailer than usual and asked him how he was feeling.

'Good-o, Missus. Nothin' to complain about.'

'Is Lily feeding you well?

'Too right, Missus. Lily dam' good cook.' He cleared his throat and looked away. 'You seen Boss Jamieson lately?'

'No, I haven't. Why?'

'Just wondered. Out at Miranda, fixin' up stockyards.' Jackson stirred the coals of his fire with a stick. 'Boss pretty unhappy. In trouble, too. Like Little Missus. Little Missus should go out there.'

'And Jackson should mind his own business!' Laura drew her brows together.

'Yeah.' Jackson was unmoved. 'That's what I bin told myself.

But somebody gotta do somethin', and that somebody gotta be you, Little Missus, or else bloody great stand-off: no good to nobody!'

Laura spoke with dangerous restraint. 'Is that so?'

'Yeah, Missus.' Jackson made a comprehensive gesture with his stick and threw it on the fire, raising a little shower of sparks. 'Makin' Boss sick: not eatin', workin' too hard. You ask Lily 'bout Mrs Mac: She out of her mind with worry, poor woman. She worry 'bout Boss; Lily worry 'bout her. That no good, Missus.' He gestured earnestly. 'No good to nobody. Someone gotta swallow their pride. Boss can't take any more. That someone gotta be you.'

Tight-lipped and tapping one foot, Laura snapped: 'Have you *quite* finished, Jackson?'

'Nah, Missus.' He looked her in the eye. 'Just got one more thing to say: You strong woman, Missus. Boss Jamieson need strong woman. Don't worry, he'll know it when he see you. You good with first aid. Boss need first aid. Better you go out to him now. That's all.' Jackson dropped his eyes to his fire, picked up a second stick and began to stir the embers, as if his visitor was no longer there.

Well, that's dissed me! thought Laura, swinging away. But beneath the fury, Jackson's words had engendered an anxiety. Jackson knew things: Things that were hidden from most people. An inexplicable truth that she could not escape. What if all he said were true? Wouldn't it be a simple way to end the agony? To find out one way or another, once and for all? If she could believe him, all she had to do was go out to the stockyards at Miranda and all would be well. *Oh, if only I could believe it!* she thought, stepping onto the verandah and making for the kitchen where Lily was dropping spoonfuls of biscuit dough onto a tray.

'Lily, is it true what Jackson just told me. That Mrs Mac is worrying herself sick?'

'Yeah, Missus. Boss Jamieson takin' things hard. Not eatin', workin' himself into the ground. Goes off every day to Miranda. Every morning, Mrs Mac pack his tuckerbox. Every night, tuckerbox still full. Then he fall asleep over dinner and don't eat that. Mrs Mac goin' up the wall about it. Any day now, she collapse. Won't be no use to call the Flying Doctor then!'

'All right, Lily. You've convinced me; you and Jackson, between you. I'd better get out there, I suppose. I'll have to go and fuel up the Land Cruiser.'

'Good-o, Missus.' Lily bent down to put her biscuits in the oven. 'I'll pack you a smoko.'

Laura picked up the first-aid kit on her way out to her vehicle. *Just in case Jackson wasn't being metaphorical,* she thought.

'Cross your fingers, Mary,' said Lily when she'd gone out the door. 'And come and help me get this smoko ready. Thank God, I bin told Jackson.'

'Yeah, it was a good idea.' Mary's eyes twinkled. 'You want me to make tea or coffee?'

§

The long drive out to the Miranda stockyards was a special brand of torture for Laura, all her memories crowding in on her: the pain in Rick's eyes when he'd told her he'd given up on her, the way he'd stepped into the plane without even glancing at her again, the finality in his voice when he'd said goodbye. 'Goodbye, Laura.' The last words she had ever heard from him. Her breath snagged on a sob, and she had to slow down because she almost lost it in some deep wheel tracks. Desperately hanging onto the wheel, she managed to keep her vehicle out of a skid and decided she'd better keep her mind on the road if she wanted to get out there at all. But her thoughts kept on straying, continually going over what might happen when Rick saw her.

In a way, it would be a relief if Jackson had been wrong, and Rick wasn't there. But, if he was, how would he react? Would he look at her with ice in his eyes and anger in his heart? Would he turn his back and walk away? Or worse, would he tell her never to bother him again? What would she do if he treated her like that this time? *Will I be able to bear it?* The tears came again. Almost, she gave up and turned back, as her resolution wavered, but something drove her on. According to Jackson and Lily, Rick was ill—suffering—at least some of it, Laura's doing. It cut her to the quick to think of it. *I must make one more try to put things right,* she thought. *For all our sakes. No matter how he treats me.*

§

At first Laura couldn't find Rick anywhere, then she saw him laying on the ground under a tree, and her heart skipped a beat. Scooping up the first-aid kit, she ran to the yard and slipped through the rails. As she bent over him, she breathed a sigh of relief because she could see that he was sleeping soundly on the groundsheet he'd spread in the shade. She studied him lovingly. He was thinner. Tiny threads of grey were beginning to appear at his temples. A lock of hair stirred in the breeze, and she put out a finger to smooth it back. At her touch, Rick opened his eyes and blinked.

'Laura!' His face lit with joy and disbelief. 'What are you doing here?' Then he saw the first-aid kit in her hand. 'Why have you got that?'

'I saw you laying on the ground. I thought … I didn't know … if you might need it.'

'No. I've gone way past that. I'm dying without you. I need the kiss of life.'

Laura abandoned her first-aid kit and dropped to her knees. She put her hands on his shoulders. 'Rick, I'm so sorry. I know what I did was unforgivable. Particularly ——'

'Sh, sh.' He stroked her cheek. 'Don't you think I know what you're like?' His mouth quirked into a lazy, loving smile as he moved his hand to thread firm but gentle fingers through her hair. 'Now, are you going to save me or not?'

'Under the circumstances,' she murmured, her lips curving sweetly, 'I suppose it is the least I can do.'

'I'm glad you've realised it at last.' He put his other arm around her and pulled her towards him, making sure she couldn't answer—in words, at least.

'Oh, Rick, I've missed you so much,' sighed Laura when she could finally speak.

'Same here, but I couldn't see any way …'

'I know. I'm so sorry, but I couldn't face my demons.'

'And you have now?'

'Yes, it's been a rough few weeks.'

'Tell me about it.' He kissed her again. 'I think I need a bit more treatment after what I've been through without you.' He lifted his head to look at her. 'But seriously, *can* you tell me about it?'

'Yes, I think so.' She pillowed her head on his shoulder, basking in the comfort of his arms about her. 'I've always known you needed an explanation, but I couldn't give it until I had answers for myself. And I couldn't find those because it was too painful to go there.'

'My poor darling, you don't have to.'

'Yes, yes, I do. And the great thing is: Now I can. If you won't let me apologise, the least I owe you is an explanation.'

'In your own time. Just that you're here is enough for me.'

'Yes, being here with you is the same for me. But don't you want to know how I came to be here?'

'If you want to tell me.' He stroked a lock of hair back from her face. 'Of course I do.'

'Jackson sent me. He said that you were making yourself ill, that Mrs Mac was worrying herself sick and that I was the only one who could do something about it.'

'Did he? He was right. I owe him, big time.'

So do I, she thought. 'He said not to worry, that as soon as you saw me, everything would be all right. And it was. He's been right about a lot of things.'

'Aren't they amazing? You know, your women have been a godsend to Mrs Mac, and Jackson with his mulga wire. Nobody gives them enough credit.'

'We will, though, won't we?'

'We will, indeed.'

'I thought I'd pushed you so far that you'd grown to hate me.'

'Hate you?' He laughed. 'I've loved you to desperation from the minute I saw you wielding a broom with cobwebs in your hair.' He was silent a moment. 'You were always so aggressive, fighting me every inch of the way. Stubbornly refusing to admit that what was between us was something that few are lucky enough to find. But then I realised that something in your past had so traumatised you, that the slightest hint of falling in love was enough to send you panicking for the scrub. I thought that time and patience would see us through it, but when I found out what you'd believed about me—what with the shock of Andy's betrayal and his mother's collapse—everything got too much for me. I just felt that I was flogging a dead horse, that it was of no use to continue.'

'And yet, despite not knowing if I could trust you, I did fall in love with you. Even though, I will admit, I fought against it because I was afraid of what my heart was saying. I was about to tell you when the last lot of cattle disappeared and interrupted me. I just had to clear out all my baggage before I could go there. That's what took me so long.'

'I knew that first day I took you to Miranda that you'd been deeply hurt by someone. What did he do to you, my love?'

Laura sat up, holding tightly to Rick's hand. 'I don't know how to tell you this. I've never been able to talk about it.' She took a deep breath. 'I was young, sheltered. I had certain romantic visions of married life.'

'Like most young girls, I believe?'

'Stephen was quite a bit older than me and so romantic. He treated me so gently when we were going out, and after we were engaged, agreeing with me to wait until we were married. Of course, now I know why! I know I was naive and stupid, but I didn't know people did those things.'

'Kinky stuff, you mean?'

She nodded. 'It was a big shock to me on my wedding night to find that he had to inflict pain to get satisfaction. I stood it for as long as I could, but after a while, I began to dread him coming near me.'

'Well, that's only natural. Quite normal, I would say.'

'You don't understand. I began to feel such guilt.' She took a trembling breath. 'I knew he was going elsewhere when I couldn't … but I closed my eyes because …And Sally! I must be stupid. I confided in her, and she supported me right to the end. I had no idea until the crash that she was going behind my back like that. Apparently, she shared his penchant for … you know. And then, when they were killed in the accident, it was obvious they were going away together. I just felt so guilty that I was alive, and they weren't—that if I'd been a bit tougher, he wouldn't have turned to other women.'

'There's no way of knowing that.'

'I should have ended the marriage, but you make promises, you know, for better or for worse, and if it was worse … well. I still loved him, even though all this was going on. I loved them both. That's why it was so hard. If they'd just talked to me …'

'Would it have made it any better?'

'I don't know. They wouldn't have had to die.'

'You can't know that, and you can't blame yourself for it. They made their own decisions. It was fate; meant to be. You can't change that. Besides, anyone stupid enough to treat you like that deserves a bad end.'

'Rick!'

'Well, it's the truth, and I'm not going to apologise for it. The thought of someone causing you pain makes my blood boil.' He sat up and took her back into his arms. 'My poor darling, you've been to hell and back, and I love you so much. I make you this promise: I will never hurt you. Will you trust me on this?'

'Yes, Rick, I trust you.' *In every way.* What a relief it was to say it and know that it was true.

'I won't let you down.' He held her gently. 'All this, the death of your husband and your friend, it must have been about the time Jonas died; otherwise, I would have known about it.'

'Yes, we didn't tell him at the time because we knew he'd make the effort to come, and we didn't want him to make such a long trip at his age. I was about to write to him to explain what had happened when I got the news of his death. After that, I just went into a dark place and couldn't see my way out. It was all too much for me.'

'They were terrible things, my darling, and terrible times. But they brought you here, to me.'

'And yet you didn't seem to want me here.' Laura raised troubled eyes to his. 'I felt that I had got in your way.'

'You did. John told you why. I told you why I didn't share Jonas's belief in your ability to rough it up here. You're so like I remember my mother—so fragile and beautiful. I couldn't bear the thought …'

'I'm tougher than I look, you know.'

'I know.' He gave a wry grin. 'I've had to learn the hard way. Come on, come back here. Let's forget about the past and concentrate on the moment. Mmm, just having you in my arms …' He lay back, pulling her down on top of him. 'You know, there's a lot to be said for Jonas's idea of throwing down a swag under a tree.'

'I don't know whether he'd approve of the use we're putting it to!' Laura laughed and sank into his arms.

'Don't you? I think Jonas would be very glad to see this day.'

'Yes, he would.' A fleeting vision of Uncle Jonas smiling down on them visited her. 'Of course, he would!'

Then, Rick was kissing her again, and Laura felt herself respond with her whole being, so that all thoughts went out the window. Time stood still until they were brought back to reality by an orchestra of curious growls and rumbles. More than fifty pairs of soulful brown eyes were watching them through the fence: a herd of Brahmans, shuffling, flicking their long ears and emitting their strange rumbling sounds.

'Rick! Look!' Laura leapt to her feet, spooking the cattle. 'The eartags! Are these my stud Brahmans? Or am I seeing things?'

Rick stood up, but before he could reply, he was addressed by an aboriginal stockman riding up on a bay horse to block the herd and turn them back to the yard. 'Found these cattle over at Gunyah, Boss.' He took off his hat to acknowledge Laura. 'Missus. Got Jonas Neumann's brand. Mind if I leave 'em here?

It's been a long trip.'

'I'll say it has! Gunyah's a good distance away. What the hell's been going on over there?'

'I dunno, really.' The man replaced his hat. 'The Stock Squad sent us in to muster it.' He shook his head. 'Cattle from all over. You know that gang they just busted? Looks like they bushed the cattle over there until the heat died down.'

'Are these the only ones with the Neumann brand?'

'Yeah, Boss. The only ones from over this way.'

'All right, you can leave them here. We'll see to them in the morning. And thank you.'

'Yes. Thank you,' said Laura. 'You don't know how happy I am to see them.'

'Good-o, Missus. Glad to be of help.' Tipping his hat to them, the stockman rode off.

Laura stared at the cattle as if they were a figment of her imagination. 'I can't believe it!'

Rick didn't reply but stood frowning.

'Rick? What is it?'

'Nothing. Just that this gang must have been bigger and better organised than any of us had supposed. Do you know how far away Gunyah is?'

'No.'

'It's a huge, abandoned cattle station in the Peninsula. These blokes did well to find your cattle. It's a surprise, but a good one for a change.'

'Yes, it is a wonderful surprise. Like a gift.'

'Almost a wedding present, wouldn't you say?'

'Rick …?'

'Well, you are going to marry me, aren't you?'

There he was, again—telling her instead of asking. But somehow, this time she didn't mind in the slightest. A mischievous smile touched her lips. 'If you ask me nicely.'

'Tonight, after a candlelit dinner, I will propose to you under the stars. Will that be nice enough?'

'It sounds divine.'

He kissed the tip of her nose and held her close. 'Come on, my darling. Let's go home.'

'My house or yours?'

'Oh, no!' A comical expression crossed his face. 'Are we *really* going to fight about that?'

'No.' Laura smiled. 'Mrs Mac needs us, and Lily and Mary practically live there, anyway. I hope you've got room for Bess and Oscar?'

'Bess, Oscar, your horses, the whole damn menagerie. Anything you like. As long as I've got you with me.'

Chapter Twenty-two

Once more, the outdoor dancefloor was set up, and all the Gulf came to Juliana, not just for one wedding, but two. Jack and Cass had previously arranged with Rick to celebrate their wedding at Juliana for two reasons: Jack's close friendship with Rick and the fact that most of their friends were from the Gulf.

It was Cass who suggested a double wedding when she heard that Rick and Laura were getting married. 'You don't want to leave it any longer or the wet will be upon us. Most of your guests will be here for ours, and it will save them another long trip and the chance of being stuck here for months. I don't mind sharing my big day with you.' She gave Laura a hug and a cheeky grin. 'Besides, Rick and Jack will be able to support each other.'

Not wanting a big formal wedding for herself, Laura was only too happy to agree. She'd already decided not to wear a conventional white wedding gown and was pleased that Cass was doing the traditional part and would take the spotlight off her. Laura wanted nothing about this wedding to remind her of her first one. There was no-one like Rick. She might have thought she was in love as a twenty-year-old, but she was convinced now that she hadn't known the meaning of the word. All previous emotions paled into obscurity beside what she felt for Rick, and everything she saw in his eyes told her that it was the same for him.

'Jack and Cass are writing their own vows.' Rick put the phone down from talking with his friend. 'Should we do the same?'

'If you like. With the best will in the world, I don't think I *could* promise to obey.'

'Now, that's a surprise!' Rick took her in his arms with a smile. 'Are you sure? Because you do realise you've messed up all my hopes?'

'Yes, I can see that.'

'Are you sure you won't change your mind?'

'What do you think?'

'That I'd better not push my luck. We'll just leave that bit out, then. Now to be serious: How do we do this double wedding? What are the rules?'

'I don't think there are any. Basically, you can do what you like: both together, one after the other.' She grinned. 'As long as it happens.'

'Well, it won't be my fault if it doesn't.'

'Or mine.' She reached up to kiss him.

'Now we've settled *that*,' said Rick after some time, 'why don't we let them go first and then follow with ours?'

'Yes. That will be best.'

'Then we'll fly out together with them on our honeymoon, so no-one will know where we're going. But I have something special planned for us. Will you leave it in my hands?'

'Bossy, overbearing …' Laura smiled lovingly and stroked his cheek. 'Of course I will! What choice do I have?'

'I will tell you all about it tonight, and it will be your choice; I promise you.'

Laura returned his deepening kiss. Whatever Rick had planned, she knew in her heart she would love it.

§

John and Nancy Neumann, Laura's parents, made a flying visit, determined not to miss their only daughter's wedding, no matter what the cost.

At dinner, the night before the wedding, Laura's mother suddenly exclaimed, 'Oh, I just *have* to tell you, we met this beautiful couple. They said they knew you. They were enquiring about the cost of a wedding in the castle. They told us they'd get back to us, but they didn't.'

'Were they both blonde and good-looking?' asked Rick.

'Yes, lovely looking: A charming couple. I think their names were Andy and Corinne.'

Rick and Laura looked at each other.

'So not island hopping,' said Rick.

'No, seeing the world instead. Will you tell Mrs Mac?'

'Probably later.' Rick's glance went to where his housekeeper was chatting to Cass's father at the other end of the table. 'It might ease her mind to know what they've been doing.' He answered Nancy Neumann's questioning look. 'It's a bit awkward—my cousin and my housekeeper's son ran away together—family black sheep, I suppose you could say. None of us have heard from them. Laura can fill you in later, in private, so we don't upset his mother.'

'Oh, I *see*.' Nancy swiftly changed the subject to a cheery reminiscence at which they all laughed. *Bless you, Mother*, thought Laura in gratitude.

The only one of Rick's family to come was Peter, full of apologies. 'I'm sorry the olds couldn't make it.' He shook Rick's hand with a rueful grin. 'They've gone on a world tour—finally taking a holiday—or so they claim. They've hired a private detective, and well, we both know they've gone to look for Corinne. I mean, I've told them to let well alone, but will they listen?' He grimaced. 'Like looking for a needle in a haystack. It's busted up the family, Rick. Bad business. But look, if I'd known you were going to need a best man, I wouldn't have agreed when Jack asked. You know, because Trish is Cass's bridesmaid, we thought …'

'Don't worry, old mate. It was all a bit short notice, but it's good of you to say so. John will be my best man. And don't worry about Corinne. I'm sure that when your parents find she is safe, they will come round.' Rick told Peter what Laura's mother had said about the beautiful couple that had visited the castle they managed in Somerset.

Peter laughed. 'I might have known she'd land on her feet.

Well, that's all right, then.'

§

Laura's outfit was an elegant silver-grey silk chiffon two-piece: the swathed top cleverly embroidered over one shoulder; and the beautifully draped neckline with tiny crystals, silver thread and pearls with a crystal and pearl-encrusted band on the slim skirt, emphasising her slender waist. A glamorous black, grey and white chiffon hat perched on the side of her head, completing the picture.

'Oh, very chic!' whispered her mother, dabbing her eyes.

The grooms and their men were standing by the bougainvillea-covered arch, waiting quietly, when Cass, delicately beautiful in ivory satin and lace, appeared beside Laura in the doorway.

'You look great, Laura,' she whispered. 'Are we ready yet?'

'I am if you are.' Laura turned to look at Cass. 'And you look great, too. In fact, the word 'exquisite' springs to mind.' Then, she greeted Trish—pretty and demure in blush rose.

John Neumann came to stand beside his daughter. 'Second time lucky, eh, Laurie?'

'Oh, Dad, I hope so. I *know* so.'

'So do I, love. You've chosen a good 'un this time around.'

Cass, preceded by her bridesmaid, went first with her father in his electric wheelchair, and Laura walked behind, arm in arm with her own father, smiling at the rows of guests.

Laura watched Jack's face light with tenderness and love as

Cass approached him and placed her hand in his. Then, she saw that Rick was looking at her with exactly the same expression, and her heart leapt with joy.

At the altar, where the Flying Padre waited, Rick moved back to make room for Cass as she stepped up beside Jack. He and Laura stood behind them on the right. His eyes told her how beautiful he thought her, while they listened to the moving vows that Cass and Jack were repeating. Soon, it was their turn to step up to the altar while the other couple sat behind.

With the ceremony over and official documents signed, they all moved onto the verandah where tables were arranged along its length for their wedding feast, with Mrs Mac, Lily and Mary serving platters of cold meats, salads, fruit and rolls for guests to help themselves. It was a merry occasion, the happiness of both couples spilling over onto all in attendance. Laura knew that she would remember it with joy all her life. A morning wedding, it had been arranged that the celebration be a lunchtime one to allow the couples to fly out before too late in the day. Otherwise, Laura was sure the party would have continued until evening; they were all having such a good time. But eventually, the newlyweds had to leave if they were going to go at all.

§

The brides, having said their goodbyes, gave their bouquets to Lily and Mary and entered the plane, tenderly assisted by their respective grooms.

'Well, that's that.' Lily watched the plane take off. 'Never thought I'd see the day.'

'Yeah,' agreed her sister. 'Good job.'

'What are we gunna do with these?' Lily looked down at the bouquets in their hands.

'Dunno. Not much use to us. Put 'em in water?'

'They're silk.'

Mary grinned. 'Won't need water, then.'

With one accord, they handed the flowers to Mrs Mac and, taking an arm each, walked her back to the house.

§

'Put us down here at Polaris, Jack,' said Rick. 'We're going bush.'

'I didn't think a luxury island resort honeymoon sounded like you, Rick. But what about Laura?'

'Rick's promised to show me all the beautiful, wild places in the Gulf.'

Cass laughed. 'How long did you say your honeymoon will be?'

'As long as it takes,' said Rick. 'I've got a fully provisioned four-wheel drive and camping trailer waiting for us on the airstrip. But if that laugh means that you think it won't take long to find all the beauty in the Gulf, then you may be surprised.'

'You can find beauty anywhere if you look for it.' Jack turned with a smile: 'But I have no fear that a relative of Jonas Neumann won't love every inch of it.'

'You've summed it up perfectly, Jack. There's no place I'd

rather be.' *And no-one I'd rather be with.*

Laura held her new husband's hand and smiled at him, knowing that not only could he read her thoughts, more importantly, he shared them.

ABOUT THE AUTHOR

Anne Rouen

Anne Rouen—the nom de plume of Lynn Newberry—is the award-winning author behind the successful historical fiction series, *Master of Illusion* and, more recently, a set of standalone contemporary historical fiction romance and suspense novels set in the Australian Outback.

Lynn is a retired Australian country woman, currently living in the North-West region of New South Wales. A graduate of the University of New England, she is a former teacher, dressage rider and cattle breeder. A life on the land, including eleven years in Outback Queensland, has mixed nicely with her penchant for writing romantic suspense in historical settings.

Lynn has recently exchanged her farm for a delightful small acreage on the edge of a village, where she writes full time. As horses and writing are her greatest passions, Lynn now embraces an idyllic lifestyle, since she has time to delve into the historical research she so loves.

Writing as Anne Rouen, Lynn self-published her historical romance/mystery series *Master of Illusion* with great success, winning four literary awards across the entire set. Book I (*Master of Illusion Bk I*) and Book III (*Angel of Song*) achieved Silver (2014) and Bronze (2016) respectively in the *Global Ebook Awards* for *Modern Historical Literature Fiction*. Book IV (*Guardian Angel*), the final in the series, was awarded Silver (2018) in the same category and Bronze (2018) for the *Global Ebook Awards Best Ebook Cover*.

Lynn has seen continued success with the *Global Ebook Awards* in 2022 with her Australian Outback cosy romance, *Winter at Medora Downs*, where she achieved a Gold Medal for the *Best Ebook Cover*, Silver for *Best Suspense Fiction* and Bronze for *Best Modern Historical Literature Fiction in a contemporary setting*.

Lynn also achieved a Highly Commended in the 2011 Rolf Boldrewood Literary Awards for her short story *The Scent of a Criminal* and a Commended in the 2018 *Thunderbolt Prize for Crime Fiction* for *The Min Min Light*.

You can find more information about Anne Rouen and read her blog at www.annerouen.com.

Other Books by Anne Rouen

Master of Illusion Series (Historical Fiction)

Master of Illusion—Book One

Master of Illusion—Book Two

Angel of Song (Book Three)

Guardian Angel (Book Four)

§

Australian Outback themed Romantic Suspense

Winter at Medora Downs

9 780099 240376